Other books by S. A. Mahan:

CHRISSIE'S RUN
THE BABY SEA TURTLE

A Pigeon's
Tale

S. A. Mahan

GROUSE MOUNTAIN PRESS
2015

Published by Grouse Mountain Press, Bailey, Colorado 80421

Cover Art by Deborah Mahan

ISBN: 1514136538
ISBN 13: 9781514136539
Library of Congress Control Number: 2015909563
CreateSpace Independent Publishing Platform
North Charleston, South Carolina

PROLOGUE

"This ain't no ordinary pigeon story. 'Course, how could it be ordinary? Pigeons ain't ordinary at all!" –Old Dude

Fact: Racing homing pigeons have been clocked flying 92.5 mph average speed on a 400 mile race!

Fact: Homing pigeons have been known to fly 700 miles in a day!

Fact: Pigeons have flown in many wars, including both WWI and WWII. They saved countless American lives!

Deduction: Noah's dove was most likely a homing pigeon!

Opinion: *The honored symbol of America's National Bird should be awarded to the pigeon because of his undaunted courage and documented sacrifice in saving so many American soldiers! What did the American Bald Eagle do to deserve this honor?*

1

MY BIRTHDAY

I wish to say that my mind is still sharp, but I am afraid that I may have lost count of the years. My beloved mate would be certain and would remind me, but, sadly enough, she passed away suddenly from a heart attack forty-eight years ago. What I know for certain is that I am either eight-hundred and thirty-something or eight-hundred and forty-something years old, I think, and the oldest pigeon living. Most pigeons today would agree with me. Of course, most of the pigeons living today are my children, my grandchildren, my great-grandchildren, my great-great grandchildren, and so on, for countless generations.

I do not think that my lack of accuracy is really that much of a problem.

The Great White Stork keeps a perfect account of a pigeon's life, and recounts every detail of that pigeon's life to him or her upon that pigeon's death. So why should I worry about exact years? I trust in The Great White Stork!

I know, dear reader, it must seem fantastic to you that anyone could live so many years, especially a pigeon. I assure you that it is true and you will find out why.

Today, countless scores of my descendants are throwing a grand birthday celebration for me. As with every one of my birthdays for the past eight hundred years, it is going to take place on Bird Island. Of course, I do not want to be late. I would feel horrible if I saw any looks of disappointment on little hatchlings faces who are even now joyously awaiting my arrival. And I love *all of my descendants' little hatchlings, even if they are hundreds of generations removed from me. They are still mine!*

I will fly in to the big event with the help of my human friends. I am far too old to make that journey on my own. I do fly around my small yard once in a while, but Bird Island is too many miles away.

Once I did make that journey alone, under the worst possible circumstances any bird can imagine. That was so long ago...so, so long ago. And so many lives depended on me then, including wonderful human lives.

I should never have survived that terrible journey across Bird Island, and to the great shore beyond. It was an impossible flight! But miracles do happen and I received help from a totally unimaginable and completely impossible source.

That is why I am writing down my story for you. I want you to believe in miracles!

Writing is difficult for me. I have to go slowly, pecking out each letter with my beak. My beak is sore, but I will persevere. I sincerely want you to know my story.

I fear that now, at long last, my years grow very short. I can feel it in my brittle old wings. Soon I will stand once again before The Great White Stork in the great, glowing halls of Valhalla, listening solemnly as he recounts the events of all of my long years. Yes...I stood before him once before when he unexpectedly appeared to all of us. It was a glorious event! When and why I was so fortunate is not for me to reveal now. First, I must tell you my story.

I will pause and rest for a bit now. My old beak is so sore.

Soon, my human friends will arrive in their colorful flying machine and we will be off to Bird Island. My thousands upon thousands of descendants will be waiting there for me, some of them are also well over eight hundred years old! It will be such a grand celebration!

When I return, and when my beak feels better, I will begin my story where it should begin. At the beginning!

In the meantime, may The Great White Stork always be with you!

2

THE BEGINNING OR, A TERRIBLE, HORRIBLE NIGHT!

He attacked shortly after midnight, when all of the lights at the ranch were turned down, the half-moon had set below the horizon, and all of the dogs were sound asleep.

The coop had carried a strange smell all day long. I could not place it, so I asked my mother earlier that afternoon.

"Don't worry, little one," she soothed me, "some of the others are just a little nervous. You smell their nerves. They get that way once in a while."

But I caught a rare glint in her eye and suddenly realized that she was also on edge. And I realized whatever that strange smell was, the odor was different from the normal, comfortable pigeon poop pungency of my home. It was the smell of fear!

All day, the old flyers whispered the news back and forth to each other with quivering voices. I was still so young that I could barely fly from one end of the coop to the other. Because of my age, I was not included in their conversations. I caught bits and pieces of information, though.

Apparently, old Rancher George had run over a wildcat with his truck the night before. George, a kind-hearted old rancher, swerved wildly into the middle of the road and tried to avoid the cat. He heard the dull thud of impact, stopped and backed up to see if the creature was still alive. Somehow, the wildcat dragged itself into thick brush and disappeared.

It was late at night, and old George wanted no part of a wounded wildcat. He decided to drive on to the ranch and hunt for its body in the morning.

All through the day, flyers returned to the coop, rang the bell, and reported seeing something bloody and furry skulking through the underbrush. Each new sighting placed it closer to the ranch, causing the smell of fear to grow stronger and stronger with each passing hour. At the evening feeding, Rancher George talked to us in his characteristic low and soothing tone.

"That bad old cat is dead," he assured us, "I hit it too hard last night. You'll be okay. Settle down now, babies, settle down."

A few old flyers cooed back to him in response. He looked at each and every one of us and then returned to the ranch house.

Night fell, but no one slept. My sisters huddled close together under my mother's warm, protective wings. I roosted a few inches away, lost in my thoughts. My father perched with the old timers, trading stories, trying to stay calm.

Well before dawn, the cat attacked! He burst into the hatch like a crazy battering ram. I could see his angry left eye gleaming red in the dark, but he never growled or made any kind of sound. The coop erupted into complete pandemonium. There were screeches and screams, with feathers flying everywhere as the cat clawed his way inside.

My eyes were fully adjusted to the dark and I saw that the entire right side of the wildcat's head and face were injured from the impact with old George's truck. His right eye was swollen shut and he moved erratically, swiping and biting at every pigeon in his way. My mother hunched over my sisters and spread her wings out to protect them. She frantically looked around through all of the chaos, trying to locate me. She saw me huddled at the very back of the coop and our eyes met.

"Fly, baby, fly!" she screamed.

The wildcat followed her scream and spotted me, huddled helpless in that dark corner. He growled and charged at me.

Suddenly, my father appeared in front him, flapping his wings and squawking as loud as a pigeon can squawk. The horrible cat swatted him out of the way. That terrible red eye focused on me! Through my panic, I suddenly remembered that there was a little pack rat hole in the lower back corner of the coop. It was such a small mouse hole, maybe too small for me. But I was highly motivated!

The wildcat lunged for me and I jumped for the hole. I squeezed and squeezed through it, feeling his razor sharp claws swipe across my tail feathers. I squawked in terror and, for the first time, heard his horrible angry screech. I squeezed one more time, and popped through the hole, out into the dark night.

I do not know what beat harder, my heart or my wings as I struggled up into the night sky. It was rough going for a few moments, and I tumbled head over tail as much as I flew. Somehow, air gathered beneath my young feathers and I ever so gradually climbed higher toward the twinkling stars. My wings filled with cool night air and soon I was traveling, truly flying for the very first time.

3

A NIGHT FLIGHT

This was my very first venture outside the coop, and I had no idea where to go. I was so scared. In my frantic state of mind, any direction was preferable to turning back to the horrors behind me.

It was a black, chilly night, and I watched as patches of fog lazily drifted through the trees like slow, ghostly flocks of pigeons. Where should I go?

The old flyers always talked about a large town that was somewhere out to the east, where old Rancher George drove for groceries and supplies.

Still, it was all I could do to stay airborne at this point. I managed to stay just about treetop level. Finally, when I worked up the courage, I looked straight up at the stars. Something deep inside of me said, "East is that way!" I made a quarter turn to the right, and headed that direction.

Fright sustained me, and I know that I must have covered some distance, but now I had to rest. Straight ahead of me, I spotted a big sprawling tree full of branches and leaves, and I aimed for it. I completely missed the first branch and tumbled through some leaves. I squawked as I bounced off another branch and, finally, my claws gripped a small limb.

I need to work on my landings, I thought to myself as I hung on helplessly, clinging upside down on the small tree limb for dear life.

Then, I started to cry. For the first time, I was able to think about the terrible attack, about my poor, beautiful mother's heroic attempt to save me from that deranged beast, and how my father had been batted aside as he charged into certain death. I thought about how poor old Rancher George would feel when he discovered the coop in the morning, how he would cry. I was miserable.

Through my tears, my senses prickled. Predators were near! I tried to quiet myself, but they either caught my scent or saw me with their super night-vision. Even as a hatchling, I had watched the terrible barn owls as they futilely tried to break into our coop at night. These owls were different. They glided quietly through the branches of the tree, giving me barely enough time to hear the air whisper through their wings.

The chase was on! They were fast, but somehow I let go and dropped away from the tree limb, tumbled, bounced off two more limbs, spread my wings and caught the air just above the ground. I hugged the dark ground and plunged head-first into some low lying brush. The owls flapped around the bushes, but they were too big to reach the spot where I had burrowed in. They screeched in anger and flew away. This happened three more times during the night; and each time I barely saved my tail feathers from certain death!

During my final rest stop, I took stock of what I knew, and what skills I might have at my disposal. Survival had just forced quite a bit of old knowledge into my young, fledgling brain. Human scientists call this ability to remember what you have not yet learned 'collective memory', and, unknown to me at this time, I was naturally accessing it in my state of panic. All animals, including humans and even bugs, seem to possess collective memory. It is, however, really strong in birds, especially in pigeons.

But please forgive me, dear readers. In writing now about collective memory I get too far ahead of myself.

As I hid from those terrible owls, I instinctively mustered up all of the collective memory I possessed. I accessed those ancestral traits and impressions, skills learned through pigeon lineages that dated far, far back. To survive, I needed all the of collected knowledge of all pigeons, living or dead. Otherwise, I was too young, too vulnerable, and too tasty of a breakfast for just about any creature that happened along.

I had a choice to make. I could try to hide out in the wild brush and take my chances scrounging for bugs, nuts and berries, or I could fly to the town the old flyers had talked about and look for other pigeons. The old flyers had said that the town was chock full of pigeons, albeit pigeons of a much lower class. Plump, dumb, and lazy pigeons, the old flyers called them. Not good for much of anything at all.

Well, if town pigeons were that plump, they had to be good at scrounging food. And there was, of course, safety in numbers. "Go to the town," the tiny voice in my head whispered to me. I wanted to heed its advice, but I wasn't yet confident enough to make that decision.

I could see a faint red glow on the horizon and knew that the sun would be rising soon. The night owls were probably still close by, so I took off and flew low toward the red dawn. Soon, I spotted a large cluster of lights on the horizon glittering in the reddish-yellow hue of sunrise. Such a strange new sight! They were the lights of the town.

4

I HAVE TO MAKE A CHOICE

When I was just a three or four-day hatchling, my dear mother lectured my sisters and me at every single feeding. We would stretch our necks up, open our beaks, screeching for her regurgitated pigeon milk, and she would speak before giving us what we wanted.

"The entire course of your lives will be determined by two or three major decisions," she would tell us. She was a homing pigeon bred from the finest line. Her distinctive regal plumage revealed a quality far above that of any of the other pigeons in the coop. I have always since wondered about my father. He was just a plain, ordinary happy-go-lucky pigeon. He must have had one heck of a great personality to attract as fine a female as my mother.

My sisters and I did not pay too much attention to mother's advice at the time; we were way too hungry. Now, so many years later, I remember her words of wisdom with great clarity.

"You will make your first big decision when Rancher George pulls you out of the coop for the first time," mother continued, ignoring our frantic squeaking, "he will carry you out to a big, open field and toss you high up into the air. You will have to decide to either fly away or return to the coop. I decided to come back, but some pigeons don't. Either way, that first big decision will send you upon your life's path."

My first big decision had been easy. There was no way I was returning to the ranch and the clutches of that crazy wildcat. The ranch was now at least a half night's journey behind me. No, I would fly east to the edge of the town, hunt for the safest place to rest and observe the town from a distance. I knew nothing about towns and I knew that I had to be extremely careful.

I was devastatingly tired. My wings had done their job for the night. I was just barely flying now and I had to find a safe place to rest.

The lights of the town grew brighter as I neared its outskirts. I crossed over a busy road and decided to follow it. It led directly to the edge of the town. To my delight, I found a thick grove of trees and settled into them. They were chock full of leaves and provided ample cover that could hopefully buy me enough time to avoid the ever present predators.

I lighted on a bushy limb, high above the ground, and remained dead still, listening. Nothing stirred near the tree. After a few minutes, I relaxed a little. As the sun continued to rise, I slept with one eye open, watching for owls and hawks. They were giant raptors that could swallow me in one gulp for breakfast. Every hour or so, I shifted on the limb and preened my frayed and blood specked feathers. My tail feathers were a mess where the crazy cat had swiped them. It was a wonder that I could fly in a straight line.

By mid-afternoon I was crying again, mourning the loss of my family. I cried at the thought of old Rancher George mourning the loss of his flock. I knew that he had worked hard for many years training it, growing the hatchlings. George loved his pigeons; just ask any of the old flyers. But, I knew most certainly, they were all gone now.

"George, you have the finest birds in all the land," ranch visitors would say. They always admired my mother, her great lineage, her perfect plumage and conformation. As George's prize pigeon, she was not for sale. He delighted in talking about her wonderful heritage. It was my heritage now; but I felt only a heavy sadness.

The landscape on both sides of the busy road was beautiful, with the first hints of autumn starting to sweep across it. It was peppered with orchard farms, streams and groves. Where the grass grew wild, it grew tall. There were newly harvested fields of wheat, with plenty of leftovers. I made a mental note; there is food here! Then something else occurred to me.

"Beauty kills," my mother once warned my sisters and me as we stretched our necks up and opened our beaks wide, "always remember this. Be very careful around beautiful places. What attracts you also attracts what wants to kill you."

Almost on cue, shadows crossed over me, cast by big birds flying above the treetops. Hawks looking for prey! They did not see me and continued on, gliding gracefully with the mid-day wind. I was terribly hungry, but even more tired. I huddled down for the afternoon and fell asleep.

5

I MEET OLD DUDE

I woke up just in time to watch the sun set in the west with a full moon rising in the east. There was a brief, magical moment when silver moon-light mixed with the reddish golden glow of sunset, filtering in through the leaves of the tree. Hundreds of cicadas started chanting, and I knew that the night owls would soon be out, looking for me.

My plan was simple; wait overnight until I saw the first glow of the rising sun in the morning, fly into town, and locate the plump, dumb, lazy town pigeons. A mild breeze tickled the trees and made the leaves chatter as the evening air grew cool. I was wide awake, and starved half to death by now. There was no way to get comfortable.

I spent the entire night listening for telltale signs that the owls were near. There might be a screech in the distance, or a horrible scream of caught prey. I was ready to flee at any instant. Nighttime lasted for what seemed like forever. Finally, the first faint glow of morning appeared on the eastern horizon. I looked out toward the road and saw a steady stream of white car lights heading toward the sunrise and town. Then, when I felt that it was light enough for me to evade the owls, I took off.

I followed the roadway, crossing and flying obliquely to it at times to see if anything flew behind me. So far, I was alone. I flew higher than the treetops, but not high enough to become a potential breakfast for a waking hawk.

The road led straight into the center of town, which was much bigger than I had imagined. It sprawled out for a long way in all directions as the light of sunrise grew brighter. I was fascinated with the cars rolling along the road below me. They were not old and rusty like old Rancher George's truck. Most of them were bright and shiny. They came in all colors, shapes and sizes. Strange folks, those humans, I thought, to have so many different kinds of machines. To me, a nest was a nest, a rock was a rock, a tree, a tree.

As the rising sun continued to break across the horizon, the lights of buildings lining both sides of the road started to flick on. Some of the buildings had bright and colorful signs. Cars pulled off of the road to line up at them. All kinds of wonderful smells drifted up through the air above those popular buildings. There had to be a lot of food down there, reminding me of how hungry I was.

By this time, white morning sunlight glinted brightly off of almost everything in sight, nearly blinding me at times. I was alarmed at first, but I learned to squint my eyes and keep flying. Presently, I came to a place where the road dipped beneath another road. I was still heading east, directly into the sun. On the far side of the crossing road, where my road emerged again, I saw a series of power lines strung high across it, stretching between two big metal poles. I squawked with astonishment at what I saw next.

Somewhere around a hundred pigeons roosted on the power lines. There were a ton of them, all facing the rising sun. A sudden thought popped into my mind: *These must be the ones that got away from Rancher George!* I circled the wires a couple of times and then flew down to join the flock.

Curiously, the pigeons roosted only on one side of the wires, overhead one side of the road. Don't ask me why; the reason was not at all obvious to me. Because they only took one side, the pigeons were forced to huddle together. There were three lines, and finding an open spot on the top line was going to be a problem.

I was only half as big as any pigeon I saw; so I went for broke and wedged myself between two rotund females roosting on the top line. They acted like they were irritated with me and pressed in on me from either side until I could barely breathe.

"Warble, warble 'chilly night'," I gasped, trying to break the ice. The females ignored me and pressed harder.

I roosted in this miserable state much longer than I would want to admit, breathing in half and quarter breaths and hoping to survive the morning. Just as I was on the verge of blacking out, and falling to a certain death into the rushing cars below, a large male flew up and, without so much as a 'pardon me', pushed the big female to my right off of the wire and took her place.

The big male turned and looked directly at me. I looked back, and was filled with a rush of horror when I saw that he was missing an eye. Memories of the terrible one-eyed wildcat came rushing back to me.

He appraised me carefully with his good eye and said, "You ought to be sleeping in your mother's nest, kid!"

I was still trying to catch my breath.

"Not sick, are you?" He asked with a deep, gravelly voice. "No? Ok. My name is Hawk-Watcher, what do they call you?"

I was too scared, and too shy, to answer.

"Look, kid," he said after a minute, "you can't stay on this wire, this spot belongs to Miriam and she'll bite your head off when she comes back."

He looked around, apparently trying to find a spot for me. When he found one, he bumped me, nearly knocking me off the line.

"See that old pigeon down there by himself on the third line?" He asked me, and gestured to an old bird that looked more like a carcass than a living pigeon, "That's Old Dude. Now listen, kid… he's a little bit eccentric; but I'll bet he'll let you perch next to him. He gets pretty lonesome."

"Brunch time?"

"Stick with **Old Dude**, little Squeaker," he answered, "I got tons to n you 'bout the ropes."

We stayed quiet for a little while, and my eyelids grew heavy.

"Well, you ain't no ordinary pigeon, I could see that right off," Old de said, waking me up. I had no idea how long I had been asleep.

"I mosied over and told ol'one-eye 'bout yer wildcat adventure the er night," he continued, "he wants to talk with you shortly."

Old Dude looked me up and down again a couple of times.

"By the looks of yer feathers, and yer body style, I'd lay odds yer e of them fine high dollar homin' pigeons!"

That got me started. I told Old Dude everything I could about y parents, and my grandparents. Then, I dug deeper into my col-ctive memory and told him the stories about my great-great-great randfather. I did not have to go into very much detail. Old Dude new the story already.

"Th-thank you," I managed to stammer meekly.

"No problem, kid," Hawk-Watcher said, "Good luck and keep your eyes to the sky."

I took a deep, weary breath and flapped over to that old bird. The closer I got, the older he looked. He had an awful, dull gray plum-age that fluttered loosely in the morning breeze. It looked like it was about to all fall out. He must have been a big pigeon in his younger days, but the years had worn on him, made him scrawny, and he was missing a lot of tail feathers.

There were a few other pigeons roosting on the third line, bunched together well away from him. As I closed in, I could see why. He smelled like the coop did when it got stale, just before old Rancher George cleaned it. I landed right next to him and noticed that he was talking, seemingly to no one in particular.

"Warble, warble," he said, paying no attention to me, "chilly mornin', downright chilly mornin'! I dang sure ought'r git back down under that bridge! Dang sure ought'r. Come on, sun. Come on, sun!" He was saying. "Come on, sun. Least I got this here little squeaker a sittin' next to me now, blockin' soma the wind."

I chanced a greeting.

"Warble, warble," I said, pigeon for 'what's up?'"

"Come on, sun," the old bird kept saying, "come on, sun. I ought'r head fer Florida or git back down under that dang bridge!"

I worked up my nerve.

"Are you Old Dude?" I asked nervously.

He stopped talking, turned and eyed me up and down. For such an old bird, his eyes were sharp and bright. They almost sparkled.

"Yer awful lucky, Squeaker," he answered me in a slightly hoarse voice, "awful lucky to land next to the likes a' me. Chance in a mil-lion! Chance in a million!"

6

SPENDING TIME ON THE WIRE

Old Dude whooped and danced on the high line. He hopped up and down on one foot and turned round and round. I guess he didn't get much company.

"By the looks of yer, yer ain't from round these parts, are yer, Squeaker," he said when he finally settled down. "Dumbest bird up here could see that, and that ain't me! That's them two big ladybirds up yonder there."

He gestured up at the two heavyset females who had given me such a problem. I have to admit, now that I looked up at them, they did look pretty dumb and dull-eyed; not like my mother, whose eyes had always sparkled with intelligence. I had already broken most of her advice, such as: never fly alone at night, never roost in unfamiliar trees, stay close to the ranch, and don't talk to strangers!

"I'm durn well purty smart, myself," Old Dude continued, his frayed feathers fluffed out proudly, "Yer lucky you came over here. I got plenty I kin learn you."

He looked me up and down, and then cocked his head to one side.

"Where yer from, Squeaker?" He asked.

I told him, as well as I could over the noise of the cars rushing by beneath us, the story of the wildcat and my narrow get away. I told him how the whole coop must have been slaughtered, my whole family. He listened intently to every word.

"That makes you one brave Squeaker in my book," finally finished. "Ever'body round here calls me Old D to meet ya."

He bobbed his head up and down, a sign of respect.

"I don't feel brave," I said. I tried hard not to cry, r the carnage in my coop. "I barely got out of there with n ers. I ran."

I lowered my head.

"Well," Old Dude said, "in my book, runnin' is the bra pigeon can do, when it's the only thing he can do!"

He cackled to himself for a minute and swayed back an the wire. The morning traffic below us was growing heavie sun was high enough to warm my feathers.

"Why do you guys roost on this side of the road and no other," I asked, "there is so much room over there."

"Glad you asked that there question, Squeaker," Ol answered, "takes a smart bird to notice all the little things li and I know'd you was smart. Why, son, you go roost over the let's say a little Toyota comes at you, ain't nothing gonna h 'ceptin you get a little breeze in yer face. Now, just fer grins, let posin' it's a full blown Mack 18-wheeler bellerin' black smoke blastin' thru at 60 plus. He's a'gonna suck you right under that bridge and smack you! And it's bye, bye Squeaker!"

It sounded like it made sense to me, even though I was not sure what a Toyota or a Mack 18-wheeler was. Old Dude got his p across; it was dangerous to be on the other side.

"Now yer take this side," Old Dude continued, "you stay all wa and comfy 'neath the bridge at night; and come morning, hello su shine! Course, on cloudy days, you stay 'neath the bridge and ho the cars can keep you warm. Now you and me, we're a'gonna st right here in the sun 'til brunch time; which ain't too long off."

7

OLD DUDE LEARNS ABOUT ME

Old Dude hopped up and down on the high wire.

"Holy hard-boiled falcon eggs!" he exclaimed, loud enough for everyone to hear, "I didn't have no idea I was a'sittin here next to royalty! Hey, one-eye! Git over here!"

I turned and saw Hawk-Watcher perched up on his high post, giving Old Dude the evil one-eye. He sat still long enough to show the whole flock who the real boss was, and then, with a look of aggravation, slowly glided down to us.

"My name is Hawk-Watcher even to you, Old Dude!" He said gruffly as he lighted on the wire.

"Amen," Old Dude cackled, "and I was already an old pigeon when I watched you hatch, buster! Yer lucky yer old grandpappy, who I grew up with, ain't still among the livin'. He'd whip you here and now fer showin' disrespect to yer elders, boy!"

Hawk-Watcher flapped his wings and crossed behind Old Dude to perch beside me. Everyone else left their places on the other wires and crowded in. Old Dude introduced some of them to me.

"This here's Limp Leg. I'll tell you later how he got his name."

"Pleased to meet you, Squeaker!"

"And that there's Black Feather."

"Likewise."

"And them big ladies you met earlier up on the high line is Miriam and Helga. I think you already are purty familiar with them!"

Miriam and Helga bobbed their heads and cooed.

"You can roost with us anytime, Squeaker," Miriam giggled.

"Yes, yes!" agreed Helga.

I shuddered at the thought of being squeezed to death.

"They landed themselves one of them special eatin' deals," he whispered back, and then continued, "an' this here is Crazy Bird. Don't mind his wiggly eyes."

And on he went, until he had introduced just about the whole flock.

"Prince Squeaker here is a'gonna tell ya'll his story," Old Dude proudly announced to the flock, "One-eye, er, I mean Hawk-Watcher done already hear'd some of it and hereby approves the followin' content of this message!"

"I'm hungry," Crazy Bird piped up, his wiggly eyes going round and round.

"Cool yer claws, Crazy!" Old Dude growled at him. "And show Prince Squeaker here a token of respect! As soon as he's done with his story, we'll all go git somethin' to eat."

So, I told my story again, including the insane wildcat, including my lineage, and including my great- great-great grandfather, to a very attentive audience. Old Dude proudly perched next to me as I talked. When I finished, everyone was enthusiastically bobbing their heads up and down in their sign of total respect.

"My word," Miriam exclaimed when I had finished, "what an incredible heritage! You are such a brave little prince!"

And that was that. These pigeons had heard my story. In the blink of an eye, every pigeon across the world would know my story: that a descendant of my great-great-great grandfather had escaped the clutches of a crazy one-eyed wildcat and certain death.

We pigeons have the ability to tap into a rare resource called 'morphic resonance' to send thoughts and ideas, intentionally or not, to each other across great distances, instantaneously. It actually seems to work on a sub-quantum level as highly charged sub-particle information leaves space and time and then instantaneously re-enters when it finds its' proper sub-quantum receptors and transfers the information to, in this case, pigeons. Even pigeons living on the far side of the world! Other birds and animals might have this ability, too. I just don't know.

I learned everything that I know about morphic resonance from a very wise old human…but more on that later.

It is getting late. I wearily perch in my room in Crystal City, carefully pecking out these words for you. My birthday party on Bird Island was a tremendous success! I had no idea how many bright eyed hatchlings would be present for the celebration of my…oh, 850-somethingth year birthday. They all cheered when I arrived, and everyone acted like I was such a grand hero. I half expected to catch a glimpse of the Great White Stork himself standing among them, but I know that I will have to wait. Not much longer, I think.

Well, before I settle down to sleep, I remember one more thing Old Dude said on that first day so long ago, on the high wires above that busy road…

"Let's eat!" Old Dude yelled.

8

THE EATIN' PLACE

"Well, Squeaker, first things first," Old Dude hollered at me above the air noise. We were flying at tree-top level along the road, back the way I had come earlier.

"I'm goin' 'ta learn ya'," he continued, "the fine art of scroungin' the best grub in town, while it's still warm-like and fresh!"

He flew closer to me, his frayed feathers fluttering in the wind, and talked lower.

"Now Squeaker, don't go a tellin' nobody 'bout this place. This is our private secret!"

"I won't tell anybody," I promised.

"See them human folks getting out'a that little Subaru?" Old Dude asked.

I was not sure what a Subaru was, but I did see two people opening the doors of a small car and climbing out.

"Them?" I asked.

"Yep," Old Dude nodded, "don't you pay no 'tention to them big-uns! We won't git even a morsel out'a them! Bigun's don't drop hardly nothin'. Look how big they are, they eat every bite of their grub! We're awaitin' on the little-uns to show up. That's our real grub-ticket!"

Old Dude and I perched on top of a big red and yellow sign that shined in the sun. Old Dude called the big, shiny building below us the 'eatin' place'. It was a building with a lot of giant windows and I could see humans perching and eating inside. Cars were driving around the outside of the place, and somebody inside was handing out bags through a side window. The whole place had such a heavenly smell to it.

As the sun climbed higher up into the sky, Old Dude cued me in on the fact that people with little-uns would soon start showing up. And they did, a steady stream of them. As soon as the little-uns were freed from their cars, they screamed and starting running around and around like a bunch of crazy little hatchlings.

"Git yerself ready, Prince Squeaker," Old Dude whispered to me with a serious sideways glance, "see that big glass coop out front?"

I did. It looked to be about half the size of old Rancher George's barn, taller than the rest of the building, and filled with all kinds of weird looking contraptions.

"That there's called the children's play area," Old Dude pointed out, "and I am the only pigeon this side of Detroit that knows how to git in there. Purty soon, the little-uns will all go out there to that play area. An' they'll be a droppin' grub left and right. If we're lucky, one of 'em will drop a sandwich. If we're real lucky, one of 'em will drop a whole ice cream!"

I bobbed my head up and down in partial understanding.

"Now, when we git in," Old Dude warned quietly, "make sure you stick right with me. An' watch out fer that mean googly eyed boy that shows up with that there broom. He'll try to hit ya with that broom sure as The Great White Stork makes the sun rise up in the mornin'. Almost nailed me yesterday!"

Sure enough, the little-uns started to flood into the play area, juggling their food in both hands.

"Now, pay special close 'tention, Squeaker," Old Dude said, "them little-uns ain't really all that hungry. Their big folks think they are and they give them tons of grub! Them little-uns is gonna set their grub down on them little tables, but don't you get near a table. That'll rouse ole broom boy fer sure. Stay low, crawl in, and get the grub that hits the ground! Plenty'll be a hittin' the ground, I promise. It's usually them french fries first."

I had no idea what french fries were, but I was hungry enough to eat anything.

"Let's fly!" Old Dude squawked, and took off ahead of me. I was amazed at him. He flew strongly, like a bird half his age.

The play area reminded me of my coop, only made of glass and metal bars and hatches so the little-uns couldn't make any escape. It reminded me of home. I realized that no matter the species, bird or man, somebody always found a way to cage you up.

The little-uns did not seem to mind, though. They were running and climbing onto the play contraptions, making all kinds of happy screams and squeaks.

Old Dude led me to a small gap at the top of the building, where one metal edge had pulled away from another beneath the roof. With pigeon-like stealth, we squeezed in.

"Now jest drop on down the ground," he whispered to me, "there's already a whole bunch of them french fries layin' there on the ground. You don't even have to peck at 'em, Squeaker. You can swaller 'em whole in one gulp!"

I followed Old Dude down into the little-uns sanctuary, and immediately had to start hopping around to avoid getting smashed by the little-uns running feet. They were everywhere!

"Keep your sights on me at all times," Old Dude warned, "eat all ya can, an' we fly out first sign a' trouble!"

I agreed, and gobbled up a whole french fry. It was a little salty, but downright tasty. I looked for more. One little-un was running along, dropping french fries like he was leaving a trail, so Old Dude and I followed him.

The little-uns really did have trouble holding on to their food. It was hitting the ground everywhere. I looked up inside the other part of the building, where the big humans were eating. They were not dropping anything. They were eating every bite of their food while they watched the little-uns.

Something big hit the ground and Old Dude rushed me over to it. "Cheeseburger!" He exclaimed, "Dee-light-ful!"

We pecked at it and I have to admit that it was downright wonderful. I was starting to get half-way gorged, but Old Dude acted like he was just getting started.

We polished off most of the cheeseburger when something caught Old Dude's eye.

"Hey, Squeaker," he said, catching my attention, "looky at that little-un over there."

I spotted what he was looking at. It was an extra small little-un with long, curly hair, carrying something big with both of her hands. She was having trouble walking and balancing the thing at the same time.

"That there's a big 'ole ice cream cone," Old Dude cackled as he explained, "vaniller, looks like to me. Now just keep on a-watchin' while this plays out, Squeaker."

Halfway across the play area, the little-un stumbled, and the ice cream started to tumble. It all unfolded before me in slow-motion. The ice cream hit the ground and the little-un went running back out to the big people, screaming and crying.

"Jackpot!" Old Dude yelled, "This is your lucky day, Squeaker! Let's grab us some dee-sert!"

The ice cream was better than mother's pigeon milk. I could have stayed all day slurping up that delicious vanilla delight. Before we were half done, though, my neck feathers prickled and I jumped, just in time to dodge the slap of a broom.

"Broom boy!" Old Dude screamed, "Watch out, Squeaker!"

Everywhere I hopped, the broom followed, swishing and slapping like the sweep of a terrible night owl's wings. I danced and dodged all over the play area, hearing the laughter of the little-uns and catching glimpses of the evil face of the broom boy. He definitely had pigeon murder on his mind.

In a daring act of bravery, Old Dude flew right into the boy's face, distracting him, and giving me my chance to get away. We met up at the gap under the roof and flew back to the red and yellow sign.

"Not bad, Squeaker," Old Dude rasped, breathing heavily, "yer showed some good solid moves down there."

"Thanks, Old Dude," I managed to gasp. I could not have escaped without him.

9

SKY GODS

Back up on the high lines, everybody traded notes about brunch.

"Not much going on at the Taco Delight," Hawk-Watcher lamented, "I picked up a scrap here and there."

"The cleaning boy missed the dumpster at Burger-Doodle," Crazy Bird exclaimed, his googly eyes rolling in two different directions, "dumped all the scraps right there on the ground. Super, smelly scraps! You can still get some of them!"

Old Dude belched and looked half asleep. We were both perched on the high wire next to Hawk-Watcher now, our brand new perches of honor.

"Not much goin' on at the red and yellow," Old Dude said, "jest that danged mean kid with the broom, nearly killed us."

He winked at me.

"The nice lady at the park fed us," Miriam and Helga said almost simultaneously, "like she always does."

"Like them big girls need it," Old Dude whispered to me. There were jealous cackles from some of the other pigeons.

"Plenty of bugs in the dirt," Limp-Leg said, there ain't never no reason to go hungry!"

"If'n yer partial to bugs," Old Dude cackled. A dozen others cackled with him.

The afternoon sun was warm, the breeze was light, and soon most of the pigeons were snoozing.

My eyelids grew heavy, but something way high up in the blue sky caught my attention. There it was, higher than I could ever dream of flying. It was silver and shiny, and left a trail of white smoke behind it marking the sky.

"A Sky God!" I whispered in awe.

That roused Old Dude out of his snooze, and he looked up to see what I was talking about.

"That ain't no stinkin' Sky God," he squawked, acting half-way irritated that I would wake him up with something so trivial, "that there's a jet, Squeaker! It's made of metal and it carries people 'round in the sky, even the little-uns. It lands at that there big airport, other side a'town."

Then he settled back to sleep.

How could I believe such a thing? That big silver bird high up in the sky was majestic! It could not be a regular bird. I knew a Sky God when I saw one.

10

SWEETIE PIE

That night, after cleaning up around some garbage bins chock full of goodies, topped off with a drink of cool water from the creek next to the road, I huddled next to Old Dude in his roost under the bridge. The odor was strong and pungent; but it was a warm roost and for the first time I felt as safe as I had felt back in my coop at the ranch.

Old Dude was sound asleep, and whispering something over and over again between his raspy breaths. I cocked my ear closer to hear what he was saying.

"Sweetie Pie," he whispered, and then breathed a raspy breath, "Sweetie Pie...Sweetie Pie..."

On and on he went. I listened for a long time, wondering about it, before falling asleep myself. I dreamed.

I dreamed that I was flying hard through a pitch black, windy sky. Salty sea water was spraying hard into my face and slowing me down. I was exhausted and scared, and lost. I had no idea where I was, only that I had to keep flying, or face certain death!

The dream changed.

My mother was entering the coop through the trap door, ringing the bell. Old George came out, called her, and unclipped the metal canister from her leg.

"She's still got the magic," old George said proudly, "longest, fastest flight yet! She flies like the wind! Good girl, Maria, good girl!"

I dreamed about my beautiful sisters who were so much like my mother. They never had the chance to prove themselves. Then I saw my brave father, whom I never really got to know.

Then I dreamed about my great-great-great-grandfather, who had proven his valor beyond a shadow of a doubt. He was flying against a horrible barrier, too. Only, his barrier was a constant rain of white, hot bullets!

My remaining dreams were peaceful enough; the one-eyed wildcat never made an appearance and I actually got some real rest.

I woke up before sunrise, as was my habit, and saw that Old Dude was still sound-asleep. As quietly as I could manage, I crawled out of his roost and flew out to watch the sunrise. There was that lovely red glow on the eastern horizon, igniting the bases of low-lying clouds with a growing, spreading river of fire. Stars twinkled in the still-dark sky above me.

Several pigeons had already claimed their usual spots on the high lines, and Hawk-Watcher manned his post above everyone. He was doing his job as lookout. I landed next to him and he acknowledged me with his one eye and a bob of his head. He was big and strong, even for a male pigeon, and armed with heavy duty wings and a strong beak. I noticed for the first time how fierce he looked in the early morning light.

"Did you sleep well, young one?" he asked me earnestly.

"Oh, yes," I answered, "Old Dude's roost is very comfortable."

"Good," he replied.

"Hawk-Watcher?"

"Yes?"

"Who is Sweetie Pie?" I asked.

Hawk-Watcher studied me with his one good eye.

"Old Dude whispered, 'Sweetie Pie' in his sleep over and over again," I explained.

Hawk-Watcher bobbed his head and sighed heavily. I could sense that this was a delicate matter.

"When Old Dude was my age," he answered finally, "and I was a little squeaker like you, Sweetie Pie was his mate."

"Oh," I answered carefully, trying now not to overstep my place. I asked, "What happened to her?"

Hawk-Watcher sighed again and shook his head.

"You have to understand, Squeaker," he said, "that beyond all of the banter between me and Old Dude, I have nothing but the highest respect for him. I always have and always will. It is not my place to answer your question. For that, you will have to ask Old Dude yourself."

I bobbed my head and decided to stay quiet. I perched with Hawk-Watcher and gazed at the rising sun.

Old Dude woke up with the sunrise. He landed next to us, stretched his wings and yawned.

"Mornin', boys!" he greeted.

Hawk-Watcher tucked his beak under his light gray wing.

"I wish you wouldn't do that, Old Dude," he gasped, "Your smell is bad enough to stop that traffic down there."

Old Dude ignored him.

"Wonderful mornin'!" Old Dude exclaimed and stretched his wings again. "Are you hungry, Squeaker?"

Enthusiastically, I bobbed my head up and down. I was always hungry.

"Good!" he said, "then let's git ourselves on down to the coffee shop. I got ta catch up on all the latest news, anyways. How 'bout you, Hawk-Watcher, wanna come along?"

Hawk-Watcher gave him the evil eye.

11

BREAKFAST AT THE COFFEE SHOP

"**N**ow, if'n the wind was outa' the south," he gestured with his beak, "we'd grab that tree over yonder."

Old Dude was teaching me his tried and true coffee shop strategy. The wind was blowing lightly from the north, with a distinct chill to it, and so Old Dude hid us midway up a young blue spruce tree. It provided us with ample cover from any danger above, and gave Old Dude a good view of what he was interested in.

Almost directly below us, sitting at an outdoor green metal table, two older men were sipping cups of steaming coffee and sharing big sheets of paper with each other.

"That there's a newspaper," Old Dude explained to me, "there's a new one ever' day and it tells you what's a'goin on in the world. It's got pictures... Oh, you ain't got no idea 'bout pictures yet, do ya, Squeaker?"

I shook my head.

The two men had long, white-gray beards, about the color of Old Dude's feathers. They were pointing at the newspaper and arguing about something.

I asked Old Dude what they were doing.

"Oh, they're arguin' 'bout polytics," he answered, "they's always arguing 'bout them polytics. Might as well argue 'bout what color the sky is!"

I had no idea what polytics were, but it did not seem to be important to Old Dude. He hopped down a couple of branches to get closer to their table.

"When the wind is right, I can git close enough to 'em to read the paper a'fore they smell me," he called up, "come on down, Squeaker!"

"What do you mean, read?" I asked. I was perplexed because something in my collective memory was tugging at me, nagging.

"Oh, yeah," Old Dude said, "don't you worry, Squeaker, I'm a goin' ta learn you how ta read. But right now, I need you to keep yer eye on them other folks out here."

He went on to explain to me what muffins and scones were and, more importantly, how crumbly they were.

"They are 'D'-double –delicious," he said, and then he concentrated on the newspaper.

Sure enough, after two or three minutes, I saw almost half a muffin hit the ground a few tables away. I swooped down next to a lady's shiny black shoes and scooped up a big chunk of it.

"Mmm…blueberry, my favorite," Old Dude exclaimed as we shared it, "good work there, Squeaker!"

"What did you learn from the paper?" I asked between bites. Blueberry was delicious!

"They's a 'nother war yonder in the Middle East," he said with a mouthful of muffin. "Vikings beat the bugsnot out'a them Eagles, an it's a 'goin'a be a long, hard winter!"

Then he kept on reading, while I searched the ground for more grub. Vikings beating up on Eagles? I had never heard of such a thing. I could not imagine how anything could beat up on an eagle.

12

I GO TO SCHOOL

"Old Dude, can all pigeons read?" I asked.

"Only the ones that's got an interest in it," Old Dude told me, "which don't count fer very many, I reckon. Then you got's this thing called smarts, which you and me got plenty of, Squeaker. Not all pigeons do."

It was about mid-morning on a pretty, sunny day, and Old Dude was flying me to a place called a school. We flew low, winding dizzily around trees and poles, but staying high enough above cars and trucks. Old Dude said to watch for a big red brick building. I was not completely sure what bricks were, but I found out soon enough.

"Now, this time o'year when the air is cool, they crack them school windows open, so's all we gotta do is sit on a window sill an' watch an' listen." Old Dude explained to me.

"Now listen up, Squeaker. Don't be a'goin inside that school or I promise you there'll be trouble fer sure. Plenty o'brooms inside a'them there schools! An' them little-uns really like us pigeons, an' they'll do their durndest to lure you in. You got that?"

"Got it."

We found the big red brick building. It sat in the middle of a big grassy field peppered with great big beautiful oak trees. There were a bunch of shiny cars parked out front, and on one side of the school there was a gravel area filled with all kinds of metal contraptions. Kids were out there, climbing all over those contraptions, swinging on them, and yelling and hollering. It reminded me of the 'eatin' place'. I wanted to go over and join in.

"Nope," Old Dude said, "that there's called the playground. We're here fer learnin' you how to read, Squeaker. Follow me!"

We circled the building twice. Old Dude seemed to be looking for something in particular.

"Let's try this 'un," he said finally, and landed on a window sill. The window was about halfway open.

The kids inside were pretty big, bigger than the ones I had seen at the eatin' place. They were sitting on tall stools, fooling around with bizarre looking gadgets on big, black-top tables, peering at glass containers filled with wonderful colorful bubbling liquids. Some were green, some were blue or yellow, and the kids were all wearing big, over-sized plastic things over their eyes and looking at the liquids carefully. Some kids were scooping up powders and dropping spoonfuls into their liquids. The room smelled awful.

"Oops!" Old Dude whispered to me, "Chemistry lab. These kids are too old. Let's keep a' lookin'."

We flapped from windowsill to windowsill until Old Dude found what he was looking for; a classroom full of little-uns.

"This is perfect!" Old Dude exclaimed. The kids had already noticed us and were starting to raise a commotion. The teacher called them back to attention.

"She's sayin' that them are just ordinary pigeons," Old Dude translated for me. I already knew a little of the human language. Don't ask me how.

"She's a' telling them that if'n they leave us alone an' do their work, we can stay."

A little boy turned around and was waving at me.

"Warble, warble," I said.

"Listen up, Squeaker," Old Dude said, "see them squiggly lines on that long white paper a' top o' the blackboard?"

He had to work my eyes onto the blackboard, right behind the teacher's desk, and to the paper above it.

"Them's squiggly lines are letters of the English language," he explained, "you put 'em together to make people words. Then you can look at 'em and talk 'em, or read em' in newspapers an' books and street signs, fer instance. Now I'm a goin' to make the sound fer each of them letters in pigeon, so's you can learn 'em. We can't talk them letters in people language, like them parrots can; but we can sure read 'em and understand 'em.

"After that," he continued, "you'll understand most o'what people say. They ain't never gonna understand you, o' course. Now, if'n you was a parrot..."

The teacher took a pointing stick and started to point to each letter above the blackboard. The kids shouted out

"A"

"B"

"C"

"D"

It was all fascinating to me. Making sounds from squiggles. Who on earth had ever come up with that? When they had finished, Old Dude turned to me.

"Now, you do it with me, Squeaker."

I did my best.

To the teacher and the kids, it probably sounded like warble, warble, coo, squeak, warble and so on. The kids laughed.

"We's a'gonna do this every day they got this here window open," Old Dude told me, "'til you git yer letters down, an' numbers, too. Then we're a'gonna put them letters together to make words, an' then you'll be a'readin' the newspaper with me in no time at all! How's that sound to ya, Squeaker?"

It sounded great to me. We sounded out the letters over and over again, while I wondered if my great-great-great grandfather had ever learned to read.

13

OUR TRIP TO SEE THE SKY GODS

Some theories concerning the demonstrated collective thought, action, and memory in pigeons postulate that it is made possible by sub-particle resonance that seems to ignore space and time. Because of this resonance, pigeons all over the world should be learning to read.

Not all of them using English, of course, but in whatever native human language they happen to grow up around and translate to pigeon language.

I discovered at my young age, however, that reading was not as easy a task as Old Dude made it out to be. He was an exceptionally smart pigeon, and I was not at all sure that I could keep up with him.

He was a harsh taskmaster, easily frustrated. But he still showed me a proper amount of respect, of course, seeing how I was a Prince and all.

"Durn yer highness hide, Squeaker!" He gasped in exasperation one day as we sat on the windowsill of the school classroom. "D-O-G, dog! What can be easier than that?"

The kids were leaving us treats of seed, bread and cookies on the windowsill. It hardly made going to the eatin' place worthwhile. Still, it was the lure of ice cream that usually pulled us away.

Old Dude danced on the sill.

"Dog" I said, finally getting it right, "D-O-G."

It was one of about twenty words we were working through.

"Ok," Old Dude said, "Spot."

"Spot," I repeated, and took a deep breath, "S-P-O-T."

"Fantabulous!" Old Dude exclaimed. "Looky here, Squeaker, ain't nobody never said this was gonna be easy, yer comin' along just fine!"

I loved Old Dude. He had really taken me under his wing, like a new father. Weeks had gone by. I was growing bigger and stronger, and more confident. I was a celebrity at the bridge, with pigeons from all over town flying in to meet me. Old Dude was basking in all of the glory.

Autumn was in full swing. The tree leaves dazzled me as they turned into a fantastic array of bright red, yellow and bronze colors. As the air grew chillier, the people below started to wear heavier clothing like jackets and sweaters. Old Dude told me that the school windows would be closing before long. I wanted so badly for them to stay open.

"Winter, she's a-comin!" Old Dude exclaimed on the colder days.

"Now, I can't have yer a'stayin' here thru the winter," Old Dude told me one lonely windy day, "not a pigeon of yer high Princely caliber!"

I protested. I was as big as Old Dude now, cramping the space in his roost a little bit. I never thought he minded.

"Oh, don't you a'worry 'bout me," he reassured me, "I got my own secret, special place I go to in the winter. Down-right comfortable thru the cold spell. But it ain't no place for a Royal pigeon."

"I don't feel Royal," I told Old Dude, "I've never done anything exceptional, and I'm not half as smart as you are."

Old Dude bowed his head.

"We'll talk to Hawk-Watcher 'bout it," he said quietly.

"Old Dude is right, Squeaker," Hawk-Watcher said after some careful consideration, "you should have no trouble at all finding a human family down south to take you in."

"Durn right," Old Dude agreed, "an' they'll learn you a lot more, too, I'm a'bettin'!"

"But I want to stay with you guys!" I whined.

"That is not an option," Hawk-Watcher declared. As the leader of the flock, his word was final.

"So when do I have to leave?" I asked, visibly shaken and sad now.

"Ah, Squeaker," Old Dude said, "t'ain't going ta be fer a'while yet! You'll be a-readin' that newspaper a'fore you have ta git goin', I reckon!"

He was doing his best to make me feel better.

"Tell ya what," he continued, cocking his head to one side, "you remember them there Sky Gods you was fawning over? Come first calm day, I'll fly you cross-town an' show you where 'bouts they land."

I agreed to that. The magnificent Sky Gods! That was one big mystery that I wanted to solve, once and for all.

Old Dude saw that his suggestion pleased me, and bobbed his head up and down.

"Al'righty, then," he said, "let's us git on down to the eatin' place an' grab some grub! I need some vaniller ice cream! You comin' along, one-eye?"

Hawk-Watcher glared at Old Dude.

"I'll take my chances somewhere else," he answered with indignation, "and I never liked broom boy! I'd like to keep my one good eye!"

"Suit yerself," Old Dude cackled, "come on, Squeaker! Cheeseburgers and ice cream's a'waitin' fer us!"

That night in Old Dude's roost under the bridge I listened quietly while he repeated over and over again in his sleep, "Sweetie Pie... Sweetie Pie..."

I had still not worked up the nerve to ask him.

Two days later, the sun was out, the sky was blue, the air was warmer, and the wind had calmed down. It was time to go visit the Sky Gods!

Old Dude and I set out to the coffee shop for an early breakfast of scone bits. Old Dude caught up on the latest coffee shop news and, to my surprise, I found that even I could make out some of the words on the newspaper.

The two old bearded men, wrapped in wool coats and wearing caps, argued politics as usual and acted like they were mad at each other.

"Always a'worryn 'bout money, them polyticians!" Old Dude exclaimed, sounding like it was the silliest thing he had ever heard of.

"All they a'gotta do," he continued, keeping one eye on the newspaper below us, "is live like us. Then, they don't need no money, or nothin'!"

I thought about that.

"But then who would make the scones and the ice cream for us?" I asked.

"Yer a'gittin purty wise fer yer young age, there, Squeaker," he said a little testily, and then he went on, "an everbody's all over the world always a' fightin. I ain't never figured out what they's all so mad about."

"Well," I said, "I sure hope it ain't about us!"

Old Dude bobbed his head up and down in agreement.

That was that. So we took off and, staying low through the trees, wound our way east toward the far side of town. By the time we stopped on a tree branch to catch our breath, Old Dude particularly, we had gone further across town than we had ever been before. I marveled at how similar everything looked, the same eatin' places, buildings, roads and cars.

"Yep," Old Dude said when he had caught his breath, "a town is nothin' but a big human nest! All towns look purty much the same; only some are bigger an' some are littler."

Then, Old Dude got kind of philosophical. That was a word he had taught me late one night when we were over-gorged with cheeseburgers.

"Squeaker," he asked, philosophically, "if'n you could be anythin' else, 'sides a pigeon, what'd it be?"

The latest newspaper articles must have turned Old Dude into a philosopher or something, I figured. I mulled his question over in my mind.

"If I could be anything else," I finally answered, puffing up my chest, "I would be an American Eagle, King of the Sky! I would rule with terror from above, while everything below me shivered in fear!"

I enthusiastically bobbed my head up and down. A great answer, I thought.

"Dag-burnit, ya young fool!" Old Dude spit out. "T'aint no eagle in the world worth a pound a'pigeon poop! And after all I done learned ya!"

Old Dude was fuming. We flew on in silence a long way to another rest stop, a small park in the middle of town. There was a tall statue of some big, important man in the middle of the park. We landed on his head. A lot of pigeons had been here before, by the looks of the amount of poop on the statue. Old Dude took a poop, too.

"That's what them polyticians are good fer," he danced and cackled, "help yerself, Squeaker!"

I followed his lead and pooped too, but my feathers were still ruffled from his earlier reaction, and he was not finished yet.

"Tain't no eagle never done nothin' fer nobody but his-self!" Old Dude finally explained to me, "You know what he's good fer, Squeaker? Eatin' us, an' rats an' skunks, that's what! Jest think 'a yer great-great-great-grandpappy and other pigeons like him! Tain't no eagle in the world could ever measure up to him!"

I had to agree with Old Dude and I told him so. Not a single eagle had ever come close to accomplishing what my great-great-great-grandfather had done. He had shown incredible selflessness, uncommon bravery, and a true love for humans.

"Take that stupid old bald eagle," Old Dude continued, "them humans made him the national bird! Well, he ain't my national bird! What's he ever done fer his country? Nothin, that's what! He just looks fierce and purty. But he's jest a selfish old raptor, lookin' fer a frog or a gopher to eat. No sacrifice or nothin' on his count. He ain't even smart enough to go to the eatin'' place like we do! No, Squeaker, yer great-great-great-grandpappy is my national bird an' he should be the humans national bird, too! And you know what, they ain't a pigeon in the world that'd disagree with me!"

"You're right, Old Dude," I admitted, "I'm happy and proud to be a pigeon like my great-great-great-grandpappy!"

"Dang right!" Old Dude agreed, satisfied.

"An' another thing. We don't eat other birds fer a livin'," he said proudly right before we took off again, "un-lestin' of course you like them chicken nuggets at the eatin' place."

I had to admit that I loved the chicken nuggets. So I had eaten other birds, too. Just like the eagles. What kind of pigeon did that make me? I must have had a worried look on my face.

"Don't ya worry, Squeaker," Old Dude cackled loudly, "I love 'em, too. Chicken nuggets! D-double-licious!"

14

MY BIG DISAPPOINTMENT

We made one more rest stop in a grove of trees just outside of the sacred abode of the Sky Gods.

"Now listen up here, Squeaker," Old Dude said as he was trying to catch his breath, "them what you call Sky Gods is actually machines called jets and airplanes. I done read all 'bout 'em. Men build 'em, and men and women called pilots fly 'em jest like people drive cars! Them pilots is also always mad 'bout money or somethin'. I done read that in the newspaper, too! More money, more money! Heck, if people could fly like us…"

One of the Sky Gods, a big silver one, flew right over us, drowning Old Dude out.

"Dang!" Old Dude exclaimed, "they sure is loud up close!"

"That there airport," he continued, "is jest over that next hill. Now listen up, Squeaker, them airports has hired a bunch of hawks to keep us away. If'n a hawk comes at you there's only one thing to do!"

I listened intently.

"Yer can't outrun him, so flip over in the air an' let him grab you by the belly."

"Ok," I said, with more than a little trepidation.

"Then, when he least s'pects it, twist 'round hard an' use yer beak to peck him where it really counts!"

What a horrible visual!

"Have you ever had to do that?" I asked Old Dude.

"Nope," Old Dude admitted, "not even sure if it'll really work, but it beats givin' up an' bein' hawk lunch!"

"Oh."

Old Dude's eyes teared up a little, as if he was remembering something sad. He had a far-away look in his sparkling eyes.

"Wanted to do it once," he said quietly, almost to himself, "but I didn't git the chance."

Then, he quickly snapped out of it.

"I did, however, Squeaker," he said as we prepared to take off again, "Gradgiate from Master Bobble's School of Pigeon Self-defense!"

He cackled as we flew over the hill and toward the airport.

The airport was a giant, amazing place, with humans bustling everywhere. There was a huge parking lot filled with all kinds of shiny cars. Beyond that parking lot sat long buildings, two or three stories tall with glass fronts that gleamed in the sunlight. Long, boxy metal arms extended out from the sides of the buildings, reaching out and attaching to grand silver Sky Gods that were perched on the ground.

We flew up over the parking lot and buildings, and landed atop of one of the boxy metal arms.

A huge Sky God sat perched on the blacktop right in front of me; so I looked for its legs and talons. What did I see? Wheels! Wheels, just like the wheels on cars. I felt a tremendous letdown growing in my heart. Old Dude was right; the Sky Gods were just machines. Was there anything that men could not build? I just sighed and stared.

"Squeaker, come on over here!" Old Dude yelled over the loud roaring noise that seemed to come from everywhere at once. He flew over and flopped on top of a smaller Sky God, one that was sitting by itself away from the building. It had loud, whirly things stuck in front of its wings. They were slowly winding down to a stop.

"This here one jest landed," he yelled, "now, looky down there!"

We were huddled on top of the big bird's tail. It was made of a hard, plastic material that reminded me of the red and yellow sign at the eatin' place. I looked down to see what Old Dude was watching.

Humans were emerging from the side of the Sky God, walking down stairs and crossing the blacktop to a door in the side of the building. What struck me as really odd was how unhappy the people looked. Why was that?

"People gen'rally don't much like ridin' in them there airplanes," Old Dude explained to me, "but they go an' do it anyways. Don't know why. Looky there, here come them pilots!"

They were the last ones out. They walked down the stairs, talking and laughing, dressed just alike in blue suits and hats, and carrying boxy black bags.

"Do yer believe me now, Squeaker?" Old Dude cackled.

With my faith in Sky Gods totally destroyed, I admitted to him that I did.

Old Dude flew me to a long, straight road to show me where the airplanes flew down and landed. Sure enough, they stuck their wheels out right before they touched down and then they rolled down the road like a car. Old Dude called the giant black road a runway.

I could see the faces of men through the front windows of the airplanes as they landed. Pilots! My admiration for Sky Gods had plummeted. The big shiny contraptions needed humans inside to show them how to fly.

I spotted four red-tail hawks circling over the end of the runway, forcing Old Dude and me to keep a low profile.

"They make a purty good livin'," Old Dude said of the hawks, "so long as they don't fly into one of them airplane contraptions!"

I tried to visualize a hawk splatting into one of those big, shiny flying machines. That would be a wonderful sight to see.

"Seen enough, Squeaker?" Old Dude asked.

I glumly nodded yes.

"Then, let's git out'a here," he said, "an' keep yer head down, son. Them hawks look hungry."

15

WINTER, SHE'S A' COMIN'

We crossed giant sunflower fields as we flew back to the city. The sunflowers had long since wilted, leaving only browning stalks and the promise of scarce leftover seeds. The sky was still a deep, clear blue, with new clouds starting to grow and billow up high. A light, chilly breeze started to blow in from the north.

As we flew low over the ground, I was startled to hear what sounded like a big pack of barking dogs above us. I looked up and saw big, long necked black and white birds flying fast toward the south in a flock that formed the letter "V" backwards.

"Danged Canadian geese," Old Dude said, panting as he flapped his wings, "dumb birds… almost as dumb as them there eagles! Let's land, Squeaker."

We landed in the middle of a sunflower field and picked through the roughage for old sunflower seeds. The pickings were slim, and my stomach was rumbling.

"They head south," Old Dude explained, "'bout same time, ever' year."

"Where do they go?" I asked, curious. This was my first look at migratory birds.

"Don't rightly know," Old Dude answered, "somewhere's warmer, I reckon. They's escapin' wintertime, but I never foller'd 'em."

"Have you ever talked with them?" I asked.

Old Dude cocked his head and looked at me like that was a pretty dumb question.

"Don't much like geese," he answered, "you kin understand 'em, but they ain't much fer conversation. Kinda reminds me of them penguins!"

"Penguins?"

"They's fat, dumb, short birds that waddle 'round on ice. Cain't fly! No ways! I seen a picture of 'em in the news-paper once."

Old Dude was on a roll again.

"Squeaker," he said with exasperation in his voice, "did you know that this here country got a Penguin Day? They's even got a Penguin Week! What fer, I ask ya! They ain't got no Pigeon Week, not even after what yer great-great-great-grand pappy done fer 'em! A Penguin Day, of all things! Why, they ain't no penguin in flying distance of this here country, 'ceptin fer the ones trapped at the zoo, o'course. They's mostly all livin' down there at that South Pole! A long way's away, I tell yer. How come they's got their day, and week, an' we don't?"

I could not come up with a rational answer, so as soon as Old Dude was rested up, we took off again. I was relieved when we reached our favorite eatin' place before dark. That meant the little-uns, all bundled up, would still be out in the play area. Their extra bundling would make it almost impossible for them to hang on to their food. Better yet, broom boy was done for the day and no one else really bothered with us.

Old Dude brought up the subject of the geese again.

"Sure sign," he said, munching on a french fry, "when you see them geese headed fer south, winter-she's-a comin'!"

I made the mistake of asking him why he called winter a 'she'.

"Ain't I never done learn'd you nothin', Squeaker?" He said, dropping his half-eaten french fry and picking up another one. He launched into a lengthy discourse on the subject.

"Now, listen, don't you believe all that crazy talk 'bout Old Man Winter," he lectured, "that notion probly come from them perfessors or polyticians. They's probly got an 'Old Man Winter' day somewhere's around here. But winter, she's a lady. An' she can be an awful mean lady at that! Ain't you never heard a' 'Mother Nature?"

My mouth was full of chicken nugget, so I shook my head no.

"Hmm," Old Dude said, "sorry Squeaker, thought I already done learned you 'bout that. But winter, she is a' comin', an' you gotta get south real soon now, like them geese, an' find yerself a people family."

"But I want to stay here!" I protested for the umpteenth time, "I like it here."

"An' I'll be 'xpectin' you back!" Old Dude answered, "don't matter, gits too cold here in these parts, an' yer feathers ain't thick enough yet fer you to be able to stay here! Now next year'll be a different story!"

That was all he would say about it, the matter was settled.

Later that night under the bridge, with Old Dude snoring loud and smelling up the place, the ground shook and I heard and felt a deep rumbling noise roll through the air. Our roost swayed back and forth, but Old Dude didn't wake up. Miriam and Helga screeched in their loft further down under the bridge. It must have been a semi rolling under the bridge that I had not spotted, I decided, or a jet flying overhead.

Jets, not Sky Gods!

I mulled over the events of the day. There was no such thing as Sky Gods! What a disappointment! I firmly decided that I would never go near an airport again.

16

THE HALLS OF VALHALLA

Early the next morning, right before sunup, Old Dude woke me out of a deep sleep.

"Today's the day, Squeaker," he whispered quietly, with more than a hint of sadness in his voice.

We flew up to Hawk-Watcher's post. Hawk-Watcher was already standing duty, scanning the early morning skies for predators.

"Today's the day," Old Dude told him.

Hawk-Watcher nodded slowly and looked at me with his fierce one eye.

"It has been an honor, Prince Squeaker," he said. Then he stretched his wings. "I'll make sure to tell everyone that you said good bye."

"Thank you, Hawk-Watcher," I said, "for everything. I feel like I'm leaving my family."

"You are," Hawk-Watcher assured me, "and we will see you in the spring!"

"Come on, Squeaker," Old Dude said, "I'm a'gonna fly with you fer a'while."

"Watch your tail feathers!" Hawk-Watcher called as we took off.

We stopped at the coffee shop to pick up some crumbs. We waited in our favorite tree, but nobody came outside. It was too cold. Old

Dude's remaining feathers were all fluffed up, and I imagined that I looked the same.

"Just be patient, Squeaker," Old Dude assured me, "somebody'll drop somethin' good to eat on the way to their car."

Sure enough, a lady in too big of a hurry and carrying way too much, dropped a scone and a pastry on the sidewalk. She muttered something to herself and ran back into the coffee shop.

"Bingo!" Old Dude hollered. We wasted no time picking up what we could and flying to safety. After gorging ourselves, perched high up on a tree branch, I worked up the nerve to ask Old Dude the question.

Well, almost, anyway. I decided to try a lead-in question first.

"Old Dude," I asked, "if you could be anything else, what would you be?"

I expected an exasperated answer from him, like 'A pigeon, yer dummy, a'course!'

What I actually received was far more surprising. Old Dude stopped eating and seriously regarded me for a long moment. Then, when he answered, he did not sound like Old Dude at all. He sounded like one of those highly intelligent college professors.

"Squeaker," he said carefully, "I have always given that question careful thought. I have always gone back and forth on my ideas and personal beliefs, but not long ago I settled on an answer that I might be able to live with. I think that if I could choose to be anything I wanted to be, I would choose to be a Viking warrior."

A chunk of pastry fell right out of my beak as my jaw dropped. Who was this pigeon? Where had Old Dude gone?

I did know that the Vikings regularly beat up on the Eagles, I had read that with joy from last week's sports page. But I was not really sure what a Viking was.

"Vikings were the greatest of warriors," Old Dude answered, as if reading my mind, "they lived in Norway, many, many years ago. They held a wonderful belief, Squeaker. It is a belief that I have taken to heart for myself."

I nodded, still not sure that this was actually Old Dude talking.

"They believed," he continued, "that if they were good enough, strong enough, brave enough, and cared for their families, they would earn the right to enter into the halls of Valhalla when they died. And there, in those Golden Halls, they would once again see all of their ancestors and all of their loved ones who had died before them."

"It sounds like a wonderful place to go," I said, thinking of my own family and of my unwavering yearning to see them again.

"But what about The Great White Stork?" I asked. "Don't all birds go to The Great Nest in the Sky when they die, to see The Great White Stork?"

"Of course they do!" Old Dude looked at me a little sharply. Then he softened again.

"I was just musing, Squeaker! I am a pigeon, of course. I want more than anything to stand tall before The Great White Stork, just like a Viking warrior was said to stand tall before his god, Odin! I do believe that I'm brave enough, I always tried to do what is right. I was very strong when I was younger and I always tried to keep my family safe!"

How could Old Dude not stand tall before anybody, I thought to myself. He had every right to stand tall!

Then, we were both silent for a while.

I was going to ask who Odin was, but changed my mind. This was the opening; this was my chance.

"Who is Sweetie Pie?" I asked Old Dude, and braced myself.

Old Dude did not answer me; instead, he dropped his head. A moment later, he took off flying.

17

I LEARN THE TRUTH
ABOUT SWEETIE BIRD

I followed Old Dude as he flew roughly southwest out of town. He had no need to follow roads or highways. I recognized that this was the same area I had flown over that chilly morning, long ago, when I had first come to town.

The sun rose higher, and illuminated a long line of red, rocky hills. We crossed the hills and entered a deep, fertile valley, still covered in dark shadows. A swift river ran through the middle of the valley, bordered on each side by thick stands of high grasses and bushes.

Old Dude headed for a grove of oak trees that stood back away from the river banks, and landed on a big branch in the nearest one.

"It was right here, Squeaker." Old Dude said to me when I caught up. He was sobbing.

"The biggest hawk grabbed her with his talons and shot right up into the sky with her. She was my mate for life, my only love. There were three hawks, altogether. They came from those red hills over there. I flew up and fought them as hard as I could, but what good can a pigeon do against three hawks?"

"When did this happen?" I asked Old Dude.

"A long, long time ago, son," Old Dude answered, looking at me for the first time. I could see the terrible anguish in his eyes.

"One of them knocked me into these trees," he continued, "knocked me out cold. By the time I came to, she was gone.'"

"I'm sorry, Old Dude," I apologized, dropping my head, "I shouldn't have asked."

"Oh yes you should have," Old Dude answered sharply, "I wanted you to know! It's just that it's such a shameful part of my past."

"Shameful?" I asked, "Old Dude, you took on three hawks by yourself and tried to save your mate! There's nothing shameful about that. At least you didn't run away like I did. They are saving your place for you in Valhalla. I guarantee it!"

"Well, Prince Squeaker," Old Dude said, "maybe so. I have to confess, I did do some shameful things, though."

"Like what?"

Old Dude dropped back into his usual vernacular.

"Well," he said, "I done snuck up into them hawk's nests more than once when they's wasn't a'lookin', and stealed their eggs. Jest like a rattlesnake!"

"That's pretty shameful," I admitted.

Old Dude cackled, his humor returning.

"Come on, Squeaker!" he said, "I'll show yer the way outta here."

With the wind at our tails, we took to the air and turned south.

"You gotta long ways ta go, kid," Old Dude instructed, "head due south fer at least a week. You'll find a good family down that way. Make sure they's got some kids; that way they won't try an' eat ya! An' make sure you don't go a'poopin' in their house! Poopin' in their house, that'll get you kicked out fer sure!"

Sound advice, coming from the smartest pigeon I knew I would ever know. I was about to answer him back when it happened.

"Look out, Squeaker!"

I felt the razor-like talons tear into my back. I was pretty big and strong now, almost bigger than Old Dude. I flapped my wings hard and simultaneously flipped and twisted around backwards with all of my might. I pecked up at the hawk 'where it counts!' He only grabbed me harder.

"Well, it don't work all the time!" I heard Old Dude yelling. I looked up to see him flapping in front of the hawk that had me, pecking at the hawk's eyes with his beak. In an instant, the hawk released me and clamped on to Old Dude. I was dazed, but I flew up to fight the hawk. Suddenly, I saw the two other hawks diving toward me.

"I'll bet these are the same three that took my Sweetie Bird!" Old Dude yelled, "There's a'goin 'ta be payback time a'comin'!"

I was not sure who would be paying back who, but I did not have a chance to think about it. As I pecked furiously at the hawk with my beak, trying to free Old Dude, one of the other hawks swiped me hard with its talons. I felt the sharp claws rip through my right wing. Then I was tumbling down. I fell into a dizzy spin and plummeted toward the ground. The three hawks ignored me and flew on with Old Dude in their grasp.

"Don't worry, Squeaker!" I heard him yell down to me as I spun round and round, "I still gotta few tricks up my old sleeve! Take care a' yerself and I'll see you in the spring!"

Then he was gone, carried away by the hawks. I splashed down in the river and flopped my way to shore; where I hid in the tall grass. I laid there bleeding, stunned, and devastated; sadly wondering if I would ever see Old Dude again.

End of part one.

PART TWO

A week or so has passed since my birthday celebration. Today, I decided to take a break from writing my story and fly out to the beach. Usually, one of my great-great-great grandkids comes along and we have some fun chasing the tiny crabs that scurry around in the sand. We don't eat them, though. As Old Dude taught me so long ago, there are much better choices on the menu when you live around humans!

Today, I decided to visit the beach alone. I wanted to stare out at the breaking waves and ponder why I, of all pigeons, have been so fortunate. I own my own luxurious urban coop near Grand Park at the center of Skynest. For nearly eight hundred years, I shared this wonderful coop with my one true love, my beautiful mate. I loved her dearly. My eyes grow misty and wet whenever I think of her now. I can still picture her as I first saw her that day on Bird Island, her eyes sparkling as she looked me up and down. She didn't seem to think much of me then. But things change.

Also, I was so fortunate to find my human family so long ago. Most of them still live in Skynest.

Now, for just a moment, I gaze up at the glow of the golden sky. I turn, and look back at Skynest, now a mix of the very new and the very ancient, gleaming brightly in the sunlight with its dazzling, colorful buildings that are actually made of crystal, quartz, and even diamonds. A memory makes me *smile. I once knew a snow goose who loved jewels. She nearly fainted when she first laid eyes on this wonderful city.*

I grow tired. Time to go home. The evening draws close, and all of my favorite eating places will be opening soon. I'll take you back to my story. Where was I? Ah, yes. Old Dude had been carried away by those terrible hawks. And I spiraled back down to earth. It was all terribly sad. And I was all alone.

18

ALL ALONE

For the better part of the day, I remained hidden in the tall, browning grass just a few feet away from a river I had spotted from high above.

I had never felt worse in my life. Aside from my real injuries, I was hurting deep in my heart. I cried constantly, my heart truly broken that I had so miserably failed Old Dude. That image of my best friend being carried away by those foul hawks was burned indelibly into my mind forever. Poor Old Dude, there was no way that he would have had any chance at all. I knew he was gone.

My right wing lay limp beside me, covered in fresh blood. I crawled back to the river's edge to let it dangle in clear, chilly water. I would do that several times a day over the next four days while it healed.

The grassy area was a terrifying place to hide. I had to constantly keep on the move, up and down the river, pausing at bushes to pick at old, dried berries. Snakes, coyotes and foxes were just a few of the many predators who came to the river to hunt and drink. I even caught a glimpse of a bobcat and a small black bear. They all smelled my blood; but I was able to keep a step ahead of them. The foxes seemed to have the keenest sense of smell and they were the hardest predators to hide from. Several times at their wicked jaws, I nearly met the Great White Stork! But each time the foxes jumped me, I miraculously escaped their sharp teeth.

Months earlier, back in town, at the small creek next to the eatin' place, Old Dude taught me how to hear and sense the approach of a predator. It always started with an uncanny quietness; even the bugs ceased their singing or whistling or chirping. Then, there was a faint rustle, or a snap of a twig. Then, longer silence, followed by another faint rustle.

The foxes were definitely the quietest of the predators, and by far the most difficult for me to detect. Compared to them, the snakes were easy, the way they slithered through the grass. All the same; those slinky, crawly monsters frightened me to death.

The noise of the river flowing nearby, with its swift current and its beautiful white water cascading down big, round rocks, helped and hindered me in my quest to stay alive. I had to concentrate on blocking its noise to hear the predators, but it helped hide any sound that I made. It also created its own cool breeze, which I used to help stay downwind of the hunters.

On the fourth day, I knew that I had to fly soon or end up on somebody's dinner plate. I flutter-hopped up into a nearby leafless tree, stretched and tested my wings while keeping a wary eye to the sky. My suspicions were confirmed when fierce shadows of raptors crossed over me, but I was never able to get a good look at them. After flapping my wings for a minute or two, I hopped back down to the safety of the grass, took a drink of water from the river, and hunted around for grass seed.

If only I had been built bigger and stronger like a raptor, I lamented, I could have whipped the hawks and saved Old Dude. Of course, he would have hated me for being a raptor...but I still could have saved him. Logic is not part of the equation when you are grieving and I was still grieving the loss of Old Dude.

I had to get moving. On the morning of the fifth day, just before sunup, I launched myself into the air, flapped hard, and headed for the ridge-line of the red hills. If Old Dude had survived, he would likely be hiding there. I crossed over to the far side of the hills. They glowed blood red in the early morning light from the east. The hawks were probably still roosting in their nests, so I wheeled around and around and looked for them.

Within moments, I spotted a few nests. Sure enough, the big birds were nestled in the shadows of the rocks. I looked for Old Dude; but what I had not counted on was being spotted myself. One of the hawks screeched out a loud warning cry and, in a minute, a whole gaggle of them rose up into the air after me. It was my good fortune that I had a head start and their wings were still stiff from a long night of sleep.

I turned south and flew hard, leaving the whole swarm of them behind me. They lost interest after a few miles and turned back toward the hills. I had no intention of returning, and instead I followed Old Dude's advice and continued to fly south.

My right wing ached horribly and I slowed down to rest it. Flap, flap, glide. Flap, flap, glide. It felt heavy and stiff, but it would hold up just fine.

At sunrise, I basked in the warming air and looked ahead at the endless stretch of ranches and farmhouses below me. From several hundred feet up, I watched as lights flicked on and people slowly walked outside to tend to their animals. Was there such a place waiting for me in the south?

I tearfully thought of Old Dude again as I flew on.

"Yer gave her the old college try, Squeaker," I could hear him saying in my mind, "now git yer tail feathers south, an' hurry! Winter, she's a comin'!"

19

MY JOURNEY SOUTH

As the day wore on, it became obvious to me that I was leaving men behind for more wide open spaces. Farms became fewer and farther between, grass was getting sparse, and trees were almost non-existent. The ground below was mostly bare of vegetation and nothing but rocky hills lay all around.

It reached the point where I became surprised when I spotted any building at all on the horizon; and I started to worry about the obvious scarcity of food and water. Why on earth would any bird head this way?

Then, when I least expected it in the harshest of places, I would spot a ranch and a windmill, a few rusty trucks, and a handful of cattle huddled around a pool of muddy water. Dogs would bark up at me and little-uns would run outside and point at me. I guessed they did not see many pigeons in these parts.

I wanted to find a town, or even a cluster of houses, but there did not seem to be any nearby. Old Dude had instructed me to fly south for at least a week or so; so I knew that I had to press on and be patient. My right wing ached.

At sundown, I found an area of rocky hills that looked to be free of hawks. Pools of water lay in crevices, glinting reddish yellow with the last rays of sunlight. I circled once, checked the area out, and landed near a pool. I rested and drank my fill of water. There were plenty of spiders and ants crawling around, so I hopped back and forth and ate as many as I could before taking refuge in the rocks higher up. There were plenty of places to hide, and the worst sounds I heard were the scratches of lizards as they crawled across the rocks. One little brown spider crawled up to me and gave me a quizzical look.

I felt fairly secure. I rested and watched bats as they darted back and forth in the failing evening light.

It was a clear night, chilly but comfortable, and I watched a full moon start its journey across the heavens. My ancestral memory tugged at me as I watched all of the familiar stars pop into view. It was a spectacular sight, unhindered by any city lights, and something primordial sang to my heart. I could use the stars, I instinctively knew, to guide me south. Tonight, however, I wanted to sleep and rest my wing.

I thought once more of Old Dude, right before drifting off to sleep. He had shown such bravery, attacking that hawk and saving my life. I whispered my thanks to him wherever he might be.

When I awoke at sunrise, I felt stronger. I hopped down the hill and indulged myself in a breakfast of bugs and water.

I took to the air on my southerly course and noticed, after an hour or two, the land below me was once again growing lusher and farms were appearing more frequently on the horizon. Toward noon, I needed to rest and spotted a small cluster of buildings nestled in a fertile valley with a creek running through it. There was a lot of barbed wire fencing everywhere, and I could see a herd of cattle in one fenced off area and goats in another.

Interested, I flew closer and circled the main house a couple of times before landing on top of its weathervane. It was a nice, homey place.

A boy walked out of the barn carrying a bucket of feed, spotted me and stopped in his tracks. Slowly, he set the bucket down and stood there for a moment, staring at me.

"Paw," he yelled, "there's a big dove sittin' on the weather vane!"

"Hot-dawg!" I heard someone shout from inside the house, "let me git my shotgun. Tell maw there's gonna be dove soup for dinner tonight!"

A man with a long beard and brown hat ran out of the house carrying a big stick made out of wood and metal. Old Dude had warned me about those. I flapped my wings and darted straight up as he pointed it at me.

Boom!

The weather vane below me clanked loudly and turned around and around.

"Dang!"

"Missed him, Paw!"

"Well, I ain't done yet!"

Boom!

This time he was closer, and a couple of hot little metal balls hit my tail feathers. They threw me off balance for an instant, but I quickly righted myself and frantically climbed higher.

"Dang!" I heard the man shout far below me.

"It's alright, Paw," the boy said, "Maybe next time."

"First dang dove I've seen in a year," the man grumbled as he walked back into the house.

Mortified, I kept climbing; this hunting for a good family was going to be harder than I had reckoned. I was so high up now that the buildings looked tiny, smaller than me.

That is when I heard the barking.

20

MY NEW FRIENDS

Straight out of the north, coming right at me, was the backward "V" formation of a big flock of geese. They barreled down at me like an airborne freight train.

"Dumbest birds in the world!" Old Dude had said more than once about geese.

From a distance, they sounded like a big pack of baying hound dogs.

Ah-honk, ah-honk, ah-honk!

I ducked down and let them pass over me. Still, their strong turbulent wake nearly flipped me over. I was going to let them fly away, but my curiosity got the best of me.

It took a little effort to turn and catch up with them. They were flat cruising! Flapping hard, I caught up to the right-wing side trailing goose. I flew right beside him and he did not seem to mind at all.

"Warble, warble," I said. Goose translation: "Whats up?"

He looked at me with his big goose face and answered.

"Ah-honk, ah-honk, ah-honk. Translation: "Same old stuff, not much going on. How about you?"

"Same here," I answered.

"I'm glad to see that you still have your tail feathers," he said, "we heard them shooting at you back there."

"It was close," I admitted, "everybody calls me Squeaker."

"Pleased to meet you, Squeaker," the goose said with genuine sincerity, "my name is Henry. I'm the leader of this flock. We let the females lead so that we can maintain a good rear flanking guard for falcons and hawks."

"I hear you," I said, "hawks carried off my best friend less than a week ago."

Henry could hear the sadness in my voice.

"Sorry to hear that, Squeaker," he said, "it happens, and it's never easy."

I watched as Henry flew effortlessly. He possessed a strong, smooth, beautiful wing stroke compared to my haphazard fluttering.

"Where are you headed?" Henry asked me.

"South," I answered, "my best friend, Old Dude, told me I could find a good family of people if I headed far enough south. And I could stay warm, too."

"Old Dude...," Henry responded, "now, that's a name I haven't heard in a long, long time."

"You knew Old Dude?" I asked, astonished.

"Everybody knows Old Dude." Henry stated, and sadly shook his head. He was quiet for a while, as quiet as a goose can be in a formation headed south.

"Hawks!" He finally exclaimed with sadness. "I always liked Old Dude."

And so I flew along with Henry. I soon learned that the geese were very accommodating; they almost immediately accepted me as one of their own. News of who I was spread across the formation like lightning and soon every goose was switching positions to get a chance to talk to me.

I received questions like: How far south are you headed? Who was your father? Who was your mother? Do you want to winter with us? We like to land in marshes, so your feet might get wet and sticky. Is that ok?

I eventually worked my way back to Henry.

"Tomorrow we will pass over a nice town," he said, "that you might want to take a look at, but you are welcome to stay with us as long as you want."

I was about to answer when he screamed out: "Hawk! Pull it in!"

The "V" formation came together and formed into a tight ball of flying geese.

"He's after you, Squeaker," Henry told me, "stay right here under my wing."

It was the biggest hawk I had ever seen, diving down out of the sky at full speed. As the formation maintained its tight ball shape, he veered off.

"He won't blow through a tight formation," Henry explained to me, "there's too much of a chance that he might break a wing."

The hawk wheeled around, climbed high and made a second dive.

"Tighten it up!" Henry ordered, "he's coming back for more!"

The formation packed itself in even tighter and the hawk veered off again. He tried four more times until, with an angry screech, he gave up and flew away.

"He's tired," Henry said, "it takes a lot of effort to dive on geese that many times. He was a powerful one, though."

I thanked Henry profusely for his protection. Old Dude had said they were dumb birds. I looked at the majestic black and white bird flying next to me.

Dumbest birds in the world? Not in my book!

21

JEWELL

I could see no marshy areas in sight, but Henry settled the flock
down for the evening in a tall, grassy field that held the promise
of seeds. Even on the ground, the flock huddled tightly together.
Henry posted lookouts, checked on everyone's well-being, and then
hopped back over to me.

"You can stay with us as long as you want, Squeaker," he said,
appraising me with his black, shiny eyes, "but we have a long, long
journey ahead of us. That town I told you about may have what you
are looking for. It is a pretty big town and it has one of those great
big schools on its south side. It is full of young people. Young people
always seem to like birds."

I thanked him again, and told him that I would follow Old Dude's
advice to look for a family and I would check out what the town had
to offer. Besides, my own city flock would be waiting to see me again
in the spring.

Henry agreed.

"You're not quite a yearling yet, are you?" he asked while appraising me, "I didn't think so. You are just the right age to catch a good
family! A word of caution, though. We've observed humans for
quite some time, and if you stay with the good ones too long, you will
become attached to them."

I did not think so. From what I had observed of humans, they honked their horns, yelled at each other, and dropped their food a lot. I could not imagine staying with them any longer than I had to. Part of me wanted to stay with Henry and his flock.

"Come with me, Squeaker," he said, "I'll show you a hidden spring of fresh water."

"Henry," called an older goose who came wobbling up to us, looking me up and down, "it's a clear night, a beautiful night. I thought we were going to stay high up on wing."

"Not tonight, Bernard, "Henry said, "tonight we will rest. We will fly through tomorrow night if we can."

"Sounds good to me, gentlemen...cheers!" Bernard said, and wobbled away.

It dawned on me that this night's rest break had been taken only for my benefit. Otherwise, the flock would have still been headed south in wing formation, ahead of the frigid air. I was humbled by their generosity.

Henry lead me through a swarm of geese, each of them honking a greeting to him and nodding to me, up to the edge of a pool of clear water gurgling up from an underground spring. The water was cool, delicious and refreshing.

"We've known about this particular spring for about six thousand years," Henry explained as I drank, "we only have to keep an eye out for predators."

"As always," I responded.

"As always," he agreed.

An elegant female goose glided over and landed beside us.

"Squeaker," Henry said, rather formally, "I want to introduce you to Jewell, my mate. She is named Jewell because she loves shiny things."

"My pleasure," I greeted her.

"Mine also," Jewell answered with a delightful, sweet goose voice. She was absolutely beautiful. "I like all kinds of pretty things and I think that you might be the prettiest pigeon I've ever seen, Squeaker!"

I was too flattered for words, and a little embarrassed. My plume fluffed up a bit. Henry and Jewell laughed a friendly, amused laugh.

"Don't be embarrassed," Henry said kindly, "you are our guest of honor tonight. Everyone knows that we have a brave little pigeon as our guest."

"It is definitely an honor for us," Jewell told Henry, "rumor is circulating around the flock that Squeaker comes from a very special lineage."

"I must hear more," Henry said, surprised, "in a little while, we will form our evening story circle, Squeaker. You can tell us your story."

Later, when I had finished telling the flock the story of my great-great-great grandfather, I realized I had won the respect of every goose present.

"I only hope that I can live up to him," I said in conclusion.

"You will," Henry assured me, "I have no doubt of that."

I went on to tell them the story of my wonderful mother, and of the horrible attack of the one-eyed wildcat.

"We heard about that," someone in the circle said with sadness, "every goose in the world knows about that terrible night by now. We are so sad for you and your family, young Prince."

The moon glowed down on us from high in the night sky, the stars pierced the black velvet of darkness like fierce, sparkling jewels. I looked around at a hundred shiny pairs of eyes staring intently back at me. Friendly eyes. And their heads bobbed up and down as a show of respect.

They wanted more stories, and I certainly did not want to finish on such a sad note, so I told them several funny tales concerning the exploits of Old Dude.

Everyone honked and cackled.

"I'm really going to miss Old Dude." Henry said. "He was such a character! But with Hawk-Watcher taking over from him, your flock is in good hands."

I had to agree with that. The rest of the evening, the geese told me tales of their ventures north in the great lands of ice, of strange creatures and mountains of crystalline ice that floated in deep, blue waters. One by one, the geese started drifting off to sleep.

"I need to go switch out the lookouts," Henry told me. I nodded and then looked up to catch a shooting star streak across the sky behind his head.

"Tomorrow you can decide what you want to do," he continued, "until then, don't worry about it. Sleep well, young one."

With that said, he disappeared into the dark.

22

A TERRIBLE DREAM

I had a terrible dream that night, one that I desperately wanted to wake up from. I was flying through dark clouds, through rain and mist, and the sky glowed orange all around me. I was flying frantically and I had some kind of idea that everything counted on me, as if a matter of life and death hung in the balance. How could I know this? I could see Old Dude's face, hear his voice urging me forward toward some unknown, but critical goal.

"Almost sunup, Squeaker."

Henry's voice roused me out of the dark dream. I looked up to see his round head and long bill silhouetted in the early morning light. Sunrises were beautiful here in the land of no people. The only other noise that I could hear was coming from the heavy breathing of a hundred sleeping geese. Some of them were stirring awake and honking. The early morning air was chilly and calm.

"You must have had a bad dream," Henry mentioned as we hunted for seed, "I heard you talking and groaning in your sleep."

"It's a dream I keep having," I told him, "over and over again."

I told him about the dream, the dark, stormy sky, and my frantic mission. Henry cocked his head to one side, and a look of concern filled his eyes.

"There is a myth among geese of dark times past and dark times coming; but no one knows when, for certain."

"Dark times?" I asked, with a sense of dread arising from the remnants of the dream.

Henry sensed my discomfort

"It's only a myth, Squeaker," he assured me, "a goose fairy tale."

I was not buying it.

"What was I saying?" I asked him.

"You kept saying: "I have to find it…I have to find it!""

"Find what?"

"You didn't say," Henry answered, "now go to the pool and get a drink, Squeaker. We will fly shortly."

I made my way to the spring pool and sipped the cool water. It made me feel better and the dream started to fade. All of the geese were up now, pecking at seeds on the ground and drinking from the pool. Shortly thereafter, we took off at Henry's command, in wing formation, and headed south.

I flew next to Henry, who resumed his position at rear guard. It was the safest place for me to be, beneath his protective wing.

It was strange. I had only met Henry the day before, yet I felt as if I had known him my whole life. Not that I had lived a whole lot of life yet, but I felt a close, special kinship with him. Like Old Dude, he was a true friend. It was not something that I even had to really figure out. It just was.

Around mid-day, I was sad to see the outskirts of a town growing on the horizon. Henry seemed sad, too.

"There it is, Squeaker," Henry said as we drew closer, "we'll fly directly over the center of town and let you make your decision. Don't worry, we've never spotted any human hunters here."

It was not a very large town, certainly not even a small fraction of the size of Hawk-watcher's city. It sprawled beneath us on flat, grassy fields, with a few low hills squatting in the far distance. I recognized the signs of a couple of good eatin' places. But my mind was still not made up.

Then I saw it on the southern edge of town. It had to be the biggest school I had ever seen; ten times bigger than Old Dude's elementary school. It was absolutely huge, with a lot of open windows. This is the place, a voice inside my head whispered to me. The things I could learn here!

Henry sensed my excitement and gave me a sad nod of his head.

"This is where we part ways, little brother," he said, "go down there and find your family."

"But Henry..." I protested.

"No but Henry!" he said firmly, "I can see it in your eyes. You know it, too! Something is waiting for you down there. Go find out what it is. Don't worry, I'll see you in the spring."

Sadness overwhelmed me. Would I ever see Henry again?

"How will I find you?" I asked, choking back the tears.

Henry laughed.

"You just ask any goose you see," he said, "they will know."

"Thank you, Henry," I choked, "for everything."

"You are welcome," Henry said, "just make sure that you look for us in the spring. Now, go on."

"Goodbye," I said as I pulled away from the giant V formation, "don't forget about me!"

"How could we," Henry called back, "you are part of our flock!"

I turned toward the school as a hundred geese shouted: "Goodbye, Squeaker! We love you!"

I circled high above the school for at least half an hour, working up my nerve. There were rows of big red brick buildings that seemed to stretch on forever. On the east side of the campus, five long, two-story buildings stretched out as long as a town block. They resembled the apartment buildings I had seen before. Students carrying books were walking out of those buildings and heading along sidewalks to other, even larger buildings. I swooped down and landed in a small, scraggy tree to get a better look.

These students were older; much older than any students I had seen before. What kind of school was this?

I took off and flew toward the long row of buildings.

"Look at that, a pigeon," I heard someone below me say.

"Probably serving stewed pigeon for lunch today," someone else commented, "he probably got away."

A cacophony of laughter followed from the other students.

I spotted a window that was halfway open on the second floor of the second long red brick building.

Go there, a voice inside my head said. I agreed, and flew toward it.

23

MY NEW HUMAN FRIENDS

I landed on the red brick window-sill and crept to the edge of the window, craning my neck to peek inside and expecting to see a classroom full of kids, but this room served some other purpose. My best guess was that this must be a human coop, judging from what I saw inside.

Two young men sat on their beds facing each other, arguing about something. One bed was neat, with its fabrics folded and tucked. The other bed looked just like Old Dude's nest, a total mess. The coop contained some things that I immediately recognized, such as tables and chairs, books and magazines, and a lot of food scraps on the floor. Bingo! The side of the coop with the messy bed was particularly littered with all kinds of delectable crumbs.

The neat young man was dressed nicely, had a kind face, and talked with a soft voice. He had darker skin than the other boy, and wore thin wire-rimmed glasses. It was the messy boy who intrigued me the most. He wore dirty, but colorful, clothes, had long knotty hair and a thick, curly black beard. He was arguing with the neat boy about something in a loud, almost booming voice. I listened in.

"Come on, dude! It's winter solstice, dude! It only comes around once a year! You gotta go to this outrageous party! Meet me at the town cemetery at seven! Free food, dancing and girls! Stupid pagan rituals that are fun! It's the best party of the year!"

I perked up. He had called the neat boy 'dude', like Old Dude! I hopped from foot to foot. How many dudes could there be in the world? This was a good sign; I had to be in the right place.

"No can do, Marshall," the neat boy said quietly, "you know how I feel about that stuff."

Marshall threw his hands up in the air and said, "Kenny! What am I going to do with you, bro?"

Then he picked up a white, fluffy pillow and threw it at the Kenny, who laughed.

"Look, dude, you are my best friend. You know I have to offer," Marshall said, "and you need to think about your self-respect. You can't hide in a cave the rest of your life!"

"Don't get me wrong," Kenny said, "I appreciate it, Marshall, I really do. I know you are trying to look out for me. I'm just not into ancient pagan blowouts, you know? I know it's just a party, but I'm just not into it."

"Just this once? For your old pal, the thespian genius?"

"Sorry Marshall, but no!" Kenny answered, standing up, "Fiona and I have other plans, anyway. Hey...look at that bird!"

I was busted! They spotted me. Might as well introduce myself, I figured. I warbled and strutted along the window sill into full view like it was my sill.

"It must be some kind of dove," Kenny observed aloud, "a pretty one."

"That's no dove," Marshall corrected him, "when you come from the Bronx like me, you know a pigeon when you see one."

"Oh," Kenny said. He jumped off of his bed and walked slowly toward me.

"Come here, buddy," he said gently, holding out his hand, "don't be afraid."

His eyes were kind, but still some fright instinct deep inside of me triggered and I flew off the sill.

I flew, circled high above the building, and thought about things. First of all, I doubted that this school really cooked pigeons for lunch. I never saw pigeon on the menu of the eatin' places. But you never knew. On the other hand, how was I ever going to get to know humans if I didn't take a chance? Old rancher George had been so kind to me and he was a human. Maybe these humans were kind, too.

I circled around in the sky for a while, watching the neat boy lean out of his window to watch me. He finally gave up and disappeared back inside. I landed on the windowsill again.

I could see Marshall crawling around on the floor, picking up chips and pizza and crumbs.

"Let's give him something to eat," I heard him whisper.

I took a deep breath, flew into the room, and landed on Kenny's shoulder.

Marshall stopped what he was doing and looked at me with amazement.

"Wow, dude!" he exclaimed, "Look at that! He must be a circus pigeon or something!"

"He sure is pretty," Kenny observed, twisting his neck to look at me, "do you have a name, buddy?"

I puffed up my feathers and answered. "Warble, warble."

"Wow, dude, he knows you're talking to him," Marshall observed, "but 'warble, warble' isn't going to cut it. If he stays, we need to give him a real name."

"Yeah," Kenny agreed, "I hope he does stay, but it's time for chemistry class. Fiona's coming by any minute."

Kenny held two fingers to me and I hopped onto them. He smiled at me.

"Yep" Marshall said, "I have rehearsal in twenty minutes. The stage is finally finished. You're coming to see me in the play tomorrow night, right?"

"Wouldn't miss it for the world" Kenny assured him, "Even if it is a week past its scheduled opening. I'll be getting home just in time for Christmas Eve because of you!"

"My pal!" Marshall smiled widely, showing his teeth through his thick, black beard.

"The Tempest!" he exclaimed, "Shakespeare! Full fathom five my father lies...!"

There was a knock on the door, and a nicely dressed girl opened it from the outside. She had dark skin like the neat young man, long dark hair, and pretty brown eyes.

"Ready, Kenny?" she asked. She carried two thick books under her arm. Kenny grabbed his books, walked to her, grabbed her books, and pecked her on the mouth. What a curious gesture! She smiled brightly up at him and then looked at me, where I was still perched on his other hand.

"Look who came to visit," Kenny said to her, nodding at me.

"How nice," she said, "but won't he mess up your room?"

"Not any more than Marshall does," Kenny said with a laugh and shrugged his shoulders. He carefully set me down on a flat, wooden table, "I don't even know if he is going to stay here."

I hopped around on the table, flapped my wings and warbled at him.

"Goodbye pigeon," he answered me, "I hope you stay."

"Yeah, pigeon," Marshall said, following the other two out the door.

"Eat anything you can find," Marshall called out as he shut the door.

I sighed and looked around the room. I had done it. I now had real human friends.

24

COLLEGE CAMPUS

How fine of my new human friends, I sighed, to allow me the free run of their coop, or dorm room, as they called it.

I took a deep breath of satisfaction and hopped around the table to explore. Kenny's side of the desk had a very neat stack of big, thick books, paper and pens, and a very nicely framed picture of Fiona. As far as humans went, I thought that she was very pretty. In the picture, she smiled right at me. I liked that, so I smiled back at her. I hopped over and worked out the letters on some of Kenny's books. The words that I sounded out were completely unintelligible to me.

A-s-t-r-o-p-h-y-s-i-c-s!

Q-u-a-n-t-u-m T-h-e-o-r-y.

M-e-t-e-o-r-o-l-o-g-y.

As Old Dude would have said about my ignorance of these titles, "You ain't that learned yet, Squeaker!"

That was for certain, but he would then always add, "But don't you never give up! Learnin' is hard, but it's the best way to spend your time, period, hands down!"

Yes, I would make it my mission to learn what these books were about. I hopped down to the floor and crossed over to Marshall's messy side, where crumbs lay scattered everywhere. They were salty, like french fries, but tasty. Marshall, I realized, must be as messy as the little-uns at the eatin place. Pigeons would never let so much food go to waste.

After eating my fill, I jumped up on Marshall's side of the desk and looked around. There were no books anywhere, just a jumble of colorful magazines. Some of them had pictures of pretty smiling girls on the covers; others had pictures of cars or motorcycles. It was an interesting assortment, but I wondered where his real learnin' books were.

He had a small fold-out computer on his desk. I had seen people use them at the coffee shop. The screen that folded out on Marshall's had a fish-lady on it, swimming up and down and in circles. How did I know about fish?

"That there is a trout," Old Dude had pointed out the shiny water creature to me at the creek, "Eagle's will try an' catch 'em sometimes, hawks and crows like 'em when they're dead and washed up on the grass."

That is how I knew. This one was different, though. It was half-fish, and the top half was a human girl. She was swimming around and around on the moving picture. I watched her for a couple of minutes until I got dizzy.

I looked at the lower half of the computer and recognized a strange layout of the alphabet. Good! I sounded out the letters a few times; it was good practice.

I was getting thirsty after eating all of the salty food, so I hopped all around the room. No water in sight!

Ok, I said to myself, time to go hunt for a creek or a pool. I flew out of the window and high above the school to look around. I scanned the skies, always mindful of hawks.

The bigger buildings at the school were arranged together to form a large square with an open area full of browning grass and trees in the center. Right in the middle of that open area sat a stone water fountain. The water surrounded a rock platform upon which a statue of a fierce-looking, bearded man stood holding books under his arm. Probably a professor or a politician and, being a new guest, I decided not to land and take a poop on his head. Besides, unlike Old Dude, I did not have anything against professors.

I landed on a branch of the tree closest to the fountain. It was a large oak tree that still had most of its leaves because of warmer temperatures this far south. The area was empty of people, except for a boy and a girl who sat together on the stone rim of the circular fountain, holding hands. They looked nice and harmless, so I hopped down next to them and dipped my beak into the cool fountain water.

"Hello, little pigeon," the girl said sweetly, and soon tossed cracker bits onto the ground below me. I obligingly hopped down and pecked at them.

"What a cute bird," the girl said. The couple studied me for a few minutes before standing and walking away

I hopped back up on the fountain's edge to drink, and looked down at my own reflection in the water. Green head, gray eyes, light brown beak; I had grown so much and I looked more and more like my mother. I had her strong, streamlined body, made for flying fast. I carried no hint of my father's rough features. How curious.

I drank my fill, warbled a 'thank you' to the fountain, and then flew back up to inspect the school. I chose a four-story building that had most of its windows open; and landed on the nearest sill.

The classroom was stark, compared to the classrooms Old Dude and I had visited months before. Just chairs, desks and a blackboard. The desks held sleepy-eyed students, as old as Kenny and Marshall, who listened as the teacher droned on and on about things that I did not understand, like "The Symbolism of Don Quixote's Quest" and the "Essence of Existentialism". It made my head spin. I flew on to visit more windows.

I recognized the contents of one classroom. It held big, black tables covered with glass things, burning flames, and horrible smells. A chemistry lab.

Kenny and Fiona sat on high stools at one table, fooling around with a glass thing full of blue liquid. Fiona spotted me in the window, tapped Kenny on the shoulder and pointed at me. I left and flew on to the next classroom. The smells were just too awful.

After looking into a few more classes, I stopped on a sill and heard a teacher talking about something that caught my attention.

"So far, our studies of Morphic Resonance," he was saying, "an instantaneous communication across great continental distances, as evidenced by the communication between flocks of pigeons from England to flocks in China, are yielding astonishing findings. Also, consider the Blue Jays, who in England were taught to open the lids of milk bottles. The Blue Jays in China instantly exhibited the same new skill."

He is talking about pigeons, I thought to myself. I might be welcome here.

"The big question is," the teacher continued, "is this a communication that defies the accepted laws of space and time? It seems to me that this communication occurs on a sub-quantum level, using an unknown medium that defies space and time."

I flapped into the room and landed on the shoulder of a girl with cropped, black hair. I liked her shiny eyeglasses. She turned to me with a look of surprise on her face, and I pecked her on the mouth like I had seen Kenny do to Fiona.

"Ouch!" she said.

The other students howled with laughter.

"My word!" the teacher exclaimed as he noticed me, "what have we here? Did one of you set this up?"

No one spoke; there was only more laughter.

"If not," he said, "this is extraordinary!"

I hopped to another girl's shoulder and pecked her on the cheek.

"Ouch!" she said quietly, "go away!"

"If the theory of morphic resonance is correct," the teacher observed, "pigeons across the world might be exhibiting this bird's unusual social behavior right now! This little guy looks like a beautiful wayward homing pigeon, a descendant of the ancient African rock dove."

He talked on and on while I hopped around the room and ended up perched on his big desk.

"Welcome, young pigeon," he said to me. He turned back to his class. "Rock doves were imported to the new world by the French in the early 1600's. They were used as food, a delicacy. As they escaped and grew in numbers, they tended to stay in cities. The city buildings reminded them of the cliff structures in Africa, their natural habitat. They flourished and, voila! We have pigeons everywhere now."

"Mmm, a delicacy," one of the boys said, "can we invite him to dinner?"

"Yuck!" several of the girls said.

"Actually," the teacher interrupted, "this looks like a special bird, from a special line." He proceeded to talk about the rich history of homing pigeons.

"If we could catch him...," he started to say. I hopped on top of his head; and then bounded out the window, leaving the laughter of the students behind.

He was right, I thought to myself as I flew away, I am from a special line.

25

MY NEW NAME

I spent the rest of the afternoon flying around the town, scoping out which eatin' places were the best targets. This town seemed to be a nice enough place to stay, although it was much smaller than the city I had left behind.

Sure enough, I located the familiar red and yellow sign, with the familiar enclosed little-un play area, so I knew that I would not go hungry. The little-un's were really revved up and running crazy all over the place, so I snuck in through an open spot on the side of the building. I watched the action carefully and before you knew it, ice cream hit the ground!

A couple of sparrows darted in behind me and pecked at french-fry bits on the ground, but they left me alone to enjoy my treat. I kept my eyes open for the local broom boy, but no one seemed to be on duty here. This place felt like it was a lot safer than Old Dude's eatin place.

After gorging myself, I roosted lazily in a nearby tree until almost dark, and then decided to head back to Kenny's room. I reached his windowsill just as the sun was setting, leaving behind pretty red and golden clouds.

Kenny must have come back sometime in the afternoon, and left again. His table lamp was now turned on and I could plainly see most of his books lined up in order. Marshall's fish girl swam around and around on his computer. I followed her around and around again until I was dizzy. One of Kenny's books lay open on Marshall's table. I took a look and saw that it contained words and definitions. Old Dude had shown me the same sort of book at the little-un's school.

"This here's called a dictionary," he had explained to me, "you can use this here book to learn you any word you can't figure out on your own."

I decided to look up astrophysics. The book's pages were heavy for me and took some effort to flip through. I was worn out by the time I found the A's at the front of the book. Here is what I found:

Astrophysics: plural in form, used with a singular verb. The physics of stellar phenomena.

Great! That really helped! I couldn't understand a single one of the big words that explained my big word. Thanks, Old Dude!

"Hey, look at that! He's reading your dictionary, dude!"

I looked up to see Marshall stumbling in through the door. He looked even dirtier and more disheveled with his long hair and beard frayed out in all directions.

"Probably more like eating it," Kenny said, coming in behind him. I was surprised at how late it felt, far past my roosting hour. I had been working at the dictionary for hours.

"Dude, you should'a been there!" Marshall told Kenny. "Full red moon, young maidens dancing around the blood red headstones, singing out to the Druid spirits! And best of all, free grub!"

"I thought you did all of that on Halloween," Kenny said with a bored voice.

"Halloween, Winter Solstice, St. Pattie's Day, who cares?" Marshall answered with a big grin. "We use any excuse we can to party!"

I flapped my wings and landed on Kenny's shoulder.

"The Tempest is on for tomorrow night, right?" Kenny asked.

"Tomorrow night, it's our first and final show, dude!" Marshall affirmed.

"Then its home for the holidays," Kenny said, smiling, "we need to decide what to do with this pigeon."

"Kenny, can't you see he loves you? He's going with you, dude," Marshall said, "and you're driving home, after all. I'm flying."

I studied Marshall with astonishment. He had long, pale, skinny arms, hairy, but definitely no feathers. How could he possibly fly? How could that be possible? I tried to picture in my mind Marshall flying and laughed so hard I nearly fell off of Kenny's shoulder.

"Well," Kenny decided, "it's his decision. He can come with me if he wants."

"Hey, pigeon," Marshall called, looking directly at me, "we came up with a perfect name for you!"

"Warble, warble," I answered.

"Walter!" Marshall said, laughing and giggling, "perfect name for a pigeon. Just like that old timey actor, Walter Pigeon! He made goofy movies in the 1940's and '50's."

"You have to spell it differently," Kenny said, "The actor's name had a 'd'! Pidgeon!"

He looked at me.

"It is a good name." He told me softly. "You can decide if you like it or not."

"Warble, warble."

Walter. A weird name, but I could get used to it.

Later, I dozed off perched on the footboard of Kenny's bed, as they called it, while Kenny and Marshall watched TV. I was vaguely aware that Marshall was messing with the TV and Kenny was telling him to leave it alone. Then, something fantastic happened!

"Hey look, there's that old dude!" Marshall exclaimed.

My eyes snapped open. I hopped over to Kenny's shoulder and looked all around the room. I did not see Old Dude anywhere. How did they know about Old Dude?

Marshall was pointing at the TV. A well-dressed young man with perfect brown hair was talking to a tall, older black man who had curly white hair and a white beard, dressed in overalls just like old rancher George. When the old black man talked, he had that same wise sparkle in his eyes that Old Dude always had whenever he decided to start philosophizing.

"How do you answer your critics who say you are just another alarmist like the Y2K people?" the young man on TV was asking the old man.

"The Y2K people were sensationalists," the old man answered with a slight frown, "they deceived a lot of people. Now that New Year 2000 is long, long gone, no one listens when a real crisis comes up. And believe me, this is a real crisis! How many earthquakes have you had this month? In places that do not have earthquakes!"

"Listen," the old man continued, "Just let me warn your viewers. This is real!"

The old man in overalls turned to look out from the TV directly at us. I jumped a little.

"Please, folks, consider your children. Let me explain what we have learned."

Marshall laughed and clicked the box in his hand. The picture on the TV changed to some weird, loud-mouthed guy chopping onions with a big shiny knife and yelling at us at the same time.

"What a whack job, Kenny!" Marshall said, laughing. Kenny yawned.

"Do you mean this obnoxious onion guy or my grandfather?" He said. "Be careful, Marshall! I might take you home to meet him someday, and you'll be sorry!"

"Don't take it personal, Kenny!" Marshall chided. "I just think your grandpa is delusional."

"Maybe, but let me ask you this," Kenny answered, "are you a good swimmer?"

"I'm a great swimmer," Marshall told him, "I can tread water for hours and hours!'

"That's not quite long enough," Kenny said, grinning back at him, "try treading water for months, or years."

He turned to me.

"What do you think, Walter? Who's the real whack job?" he asked.

"Warble, warble," I answered as I lazily flopped over to Marshall's shoulder and tried to catch the popcorn he was tossing in his mouth. Marshall could not stop laughing and reached up to pet me. I was tired and my head started to nod.

"That's what I think," Kenny agreed, "time for bed."

I flapped back over to Kenny's footboard while he climbed into his bed. He yawned and smiled warmly at me.

"Goodnight, Walter," he said.

"Warble, warble."

That settled it for me. Humans were not bad. Not bad at all!

26

ROAD TRIP!

Two days later, Marshall said his goodbyes and caught a taxi to the airport.

"See you after break," he said to Kenny, and then winked at me.

"Walter, you are going to love riding in Kenny's bug," he said, laughing.

Terrible confusion flooded my brain. I twisted around on Kenny's shoulder and watched Marshall carry his bags away. How on earth could Kenny and I fit into a bug? Bugs were little bitty critters that scrambled away from you screaming in terror while you pecked at them. That is, when you could not find anything tastier to eat. I just could not picture Kenny and me riding in something that small. It was impossible.

I made up my mind that I would fly alongside, at a distance, and observe while Kenny performed this marvel. Knowing what I did about the speed of crawling bugs, I surmised that we would not be traveling very fast or far. Kenny grabbed his bag and we headed outside to the gigantic college parking lot.

"It's that yellow bug over there," Kenny said, pointing to a little round, yellow car. Why, it was not a bug at all. That jokester Marshall had fooled me again.

"They call it a Volkswagen," Kenny explained to me, "or VW bug for short. It's a German car, Walter."

Even for a car, it was still a little small; but I could see that we could both fit inside of it with no problem at all, even with Kenny's bag."

Kenny threw his bag into the back seat, and then draped a sheet of plastic over the right front seat.

"You'll ride shotgun, Walter...here," he said, pointing at the plastic, "just in case you have an accident along the way. It's a long drive."

I dropped my head. I felt humiliated and crestfallen. I had carefully followed Old Dude's advice to always poop outside, never in a human's home. Standing on plastic for just a few minutes is torture to a pigeon. No, I decided, I would not do it!

All around us, students were packing bags into their cars. Kenny waved to a few of them. Fiona ran over and pecked Kenny on the mouth, and then patted me on the head. I had no trouble imagining how pretty she must look to Kenny.

"Have a Merry Christmas, Kenny!" she said cheerfully, "and you, too, Walter!"

"Warble, warble!"

"He's so cute," Fiona gushed, "do you think he'll be back with you after break?"

"That's entirely up to him," Kenny told her. I liked that about Kenny. He never really tried to control me, other than his effort to make me perch on this stupid plastic.

"Merry Christmas!" Kenny told Fiona, pecking her on the mouth again. He reached into his coat pocket and handed her a small, brightly wrapped package.

"Don't open it until Christmas day," he told her. Fiona reached into her bag and pulled out a package for him.

"I love you," she said as she handed it to him.

"I love you, too," Kenny said back.

"Not until Christmas!" Fiona said, wagging her finger.

"I promise," Kenny said. We watched her as she ran to her car, her beautiful black hair bouncing in the sunlight. Kenny sighed. I could tell he was in love; I was in love with her, too.

"Warble, warble," I said, consoling him.

"Thanks, Walter, let's get going."

We jumped into the bug and were on our way. Kenny's bug made a series of funny, coughing noises as he fired it to life. It sputtered for a minute and then settled down to a steady rumble.

"So far, so good," Kenny muttered under his breath, "Grandpa fixed it last summer."

I sat quietly on the plastic covered seat until Kenny pulled out of the parking lot and onto the road. With Kenny concentrating on his driving, I seized the opportunity to hop over to his right shoulder.

"No, Walter," Kenny said, and reached up to grab me, but I was too quick for him. As his hand came up, I crawled around his neck to his left shoulder. Back and forth, shoulder to shoulder I hopped as the bug puttered down the road.

"Walter!"

"Warble, warble!"

Kenny finally gave up, and I settled down on his left shoulder and enjoyed the ride. Kenny kept the windows open to let the cool breeze blow in and I could feel it flowing through my feathers. It felt like I was flying through the air. I tried to watch every single road stripe as it passed beside the bug, but it made me terribly dizzy after a minute or two.

What a magnificent machine the yellow bug was! I laughed at myself for being so confused about it. It glided down the desert high-way like a giant bird of prey. I was certain that it could outrun a hawk; and I marveled at the ease with which Kenny operated it.

Humans are amazing creatures! They build such incredible machines, and then continuously complain about them. If Old Dude and I had owned one of these wonderful bugs, imagine the possibilities!

The desert stretching out around us was a pretty, empty place, except for little prickly bushes, and an occasional ugly buzzard and, every once in a while, a long string of signs popped up alongside us. Ten – More – Miles –– To – Calvin's – Corner – Gas – Burgers – Candy – Soda – Beer.

I read every one. It was fun, and helpful, to practice my English.

Occasional cars swept past us heading the other way and I twisted my neck backwards to watch them fade into the distance. Then, a big sixteen-wheel semi blasted by and Kenny struggled to keep the bug on the road as the semi's wind wash smashed into us. I flapped my wings and struggled to stay on his shoulder.

"Semi's," Kenny muttered.

"Warble, warble."

Old Dude had been right. Perch on the wrong side of the wires and a sixteen wheeler plows by under you and its bye, bye you, pigeon!

27

ROAD TRIP, PART 2

The highway cut a black, straight line across the sandy desert floor, as far as my eyes could follow. The ground to either side of the road was as flat as the runways I had seen at the airport. Except for the very occasional car or big truck that would rush past us headed the other way, causing the Bug to shudder and me to jump and squawk, I felt like Kenny and I were the only boy and pigeon in the world.

Kenny had been right, it was a long drive. We headed south and east all day long, stopping occasionally so that Kenny could stretch and I could fly around the Bug a few times and poop in the desert. There were curious sights to see during the stops. I liked looking at the lizards that tried to hide under the prickly bushes, and I was fascinated by the funny large, black beetles that stood on their heads and soaked up the sunlight.

"Watch out for snakes, Walter," Kenny warned me with concern in his deep brown eyes, "they hide under the sand and pop up if you get too close to them."

Great White Stork! That settled me down. It seemed like no matter where you go in the world, something patiently waits to make a lunch out of you.

"Ever' things out ta eat you, Squeaker!"

The Bug performed without a glitch and Kenny was obviously very satisfied with it. It hummed along the highway like it was happy to be out of the student parking lot.

As the rhythmic white lines of the highway passed by us and hypnotized me, my mind drifted back to that television program that Kenny and Marshall had watched the other night. Who was that old, bearded rancher man and what had he been warning about? It was a mystery that I really wanted to solve; but lacking the communication skills, it was impossible to ask Kenny. He definitely seemed to know something about the whole matter. I did not place much weight in Marshall's whacky opinions, and I was still peeved at him for switching the TV off.

"You can't believe that tripe!" Marshall had exclaimed to Kenny the next day, in between reciting lines from ""The Tempest".

"Read his book," Kenny answered, and sighed.

"'Full Fathom Five Thy Father Lies, of His Bones are Coral Made'... look Kenny, the debate is over! Over twenty thousand scientists disagree with your grandfather, the mighty Sir Alfred! Twenty thousand!"

"And over twenty thousand scientists are dead wrong," Kenny answered quietly while turning a page of his book on nanotechnology, "and you are dead wrong, too, Marshall."

"'Those are Pearls That Were His Eyes: Nothing of Him That Doth Fade, but Doth Suffer a Sea Change'...Sir Alfred! Where did he get a title like that, Kenny? From a box of Cracker Jacks?"

"From King William of England, dummy!" Kenny answered, engrossed in his book.

"'Into Something Rich and Strange, Sea Nymphs Hourly Ring his Knell... What do you think Walter?" Marshall asked, looking at me. I was perched on Kenny's shoulder.

"Warble," I answered. I did not have enough information on the subject to have an opinion, but I was listening with interest.

Sir Alfred, I now thought to myself, watching the highway lines go blink, blink, blink. What a wonderful name! I wondered if there were any 'Sir' pigeons in the world. My great, great, great (and more) grandfather should have been a Sir, but I had never heard anyone give him such a title.

Kenny was alert, driving and listening to some lady on the radio whine loudly about her broken heart. I closed my eyes and drifted off to sleep. I dreamed.

I dreamed that Old Dude and I were playing together, soaring high through thick, billowy white clouds. The sky, in contrast, was the deepest beautiful blue I had ever seen. Old Dude looked as young as me, and he was laughing.

"I knew yer would do well, Squeaker!" He called to me over the whoosh of the wind. "Yer a fine young pigeon now, son. Keep on a' keeping on, yer picked yerself the best family ever!" He soared ahead of me, and gently rolled across the cloud tops toward a golden setting sun. He flew so fast, I could not keep up with him as he disappeared into the golden light.

Kenny woke me up. "We're almost there, Walter," he said. The sun sat low on the western horizon and we were now driving across rolling, grassy hills dotted with occasional short, stubby trees.

Kenny slowed the bug down and pulled into a service station.

"Gotta get some gas, Walter," he told me, "you'd better stay put. There might be cats around here."

"Warble, warble."

"Here you go." He placed a little bowl of water and a dish of cracker crumbs on my seat. I was hungry, thirsty and grateful.

"Another tank of gas," he said happily when he finally climbed back in. He carried an open can of soda in one hand.

"Sorry about the radio, it's old, but it works," he said.

He fired up the bug and switched the radio back on. At first, it sounded like a rattle snake, hissing and rattling; but Kenny twisted its knob and finally found a station where some poor guy was howling in pain to slow, twangy music like he was caught in the talons of a red-tailed hawk. I felt sorry for him.

"Nothing but country music." Kenny told me apologetically. "Ahh, Walter! There's nothing like life on the open road!"

And down the highway we rolled.

28

I MEET GRANDPA

Within the next hour, I could see the lights of a small town ahead as the sun started to set.

"Let me tell you about my family," Kenny offered as we drew near the town's city limits.

"Warble, warble."

"Well, Walter, you have my Grandpa," he started, "and Grandma passed away a few years back. Grandpa really runs the place. Then there are my parents, George and Janine, and my little sister, Dottie. Grandpa is working on a big project. Dad oversees the farm chores and helps Grandpa."

That is what I really liked about Kenny. He had a way of talking to me as if I were his equal. It was as if he was convinced that I could understand every word he said, which I could, for the most part.

"Just wait until you see Grandpa's big project," Kenny continued, "it's incredible. Now, I have to warn you about our big black cat, Bear. He's got a pituitary gland problem, and he is twice as big as any other cat I have ever seen. He shouldn't be a problem for you, Walter, because he's pretty clumsy. He can't climb up trees or anything; he gets about halfway up them and falls down. If he tries to bother you, just fly up a tree or get on the roof or something. You'll be ok."

"Warble, warble."

"Do you like dogs?"

"Warble, warble."

"Good. We have a brown female dachshund named Schatzie. She's really friendly, and I'll bet the two of you will get along just fine."

The town lights were growing nearer. I could just make out the buildings and trees in the town.

"We have some chickens, a milk goat named Myrtle, and a billy goat named Jack. Watch out for Jack!"

We drove a little further and pulled into town.

"Welcome to Jerome, Texas," Kenny said.

There was not much to be impressed with. We passed the town square and shot out of the other side of town in the blink of an eye. I was disappointed; not a single familiar eatin' place in sight. There might be tough pickin's ahead, as Old Dude would say.

A mile past town, we slowed down and turned onto a dirt road next to a mailbox with the name 'Jerome' printed in fading letters on it. About a hundred feet up the dirt road, I spotted a white farmhouse with a big wrap-around porch, and a big, red barn that stood back just a little further. The farmhouse and barn were both lit up with festive strings of colorful lights; and a well-lit, colorful tree glowed in the center of the house's big front window.

"Look at those Christmas lights, Walter," Kenny exclaimed as we drove up the dirt road.

We pulled up to the house and a lady ran out to greet us. She had long black hair and wore a nice, dark red checkered dress that billowed out in the evening breeze as she circled the bug to reach Kenny's window.

"Merry Christmas, honey!" She screamed, reaching in to hug Kenny's neck. "How was your drive?"

Merry Christmas, Mom!" Kenny said happily. He patted the top of his steering wheel. "The yellow beast made the trip just fine, not a hint of trouble."

By this time, a large black man wearing a green cap with the yellow words 'John Deere' on the front of it joined Kenny's mom. He had a weathered face, a short black beard and bright brown eyes.

"Merry Christmas, son," he exclaimed with a smile, and reached through the window to shake Kenny's hand. So this was George and Janine, I surmised, Kenny's parents. They looked like wonderful people, all dressed up for Christmas Eve. George wore a pretty red shirt and dark slacks for the occasion.

"You're just in time for Christmas Eve dinner," Janine exclaimed, "let's get you inside before it gets cold out here."

Kenny opened his door. A little shy, I hopped over to the plastic covered passenger seat and perched on top of the headrest.

"How is Dottie?" Kenny asked.

"Oh, she can't wait to see you, Kenny," Janine gushed, "she's inside lying on the couch, waiting for you!"

"And who is this little sidekick?" A gentle, deep rumbling voice asked through my passenger side window. It startled me so badly I nearly fell off of the headrest. I turned to see a big black man with a ruddy weathered face, merry brown eyes, a white beard and salty white hair. He smiled broadly and his eyes sparkled as he looked at me.

Kenny laughed.

"That's Walter, Grandpa," he said, "I'll tell you all about him."

"Walter Pigeon," the man with the white beard said with a deep, merry laugh. He leaned in through the bug's window and spoke with a quieter voice.

"I have waited so long to meet you, Walter," he said, "we are going to be great friends. Please, call me grandpa."

His sparkling eyes were deep and hypnotic. What kind of vast intelligence lay hidden behind them? It was real, I could sense. And he looked oh so familiar to me.

I looked into his eyes, bobbed my head, and said, "Warble, warble."

"He likes you, Grandpa," Kenny said, laughing.

Grandpa smiled again. A great, wide smile!

29

KENNY'S FAMILY

Kenny's family wasted no time helping us out of the Bug, including Kenny's big overstuffed bag, and into the house. They moved as rapidly and efficiently as Henry's snow geese.

"Let me get that," Janine said.

"I've got it, Pop," George said to Grandpa as they wrestled over Kenny's bag.

I perched on the plastic, proud that it was still clean, until Grandpa presented me with two strong fingers.

"Come along, Walter," he said.

I hopped on, and into the house we headed.

"You can understand what I'm saying, can't you, Walter," Grandpa whispered to me as we walked.

I bobbed my head and answered, "Warble, warble."

"Excellent" he said, smiling, and stopped on the front porch, "why don't you fly around a little, stretch your wings, and I will leave the kitchen window cracked open for you. Oh, and watch out for our big black cat!"

I knew that the cat he was referring to was Bear, the one Kenny had warned me about. I had no idea what a kitchen was. I would just have to fly around the house and look for it.

With a last "warble" to Grandpa, I flapped my wings and took off toward the barn. There were several large bushes nearby, so I picked one, roosted and did my business. Then I took off and headed behind the barn to get a look around.

There was nothing but a tiny wooden shack out back behind the barn, with one locked door and a dark window.

I circled the farmhouse and spotted the window that Grandpa had left half-open for me. As soon as I landed on the sill and peered inside, I became overwhelmed by the wonderful smells drifting outside with the warm air from the kitchen. It was heavenly and intoxicating at the same time.

"There he is!" Janine called out. She was wearing a white covering over her checkered dress and stirring something in a big pot with a big wooden spoon. Other steaming pans held all kinds of wonderful looking food.

"Purty good fixin's!" Old Dude would say. My feathers puffed up in anticipation of the coming feast.

Kenny walked into the kitchen, saw me and pointed to a tall, oblong white box.

"Watch how smart he is, Mom." Kenny whispered to his mother Janine, loud enough for me to hear. He looked straight at me and motioned at the top of that white box.

"Walter," he said, "this is the refrigerator. This is your perch. When you are in the house, you have to stay here on top of it."

I half-heartedly flapped my wings and headed for the refrigerator. It was taller than Kenny, so that when I landed on top of it, I was looking down at him and his mother. There was a newspaper placed up on top. At least they were thoughtful enough to give me something to read. Next to the newspaper sat a bowl of birdseed and a bowl of water. Birdseed! In the middle of all of this food with all of its wonderful smells? Who did they think I was? My heart dropped as I sniffed at the seed.

"Slim pickin's!" Old Dude would say.

I dutifully perched on the top of the refrigerator and read the headlines of the newspaper. Snowstorm in New York Bronx! The accompanying photo showed humans running like crazy around a street while being pelted by something white and flaky. There was nothing else in the headlines, just boring stuff about wars. I took a look around the kitchen, recognized the sink and the stove from pictures that I had seen before. The kitchen door opened up to a larger dimly lit room. A long, red cloth covered table took up the center of that room, with a half-dozen dark wooden chairs carefully placed around one end of it. It was lit only by candles, and covered with shiny plates, silverware and glasses, not to mention several bouquets of red flowers. The table had a warm, inviting look to it.

Grandpa took his seat at the table. Propped next to him, on a big soft chair filled with blankets and pillows, was a frail wisp of a little girl. She reminded me of a new born hatchling in a nest. Her skin was very sallow, she had big brown eyes like Grandpa, and long, black hair. She wore a soft plush red dress and had a matching ribbon in her hair. That must be Dottie.

"He is smart!" Janine said, startling me. "He hasn't moved from his spot, Kenny."

"He is real smart, mom," Kenny agreed, "wait until you've watched him for a while."

"Help me with the dishes dear, everything is ready to serve."

Soon, pretty music was playing in the background, and the entire family was seated at the table wearing, as Old Dude would say, their finest duds. Janine and George sat together on one side of the table, Grandpa at the end, and Kenny sat next to Dottie on the other side.

"Merry Christmas Eve!" Everyone but Dottie announced, lifting their red liquid filled glasses.

"Warble, warble!" I called out from my newspaper.

Everybody laughed. I could hear a dog barking from another part of the house. That had to be Schatzie the dachshund, I deduced.

"Let us bow our heads and pray," Grandpa continued, "Dear Lord,…"

Just at that moment, I caught the sly movement of something tremendously big slinking across the kitchen floor. I looked down into the giant green eyes of the biggest black housecat I had ever seen. He was nearly as big as the one-eyed wildcat of my nightmares. Bear! He glared up at me with nothing but obvious malice on his mind. I danced nervously on the newspaper while I watched him devise his plan.

30

CHRISTMAS EVE DINNER WITH THE

JEROMES

Grandpa continued his prayer in the peaceful comfort of the dimly lit room, with nothing short of a feast spread out in front of him.

As far as Bear was concerned, I was his feast for dinner. He carefully watched me dance around high up on top of the refrigerator, looked around the kitchen for any potential witnesses, and then stared directly back at me with his giant green eyes.

"Don't worry too much about Bear," Kenny had said earlier.

Right! Thanks, Kenny!

A tall chair sat against the kitchen wall, right next to the refrigerator. Bear looked at the chair and got an inspired look in his evil eyes like a light bulb had just popped on in his head. With the grace of a fat turtle crossing the road, he clawed and struggled his way up onto the chair, looked up at me, and grinned.

Could he make the jump up to me?

Kenny had told me how clumsy he was; but all he had to do was stretch out to almost reach the refrigerator top. No way was I going to hang around and find out. I flew off of the refrigerator, out of the kitchen into the dining room and across the long table, carefully weaving back and forth between the burning candles, and landed gracefully on Grandpa's right shoulder.

"Amen!" Grandpa said, and turned to look at me. Dottie looked up and smiled at me.

"Dear, dear," Janine said as she reached for another bottle full of shining red liquid. George shook his head.

"Walter!" Kenny said reproachfully.

Then there was a howling cry and a loud crash in the kitchen. Kenny turned around in his seat to take a look.

"It's Bear, mom," he said, "he was trying to jump up on the refrigerator."

"Good move, Walter!" Grandpa said, smiling down at me.

Kenny was already up and walking by us carrying Bear to another room. His big green cat eyes glared maliciously at me. Next time, his eyes seemed to say.

"I'll put Walter back up on the refrigerator," Kenny said as he returned.

"No, no," Grandpa countered, "Walter is part of our family now. He can sit here on my shoulder."

And that was that.

When no one was looking, Grandpa snuck me tastes of every delightful morsel on his plate. Janine filled everyone's tall glass with the red liquid, except for Dottie's. Dottie hardly touched her food, but continued to smile weakly at me.

"Dottie, you must eat," Janine told her, "I know the medicine makes you sick, but you have to eat."

Grandpa offered Dottie a spoonful of something delicious, but she folded her arms and frowned.

"Come on, honey," he pleaded.

"How's the project coming along, Grandpa?" Kenny asked.

Grandpa took a sip of his red liquid and looked at George, who smiled back.

"It's finished, Kenny," Grandpa said, "your dad and I are now well into the testing phase."

"I'll be able to help," Kenny said, "I made A's in astrophysics and nanotechnology this semester."

"Why, Kenny!" His mother declared. She and George clapped their hands.

Grandpa smiled at Kenny.

"I knew you would!" he exclaimed, and raised his glass. "To Kenny, a true Jerome!"

"Here, here," Kenny's parents cheered in unison, joining Grandpa with their glasses.

The music playing in the background was so soothing and pretty. It was not anything like that loud claptrap noise that Marshall cranked up back in his dorm room. It calmed me and I started cooing to it.

"That's a good Walter," Grandpa whispered.

A dessert of delicious pecan pie followed dinner. Grandpa made sure that I received my fair share, and offered me a sip of his water. He called the red liquid in his other glass 'wine'.

"You're not quite ready for that, Walter," he assured me.

After dinner, the family gathered together on the couch and chairs in the front room next to the colorfully lit tree. Brightly colored packages were spread out beneath its glowing branches.

"It's called a Christmas tree, Walter," Grandpa explained to me as George and Kenny made Dottie comfortable.

Grandpa picked up a large, black book from its holder on a lamp table and opened it up.

"Now," Grandpa announced, "it's time to tell the story of the first Christmas."

It was a fascinating story, and vaguely familiar to me. I loved the part where everybody followed the bright star in the sky. Why, that is also what pigeons do, they follow stars! Geese, too!

Grandpa finished the story and George announced that it was time to observe the family Christmas Eve tradition. Everybody would open one present. Grandpa hurried to the tree, picked up a package, and carried it to Dottie. As I flew across the room to Kenny's shoulder, Grandpa helped her open it.

It was a computer of some sort, similar to Kenny's with the exception that it did not fold open. It was just a flat screen that had all of the alphabet keys on it.

"Now you can talk to us, Dottie," Grandpa explained to the pale little girl, "just type in what you want to say and see what happens."

"Dottie's been sick since she was six," Kenny whispered to me, "she has not spoken since then. It's the cancer. Two years."

Dottie busily typed and the letters showed up on the screen. "Thank you, Grandpa! I love you!"

"Okay, now push this button," Grandpa pointed out with his large, weathered hand.

Dottie pushed the button and I heard a little girl's voice say "thank you, Grandpa, I love you!"

George and Janine gasped. Janine had tears in her eyes.

"Oh, dear!" she exclaimed.

Grandpa smiled and kissed Dottie on her forehead.

"You're welcome, honey," he said, and then turned to us.

"Built it all myself," he proudly explained, "I synthesized Dottie's voice from some old videos we had stashed away. Worked like a charm."

Dottie typed in something else on the computer and pushed the button.

"Hi, Walter!" her little voice said, and she smiled weakly at me.

"Warble, warble," I said back. I cocked my head and studied her computer for a long minute. It held great possibilities!

Hmm...

31

DOTTIE

W hat a fine family the Jeromes made. They handed each other gifts, cheerfully opening them and singing quietly to the Christmas music I enjoyed so much. While Janine brought in a tray of nicely decorated cookies and a pot of hot cider, I heard the words to 'Hark the Herald Angels Sing', then, 'Joy To The World' quietly sung as Kenny opened his present to find a new light green fleece jacket inside.

"Boy, do I need this," he said, and thanked everyone.

George opened a box containing a new pair of leather work boots. Janine opened a small bottle of sweet smelling perfume.

"Thank you, dear," she said, smiling, to George, "it's my favorite."

I sat on Grandpa's shoulder and listened to 'Oh, Little Star O' Bethlehem' while he opened his present. It was a book with the title 'Albert Einstein.'

"Dear old Albert," Grandpa whispered quietly to me under his breath, "He was such a good friend to me, Walter."

Dottie fell sound asleep. When the time came, Grandpa gently lifted her frail body off of the couch and carried her to her bedroom. Her thin arms dangled limply in the air as he slowly walked.

Grandpa Jerome was a big man, as far as men went, and he looked to me to be strong enough to pick up the whole couch if he wanted to. He moved as gracefully as a cat; not like Bear, of course, but a real cat. Like the alley cats I had seen in town. I knew from the look of his white beard that he had to be old; but his big brown eyes sparkled like those of a young man, or even a child. He was a wonderful man, full of life.

Dottie's bedroom was decorated as colorfully as a rainbow, in full majesty after a spring storm. Flowers and butterflies, birds and animals covered the walls. Multitudes of stuffed animals, bears and tigers, giraffes and elephants, surrounded her bed. Horses and penguins, dogs and cats, I had seen pictures of them all at Old Dude's school. As I looked at them, even the stranger ones, I felt some faint, distant memories of experiences far in the past, of an ancient life of flying high above the elephants, gorillas and giraffes in a far off, distant land. It was that 'collective memory' tugging at me again.

I searched the pile of stuffed animals to make sure that a real one, a giant evil black cat, was not hiding in there somewhere. I saw no evidence of him.

Grandpa laid Dottie gently down on her bed and kissed her forehead. He then moved aside so that Janine and George could take over making their daughter comfortable for the night.

"Thank you, Grandpa," Janine said with a kiss.

"Come on, Walter," Grandpa whispered to me, "let's step outside for a moment and take in the beautiful night."

I hopped from the top of Dottie's dresser to his shoulder and we proceeded out of Dottie's bedroom, through the front room and out the front door. I looked up into a clear night sky full of bright, twinkling stars. Grandpa pulled a beautiful redwood pipe from his jacket pocket, stuffed it with a fragrant tobacco, and lit it up.

"It's called a pipe, Walter," he explained to me.

"Warble, warble."

I recognized a pipe when I saw one. I liked pipes. The old professors who drank coffee and read the paper on the patio of the coffee shop smoked them. Old Dude used to hop around trying to avoid the sweet smoke so he could read their paper.

"Durn pipes!" he would exclaim in frustration. I would hold my ground and enjoy the spicy clouds of smoke billowing up around me, then. Not only was it pleasant. It also had the wonderful effect of blocking out Old Dude's strong body odor.

"What a night!" Grandpa exclaimed. He raised his right hand and motioned it around in circles.

"Go ahead, Walter," he told me, "fly around the house a few times. Stretch your wings."

I took to the air and enjoyed the brisk chill of the night. I circled the house, keeping an eye out for barn owls.

When Grandpa was finished with his smoke, we returned to Dottie's bedroom. The lights had been turned out, leaving only the glow from the open bedroom door and silver glint of the moon outside shining in through Dottie's window. The sparkling eyes of a hundred stuffed animal eyes gleamed up at me.

Grandpa dropped to his knees beside Dottie's bed, clasped his hands together and bowed his head.

"Help me pray, Walter," he said quietly. I truly believed that his prayers would reach The Great White Stork also, and I followed along.

"Our Father..."

"Warble, warble."

"Who art in heaven..."

"Warble, warble."

"Hallowed be thy name..."

"Warble, warble..."

And so it went. Grandpa prayed for a long time. "Please, Lord," he prayed," find it in your heart to heal this little girl......" He prayed for his family and for me. He prayed for some things to happen and for some things not to. "All according to Thy will," he prayed. I did not understand everything, but I sensed by the intensity of his voice that it was very important. Finally, he was finished and looked me in the eye.

"Prayers said on Christmas Eve are very special." He whispered. "I knew you were coming, Walter. I've known it for a long, long time;

even before you were born. I know that you are here to help us. I once had a very strong vision about you; you were flying as hard as you could through terrible darkness, struggling to save us."

"Warble."

"That's right! You were flying to help us. And in my vision, you were not alone."

"Warble?"

Grandpa smiled. "In my vision, there was a bright, glowing pigeon flying along on each side of you."

He offered me his two fingers and set me down on Dottie's dresser. "I'll be right back, Walter," he said, "I forgot something.""

When he returned, he carried in a tall brass perch and a handful of newspapers.

"Your Christmas present!" Grandpa announced. He set the perch down next to Dottie's bed and arranged the newspapers around its base.

"Stay here with Dottie, Walter, and watch over her. She really needs your help."

"Warble, warble."

I hopped up on to the perch. It contained a flat, soft area on one side where I could roost comfortably and a brass bar on the other.

"Don't you worry about that cat," Grandpa assured me. "He's going outside for the night. If you see the dog, don't worry about her, either. She won't hurt you."

"Warble, warble."

"Merry Christmas to you, too, Walter," Grandpa smiled as he left the room.

When little Dottie opened her eyes early on Christmas morning, I was the first sight that she saw; a pigeon perched on a shining brass pole, haloed in the full glow of the early sunlight streaming in through her east facing window.

She smiled at me.

32

CHRISTMAS DAY

I am typing furiously now, my dear friends! The thought of Christmas always invigorates me, and for me this was the most special Christmas of all! Especially because this was the particular day that the mystery began. It all started with the tiny building out back.

It was called the shack. I flew all the way around the little building that sat in the middle of a big field behind the farmhouse, looking for a clear window to peek inside. There was none.

I studied the tiny shack all through the morning, sat on top of it, tried to sneak in when Grandpa or when George entered it. My efforts were all to no avail. I was not allowed inside because of something George called 'contamination'! I would have to look that word up in the dictionary.

It was a huge mystery to me. Where was Old Dude when I needed him? He could probably explain what the shack was. I watched in vain as Grandpa, George and Kenny went inside and emerged tired and worn out later that afternoon. I declare, there wasn't enough room for all of them to fit inside!

"You're doing great, Kenny," Grandpa said, patting Kenny on the back as they came out, "you'll make a fine scientist."

I spent a large part of Christmas day sadly perched next to Dottie's bed. She slept a lot and took a lot of medicine. I was heartbroken when I learned that her beautiful long black hair was not her own.

"It's called a wig, Walter," Janine kindly told me as she held it up in the sunlight and brushed it while her daughter slept.

"Dottie lost all of her hair," Grandpa explained to me later, "when she started taking her medicine."

What kind of medicine does that? I had been under the impression that medicine was supposed to do good things for you. This stuff made all of her hair fall out? No wonder she felt so puny, she was probably too angry to talk to anyone.

"It's a good medicine, Walter," Grandpa continued, nearly making me squawk. This would not be the first time that I had the overwhelming impression that he was reading my mind. Even when he was sad, Grandpa's big brown eyes sparkled while he quietly studied me. We were swinging softly in the front porch swing in the late afternoon, something that Grandpa enjoyed and did often. I perched on his left knee and looked up at him. Inside, Janine read Dottie's favorite book to her about the strange going's on during the night before Christmas. A fat, jolly old man flew a big red sleigh pulled by reindeer and delivered presents to every child who had been good during the year. The whole story sounded like a pretty far stretch to me, but after learning all kinds of amazing things from Old Dude that had turned out to be true, who knew?

The funny thing was, the pictures of Santa, that was the jolly old man's name, were the spitting image of Grandpa in an almost uncanny way, except that Santa was white. Grandpa was not as fat as Santa, of course, being a rancher and all, but the resemblance was remarkable.

"Dottie is very sick." Grandpa told me sadly. "Our prayers, and her medicine, are the only things keeping her alive."

When Dottie was awake, which was several times that day, I would hear her computer say "I love you Walter" and I would look to see her smiling weakly up at me. I would land lightly on her shoulder and rub my head up and down on her cheek.

You can save her, Walter.

Where did that come from? It was like the distant rumble of a familiar voice deep inside my head. What did it mean? Christmas night, and every night afterward, Grandpa and I knelt beside her bed and prayed for her.

All Christmas day, Bear, the cat, worked and plotted ways to get to me, but I quickly learned how dumb he was. It was funny and serious at the same time. I always kept in mind that he might get lucky.

He fell off of everything he tried to climb. That afternoon, as I sat on the branch of a leafless tree, Bear stealthily climbed up its trunk. I pretended, of course, not to watch him.

Halfway up the trunk, Bear fell off and landed flat on his back with a loud, painful howl. He fell out of the tree! I did not think such a thing was possible. That was like a crazy pigeon pulling in his wings on purpose and dropping to the ground! Bear rolled over and stood up, grumbling to himself in cat language, and waddled off to hatch another scheme.

Also on Christmas Day, I met and made friends with Schatzie, the family dachshund. She was genuinely elated to meet me. She jumped up and down, panted with her tongue hanging out, and tried to lick me. I had to hop around quickly to avoid being drenched by the waterfall of her pink, lapping tongue.

Schatzie was a sweet creature, but also every bit as dumb as Bear. She had a big, red ball, and constantly begged me to push it around the yard with her. I obliged, and we spent hours pushing the ball, avoiding Bear, until I could hardly stand up. Schatzie never grew tired of the game. She was a perpetual ball pushing machine.

In the barn, I watched in fascination as Janine milked Myrtle, the goat. Myrtle had a kind, gentle nature and I sincerely wished to learn goat language. She would happily hop up on the milking bench and wait for Janine's expert milking hands.

Language was a problem for me. I knew pigeon, of course, and human, although I could not speak it, goose, and that was about all. You would think that with all of our vast collective memory, pigeons would know more languages. I just found that not to be the case.

Goat language would have come in handy in my dealings with Jack, the billy goat. He was a mean one, and I had a few choice, ugly words reserved for him. He would stare at me with his stoic, golden-slitted billy goat eyes and then try to run me into the ground with his ramming horns. I had to be content to warble indignantly and fly away from him. Like Bear, he was always plotting ways to get me.

So, holidays continued and then New Year's Day came and went. It was time for Kenny to return to school. Was I going back with him? I liked my new home and I really did not want to leave Dottie or Grandpa. But I also loved Kenny; so I was torn.

Grandpa quickly settled the matter. "Walter has to stay here," he told Kenny, "Dottie needs him and I have work for him to do."

Kenny was sad, but agreeable, and bid me goodbye. I sadly watched him wave goodbye and drive down the dirt road in his wonderful yellow bug.

"We have a lot of work to do, Walter," Grandpa informed me, his big, strong arms folded across his chest.

33

SCHOOL TIME

Janine was a teacher at the school.

"You should come with me today, Walter," she told me on the morning of the first school day following the holidays. Both she and George had started talking to me the way Grandpa did.

"The kids would love to meet you," she said. Grandpa nodded his approval at breakfast. I was sitting on his shoulder, finishing up a syrupy piece of pancake he had just snuck to me.

Janine drove a giant car, a brown Pontiac station wagon, and so we climbed in after breakfast, me perched on her shoulder, and drove to town.

"Now you will need to behave yourself, Walter," she warned me in a distinctly teacher-like tone, "and stay where I tell you to stay."

"Warble, warble," I agreed.

Janine was all made up like the teachers I had seen in Old Dude's school. She wore dark red lipstick, was dressed in a long, dark dress, and carried her long black hair all bundled up on top of her head. She looked like she meant business.

By any standard that I knew, Jerome, Texas had a very tiny school. It was a small, white wooden building containing just two classrooms separated by a door in the center of the inside wall. Out front, right above the front school entrance, a sign read: Jerome School, est.

1898. As we parked in a small lot across the street, Janine explained to me that it was a very old school, well over a hundred years, and that one room taught grades one through six. The other room was her room and held the students for grades seven through twelve. It was one of the very few two-room schools left in the country.

"I specialize in science, Walter," Janine told me, "but I teach everything."

In my eyes, Janine grew taller and taller. What a smart lady! I could learn a lot from her.

Confirming my suspicions about the small size of the town, there were only a handful of students in each room. Janine's students walked in and surrounded her desk, looked at me perched on her shoulder, and laughed. Janine greeted each one of them by name: Sam, Tracy, Julie, Scott, Brian and I forget who else. There were fourteen in her class in all, half grown little-uns to almost big-uns.

After a few minutes, Janine ordered the children to their desks and everyone stood facing the flag ready to recite the 'Pledge of Allegiance'. I did my best to follow along; America was my country, too. Then, she had her students take their seats and told them all about me and how I had ended up in Jerome.

"Professor Jerome calls Walter a homing pigeon," she said finally, and continued to teach them about that.

Professor Jerome? Who on earth was Professor Jerome? I did not know about any professors. While Janine lectured about the science and history of homing pigeons, I took off to look around.

The girl named Tracy wore a bright green dress, my favorite color, and had her hair tied together, hanging in a ponytail down the middle of her back. The temptation was too great. I landed on her shoulder and started pulling at her hair. The kids howled with laughter.

"Walter, come back over here and behave!" Janine scolded me with Hawk-Watcher-like authority.

Yikes! I had never heard her voice sound like that before. It was time to bail.

I flew through the open door into the other classroom. A younger lady teacher held a tight reign over a dozen little-uns. She looked up, startled, and the kids laughed as I made my entrance. So this was grade one through six.

I was pretty comfortable at grade level five and sat on the shoulder of a boy who had his book open and was reading about the Oregon Trail.

Behind me, I could hear Janine and the young teacher, Miss Dixon, whispering to each other. The boy I was reading with looked up at me with his big, brown eyes and grinned. I warbled back.

"Ok," I heard the teachers whisper to each other.

"Walter, you are officially one of Miss Dixon's students," Janine told me," but you have to behave yourself. And it will be only for the morning session. Grandpa needs you in the afternoons."

"Warble, warble."

I could live with that arrangement. And I behaved myself. I only knocked two pencils off of desks that morning. And I liked Miss Dixon. As far as humans went, she was very pretty. After the morning session, I made the short flight back to the farm. I was happy that there were no hawks in sight, although I did spot one fat, ugly buzzard picking at something dead on the side of the highway.

Dottie's window was half-open, so I flew inside and landed on my perch. Dottie was propped sitting up on pillows reading a book. Being only eight, she was not as far along in her studies as I was. She smiled, set down her book of fairytales, picked up her computer and started punching the letter keys.

"Hi, Walter, "her voice said through the machine, "I love you!"

"Warble."

Having just been to school, I was still in a scholarly frame of mind. I hopped down to her bed and carefully studied her computer. I knew how to spell. I knew a lot of words.

Hmm!

I carefully eyed the keyboard. There were a few symbols on it that were foreign to me, but maybe that was ok. This just might work.

I pecked hard at the keys, one at a time, until I was satisfied with what I saw written on the screen. Dottie watched me with her surprised, undivided attention. Then I pecked at the big button. Nothing happened. I pecked harder with no luck. A big, weathered hand reached down in front of me and pushed the button.

"I love you, too, Dottie," the machine said in Dottie's voice. Dottie smiled brightly at me.

"So what have we here?" the owner of the weathered hand asked in his deep, familiar voice. I looked around to see Grandpa standing there, with his big arms folded, wearing a huge smile on his face.

34

JOHN WAYNE

George stood in the kitchen, wearing his farm clothes and eating a peanut butter sandwich.

"George," Grandpa said, "sit with Dottie this afternoon. Reading and math are on the schedule for her. Walter and I have some work to do."

"Sure, dad," George said, and held out a piece of sandwich to me. He looked so much like Grandpa, even with his jet black hair and younger face.

Grandpa took me out to the little shack. Inside, it was packed with keyboards and screens, a desk, a lamp and chair, shelves full of books and shelves full of wires and gadgets.

On top of the desk, nestled in amongst a mountain of paperwork, sat a framed photograph of Kenny and Dottie. Kenny was a young boy in the photo and Dottie, holding his hand, was a real little-un. She smiled brightly at me, with beautiful curly black hair and no hint of the sickness.

I turned and scanned the titles of the books on the bookshelves. I recognized 'Astrophysics' and 'Nanotechnology'', but most of the long titles eluded me. And there was no dictionary in sight. Rats! Or as Old Dude would say: Hawk-poop!

One of the titles did intrigue me, especially the name of the book's author. The book was titled: "The Effects of Gravity on Earth Core and Field Magnetics." Whew! The name of the author was none other than Sir Alfred Jerome. Sir Alfred Jerome!

It was all rushing back to me. The black, white bearded man in overalls talking to the wiseacre young man on Marshall's television that night at the dorm. There was a connection here!

"Do you like that book, Walter?" Grandpa asked as he cleared the papers off of his desk and dumped a bunch of gadget parts on it.

"Warble."

"Oh," he said, shaking his head, "that isn't going to do!""

He sat me down at a keyboard in front of a blank screen with only a little green square flashing on and off in its top, left hand corner.

"This is a light touch keyboard, Walter," Grandpa explained, "type what you want to say here and I'll read it, ok?"

"Ok, Grandpa," I typed.

Grandpa laughed and went to work at his desk with a pen-like instrument that glowed red-hot at its tip.

"I'm building you a computer like Dottie's," Grandpa explained as he worked feverishly. Little metal, plastic and glass parts clattered and clanked on his desk as he moved them around.

"I'll make it lighter on the keys and the talk button for you," he continued, "I really want to talk with you, Walter."

I typed on the keyboard in front of me. Grandpa leaned over in his chair and watched me.

"That is your book over there, you are Sir Alfred Jerome, aren't you?" I typed.

"That is correct," Grandpa affirmed, "and that book is one of my proudest achievements."

"Marshall says you got your 'Sir' in a box of cracker-jacks or something," I continued. Grandpa paused at what he was doing and frowned.

"Is that so?"

"Marshall says that only a whack job would believe…," I started to type, but Grandpa interrupted me with a raised hand.

"That's fine, Walter," he said, "I get the picture."

Grandpa continued to work at his desk.

"All of these terminals, Walter," he said, sweeping his hand around the room as he worked, "are tied into telescopes and mainframe computers across the world. A telescope is a beautiful instrument that we use to look more closely at the stars and planets above us.

"That one over there," he gestured at a computer in the far corner of the shop, "is very special. It is connected directly to Heaven Sight, a big space telescope high up in the sky that belongs to Star Watcher Corporation. Its owner, Sam Locklear, is one of my best friends and gives me two hours a day to use his telescope for my research."

"It was Heaven Sight," Grandpa said, leaning back over and looking at me, "that verified my early assumptions and then confirmed my later theories."

Grandpa continued to work. He was obviously a master designer. Soon, the machine started to look like Dottie's.

"I've written over seventy books, Walter," he said as he continued to work, "Most of them on physics and astrophysics. I love those fields."

He laughed a little; a sad laugh. "I remember as a boy telling my friend, Albert, 'don't publish that theory, it leads to dangerous places. You never know who will pick it up and run with it.' And look at us now, so many, many years later, and in such deep trouble from our own inventions. The world is a strange place, Walter."

He continued his work

"Dottie is so terribly ill, Walter."

"Can't you help her?" I typed.

"One of my brothers is a world famous cancer doctor. He told me that there is no hope for Dottie, the cancer is too advanced."

He stopped working for a moment and looked at me with sad eyes. "What do you do with a diagnosis like that? Give up?"

I typed hard on the key board.

"Old Dude told me to never give up!" I typed.

"That's exactly what I think," Grandpa agreed with vigor, "never give up! I have prayed for two years. If there is no natural solution, there has to be a supernatural one! It was my vision of you, Walter, that really gave me hope. Somehow, I believe that Dottie's life is going to depend on you!"

"How?" I typed.

"I don't know," Grandpa said, shaking his head, "but the answer will be obvious to us when the time comes."

He turned back to the desk for a little while longer.

"There," he finally said, "this is going to work, Walter, but first we need to choose a voice for you."

He turned to another computer and worked the keyboard. The computer talked back and I heard voices like "How do you do," or "Frankly, my dear, I don't ..." They were neat voices, but we nixed each one. Grandpa kept pulling up more.

"The only thing we have to fear, is fear itself!"

"Hey, Moe!"

"I am not a crook!"

"It's a beautiful day in the neighborhood."

"I'm singing in the rain, just singing in the rain."

"His name is Harvey. He's invisible."

"Fill your hand, Pilgrim!"

Wait a minute!

"Warble, warble," I said.

"By George, good choice!" Grandpa agreed, "No one has a better voice than the Duke! So be it, Walter."

He worked a little longer and then the computer was finished. He had me try it out.

"Hello, Sir Alfred," the voice came out with its southern drawl.

"Call me Grandpa, Walter," Grandpa said, chuckling, "tell me, Duke, what do you want?"

"I want to learn," my new voice drawled.

"What do you want to learn?" Grandpa asked me with a smile.

I typed.

"Everything." I typed. "But first, I want to know what you really have inside this shack, Pilgrim!"

35

THE GREAT QUESTION

Grandpa laughed cheerfully.

"All in good time," he said, "I have other work for you, first."

Just then, George opened the door and stuck his head in.

"Janine's home," he said, "how's it coming, Dad?"

"We're finished for now."

I typed rapidly on my new computer and pecked the button.

"Howdy, Pilgrim!" I said.

George nearly dropped to the ground.

"Dang!" he said, looking at me with astonishment. "That's John Wayne!"

After a few weeks, Grandpa decided that it was far too dangerous for me to fly home from school after the morning sessions.

"He is just too vulnerable," he told Janine, "and I would never be able to forgive myself if anything happened to him."

Janine agreed with Grandpa. She worried about me, too. From now on, Grandpa would drive the truck into town and pick me up. I was not at all crazy about the new plan.

"How am I going to fly enough?" I asked Grandpa via my computer, "I'll get big and lazy like all of those New York pigeons Old Dude told me about!"

Grandpa laughed.

"Don't you worry, Walter," he assured me, "I'm cooking up something special for you."

I loved school. The kids started sneaking me candy and snacks behind Miss Dixon's back. I really was starting to get heavier. In weeks, I soaked in everything that sixth grade had to offer and I flew over to Janine's classroom.

Seventh grade was quite a step up. In history they were busy studying World War I, which immediately captured my attention. I sat on Brian's shoulder and looked in horror at picture after picture of the war.

"The trenches were cemented with mud," Janine lectured the class, "both sides fought day and night, month after month for inches of ground. Mustard gas drifted like a spirit of death through the trenches, burning out the lungs of soldiers who did not have enough time to put on their gas masks. Thousands of men died; young men, not much older than some of you."

It was sickening. For pigeons like me, this was called 'The Great Question.' It was the question that I had unwittingly asked Old Dude one day as we perched above the two arguing professors at the coffee shop.

That particular day, they were arguing about the war in the Middle-East.

"War," Old Dude explained to me, "is when one big bunch of men git together and go shoot at another big bunch of men 'til they durn near kill each other off."

I asked the Great Question.

"Why do they do that?"

Old Dude shifted uneasily on the tree branch.

"Well, Squeaker," he answered, "we's a'been watchin' men fer a long, long time now. Ever since they was a'livin' in caves an' eatin' berries, I reckon. An' that's ages ago! An' they's always a'been fightin' against each other. Bigger wars, nowadays. They kill lot's of each other, and a lot of innocent critters like us pigeons, too. Don't make no durn sense at all!"

"It sure doesn't seem to," I agreed.

"Far as I kin reckon," Old Dude continued, "people are crazy an' that's all there is to it. Even them human Viking warriors, far as I kin tell. Now, you take hawks, fer instance. Hawks is always eatin' us pigeons; but does that make me want to go and kill all the hawks in the world? Heck, no! Don't mean hawks is bad 'cause they git after us; means they're hungry, that's all! An' we're mighty tasty morsels fer them. Ain't nothin'crazy 'bout that. I jest don't want them a'eatin'me!"

I kind of understood.

"Now, you take people," Old Dude continued, "they don't eat each other, they jest kill each other an' leave everbody layin' right where they drop. I done seen it myself when I was a squeaker like you. People is just crazy, that's all!"

Well, I thought as I listened to Janine's lecture, Grandpa did not seem to be crazy, nor did Kenny, or George, or Dottie. Marshall... well, he might be crazy.

That night after dinner, Grandpa and I sat on the front porch swing, enjoying the chilly, moonless night. Grandpa seemed to be deep in thought, puffing on his pipe while I sat quietly, pondering the Great Question. My computer sat on the swing in front of me and I started typing.

"Grandpa," I asked, "how many is a thousand?"

Grandpa stopped smoking and looked down at me.

"Do you know how many a hundred is, Walter?" He asked. I bobbed my head yes.

"Well, then," he said, "a thousand is ten times a hundred."

Wow, I thought. A hundred was roughly as many geese as there were in Henry's flock. Henry had told me that himself. It meant that a thousand was ten of Henry's flocks. That was difficult to visualize. Ten of Henry's flocks would block out the sun if they all took to wing at once.

"And then you have ten of the thousands," Grandpa continued, "for ten thousand, and ten ten-thousands for one hundred-thousand, and ten one hundred-thousands makes one million. Do you understand, Walter?"

My head was throbbing, but I did understand. I nodded yes.

"Then," Grandpa continued, "if you take one thousand millions, you have one billion. Look up at the stars, Walter."

Grandpa and I looked up at the dark night sky together. There were more twinkling stars up there than I could count.

"That thick, bright band of stars," Grandpa said, waving his arm across the sky, "is called the Milky Way, our galaxy, Walter. It contains billions of stars. And it is not the only galaxy up there. There are actually billions of galaxies up there, each filled with billions of stars."

My head was spinning now; it was all beyond me.

I started typing again. This was such a good conversation, I decided it was time to ask Grandpa the Great Question. The Great Question had been discussed among pigeons for thousands of years. It was a question that vexed us. We could not find an answer. Maybe Grandpa knew.

"Why do thousands of men make war with each other? Why do thousands of men go and die?" I asked.

Grandpa listened to my question and gazed out toward the dark horizon.

"Hmm, you are a deep thinker, little bird." He said, rubbing his beard. He had that sad look in his brown eyes.

"Try millions, Walter," he said, "Millions of men go to war; millions of men and women kill each other."

"Why?" I asked.

Grandpa pushed at the ground with his feet and started to gently swing the porch swing. I waited patiently for his answer.

"Because perhaps, in a way, men are insane, Walter," he finally answered in a quiet, sad voice.

"All men?" I asked.

"Most men," he answered, "not all, but most. There are a few, a very few special ones who are not. We usually call those men and women 'enlightened'.

"Are you one of those?' I asked, hoping for the answer I wanted to hear.

Grandpa gave me a humble look.

"I would never, ever presume to be," he said, "but I would like to be. That is why I pray. You see, Walter, it is the sad nature of men that they are driven by thoughts and desires in their heads. The thoughts bounce around their heads like raging monkeys, telling them that things like cars and televisions, money and land, will make them happy. But they never have enough. They want more and more. Sadly, the more of everything they have, the unhappier they become; and their thoughts tell them to get more and more. They make enemies of each other by wanting to possess what each other has, or to control each other so that they get what they think they want."

Grandpa sighed.

"You see, Walter, men's desires trap them," he continued, "their thoughts make them want more and more of what makes them unhappy. It is insanity. Eventually they create war to try to take from their enemies what they think will make them happy. Even if it means taking their enemies' lives."

It was a terrible idea. Like Old Dude used to say, "*Them folks is never happy!*"

"There has to be a solution," I typed.

"Oh," Grandpa agreed, "I believe there is. I believe that men have to quiet those desires, quiet their material wants and raging thoughts, and let the light of what I call the Peaceful World filter into their heads. It is a world that exists beyond men's insane desires. It is the only place where they can truly be happy."

The Peaceful World. It sounded wonderful; but was there really such a place?

"Have you seen the Peaceful World, Grandpa?" I asked

Grandpa smiled down at me. "Yes, Walter, I believe that in my dreams I have, and it is a lovely place."

I closed my eyes and tried to visualize the Peaceful World. I saw myself perching high atop the pole with Old Dude and Hawk-Watcher, enjoying the beauty of the morning sunrise. I saw myself and Old Dude going to the eatin' place with no evil broom boy in sight. The Peaceful World. In my vision, Old Dude turned to me and spoke: "*Valhalla!*"

"Grandpa," I typed, "I don't like war."

"Neither do I, Walter," Grandpa agreed, "Neither do I."

In the weeks that followed, Grandpa trusted me to watch over Dottie for short periods of time while he worked on his project. George usually either worked the farm or put on clean, white overalls and disappeared inside the shack.

Dottie and I had conversations through our respective computers. I could tell that she wanted to talk out loud, she just could not manage to do it for some reason.

"What does it feel like to fly?" She would ask me and look at me inquisitively with her beautiful brown eyes. Flying was so natural to me, I had not given it much thought.

"I like to fly," I told her, "because when I am up high in the wind, I feel free. I can see everything and go where ever I want."

It must be hard, I thought to myself, to be locked on land the way people are. The idea of it was suffocating to me, and I immediately felt even sorrier for Dottie.

"I wish I was a bird like you, Walter," she typed, "then I would be free!"

"I wish so, too," I told her, "then we could fly together high up in the sky. Just close your eyes, Dottie, and watch us fly in the clouds with each other."

Dottie closed her eyes. In a minute, she snapped them open again. "Are you ever afraid when you are flying?" she typed.

"Only when hawks are after me," I told her truthfully.

"But I love hawks," Dottie answered, puzzled, "I think they are beautiful."

"They are beautiful," I typed, "and I suppose that they do have their good points."

I let it go at that.

Dottie's reading skills improved every week. I would question her on what she read and she would type in her answer. She tired easily, however; and I was so far ahead of her that she would become exasperated with me.

"It's not fair," she would type, "a person is smarter than a pigeon!"

Tell that to Old Dude! I would coo and warble at Dottie until she smiled, and then she would fall asleep.

Schatzie, the dachshund, made up a game that she called hide anything she could find in the yard from Walter. She was a world-class digger. She could bury a bone quicker than you could say: "Hey, look at that hawk smack into that tree!" Then she would wag her tail, jump up and down on her squatty legs and bark at me to go find the buried bone, ball, rock or whatever. I always held out hope that it was Bear the cat. The game was far too easy. I had a distinct advantage over a short four-legged land dweller like Schatzie, whose field of vision was limited to a few inches in front of her long, wet nose. I could take off, fly high up above the backyard and spot her diggings. Then, of course, I had to make a big show of hopping around on the ground for an hour or so, looking here and there, before finding the prize. It delighted Schatzie to no end, and off she would go to hide something else.

My nights, after dinner and prayer with Grandpa at Dottie's bedside, were spent in the workshop until the wee hours of the morning. It was my chance to tell Grandpa all about my life. I told him everything, from the terrible attack of the wildcat to meeting Old Dude and Henry, and of course, of finding Kenny.

Grandpa listened intently while I described my wonderful mother and father, how they sacrificed themselves to save me. I told him the story of my great, great, great grandfather and watched as he nodded his head in appreciation

"You are a member of a fabulous species," Grandpa commented, "if only men could be more like you."

"Walter," he continued, "I have studied all about the evidence of a great collective memory that pigeons share. Men have a collective memory, too. But as I told you, our egos, our raging monkeys, usually consume all of our attention. Our collective memory is very hard to detect. Can you detect yours?"

I bobbed my head yes.

"I want to explore it," Grandpa said, "it may contain clues that can help me access more of mankind's collective memory. I have had some success already, but I think that you might be the expert. It might not work, we would have to take you a long way back in time. Would you be willing to do that?"

I bobbed my head enthusiastically.

'What would you like to know about the woolly mammoth?' I felt like asking. I could not wait to get started.

36

THE SECRET OF THE SHACK

A nother month passed, and ten big trucks rolled up our dirt road, leaving a big brown cloud of dust in their wake. They were flat-bed trucks with side rails, each carrying dozens of long metal bottles that clanked loudly as the trucks bumped along.

It was a fine, green spring day with winter long gone, and Kenny was due home for spring break in a few weeks.

As the last truck pulled onto our road, two sheriff's cars, lights flashing, followed it in. As George directed the truck crews to unload the bottles and wheel them on dollies into the barn, Sheriff Tim, that was his name, walked directly up to Grandpa. He stood in front of Grandpa with his hands on his hips and spat black tobacco juice out of the side of his mouth. He was a tall, lanky fellow, and his broad brimmed hat shaded his eyes.

"Hi, Walter," Sheriff Tim said to me as I perched on Grandpa's shoulder. Everybody in Jerome knew me, including Sheriff Tim.

"Dang it, Grandpa," he exclaimed, "this all looks danged suspicious, dang it!"

"It's only helium, Tim," Grandpa said quietly, his big arms folded, "for my science project."

"I know that, but Homeland Security is breathing down my neck! They're checking you out, Grandpa. If I'm lyin', I'm dyin'! They want to know everything about you and your program. They sent me out here to spy on you, dang it! I hate that!"

Spit.

"Haven't they seen me on TV?" Grandpa asked, "Haven't they read my books? Why don't they just call me?"

"You know how they are, Grandpa, they don't work that way! You'd better go ahead and let me take a look inside that shack of yours!"

Spit.

"Do you have a warrant, Tim?" Grandpa asked, getting serious.

"Course I got a warrant," Sheriff Tim said, pulling a folded piece of paper out of his pocket, "because you've trucked enough gear out here to build a rocket!"

Spit.

"Well, Tim," Grandpa sighed, "put that warrant up. The project is finished anyway. Come on, I might as well show you around."

"Warble?"

"Yes, Walter you can come in, too."

Hallelujah!

Grandpa walked Sheriff Tim to the tiny door that led into the shack. He punched in a number code on a keypad mounted on the right side door.

"No spitting inside, Tim," Grandpa told the Sheriff, "leave it out here or hold what you've got."

Sheriff Tim spit a big wad of tobacco out into the green grass and followed us inside.

How can I describe what happened next? The shack door closed and we started to sink. We went down for a long ways and finally stopped. The opposite wall of the shack, papers, computers and all, swung out into a vast room.

Sheriff Tim gasped, and stepped forward through the opening.

"Careful, Tim," Grandpa warned. Sheriff Tim ignored him.

The wall of this room was grayish and sleek, like the skin of a fish. Sheriff Tim ran his hand along its sleek surface. When he pushed on it, it gave way and regained its original shape as soon as he released it.

"What the...," Sheriff Tim said in surprise, "I feel a current running through it, like an electrical vibration or something!"

"It's called nano-skin," Grandpa explained, "it has its own life and memory."

"Dang!" Sheriff Tim exclaimed, "ain't it too soft to do anything serious with?"

"Oh, it's many times stronger than steel or any other material you can think of," Grandpa said, "don't be fooled by appearances."

Sheriff Tim looked Grandpa up and down.

"So the aliens aren't up there," he said, pointing at the sky, "I'm looking at one of them right here in front of me!"

Grandpa laughed.

"Welcome to Skynest One, Tim," he said.

"Just wait until she spreads her wings," Grandpa said, "like a giant bird."

"Can I go further inside?"

"I'd rather you didn't for now," Grandpa requested, "the instruments inside are delicate and George is still running the final calibrations. How about next week?"

Sheriff Tim took one last look.

"So this is what you've been carrying on about for the last ten years," he said, "ok, Grandpa. Thanks for the look-see."

Grandpa ushered him to the door. Outside in the barn, George and the work crews were halfway finished with off-loading the bottles of helium.

"Now, listen, Tim," Grandpa said as he closed up the shack, "I've reserved space for you, Sarah and Joey. When the time comes, and you'll know when it does, you get your family out here as fast as you can!"

Sheriff Tim crammed another plug of tobacco in his cheek.

"Thanks! See you 'round, Grandpa," he said as he left. "Bye, Walter."

"Warble."

37

THE FLIGHT SIMULATOR

Long gone were the days when I could take off and soar over the wide, flat Texas plains. Grandpa made it clear that he expected me to stay within a stone's throw of the farm house. No questions asked!

I complained that his rule denied me the chance to really stretch my wings and get exercise, that I was built for long distance flying.

"I have to fly, Pilgrim!" I typed on my computer sitting on Grandpa's desk. He was reading a book entitled, 'Advanced Aerospace Design.' I pecked the talk button.

"I know, John Wayne!" he said with a sigh, "I just can't take the chance of a stray predator getting you!"

"But, I graduated from Master Old Dude's College of Pigeon Self-Defense!" I typed.

"And look what happened to Old Dude," Grandpa answered with a hint of irritation in his voice.

I dropped my head. Grandpa frowned.

"I'm sorry, Walter," he apologized, "that was terribly insensitive of me."

He put down his book. Several new books were stacked on his desk, including 'The Fundamentals of Celestial Navigation' and 'The Fundamentals of Morse Code Transmission'."

"Come on, hop on my shoulder," he said to me, "let's take a walk over to Skynest."

Grandpa coded open the shack door and, after descending, we walked down the inside of the giant, inner gray structure until we were deeper inside than I had ever been before.

We arrived at a large black box that was about as tall as Grandpa and as long and wide as Janine's Pontiac. Grandpa walked me all the way around it, and at the front end I could see a motor and a big fan. The opposite side of the box had an open window, about two feet square. I looked through the window and spotted a perch inside. The rest of the box's interior was pitch-black.

Grandpa smiled at the contraption and gestured at it with a grand, sweeping hand.

"This, Walter," he said, his brown eyes sparkling proudly at me, "is your new flight simulator. I designed it especially for you!"

Flight simulator?

"See these gauges," he continued as he carried me to the front end of the machine.

I was now studying at the grade level eleven at morning school, and I fully understood gauges and graphs. On the gauges, I could read wind speed in knots, gust factor, and directional shift in degrees. The top speed on the airspeed indicator was one hundred and twenty knots. Fast! There was also a small, flat computer mounted next to the gauges, along with other gizmos that I did not recognize.

"I programmed in directional wind shifts to test your ability to stay on bearing over long distances," Grandpa explained, "This simulator should be able to help you perfect the skills you already have. From what I have learned, racing pigeons like you possess a strong internal compass that they use when they can't rely on the sun, stars or even the earth's magnetic field. We'll test that theory, Walter."

"Warble," I answered with a little trepidation. It all looked intriguing to me, but also dangerous.

"Let's give her a trial spin," Grandpa suggested with delight. He carried me to the box's open side window and lifted me inside.

"Grip this side perch while I slowly crank up the wind in your face. When I shout 'Go!' then you jump out into the middle of the box and fly!"

Timidly, I took the perch. I looked back at Grandpa's strong, weathered face. He looked like the master of all things, framed in that black window.

"This is your exercise machine, Walter," he said, "it will make you strong!"

I danced on the perch while Grandpa fidgeted with the controls at the back of the machine.

"Almost ready!" he called out.

The box whirred to life. I could feel a breeze blowing down through the middle of the box, right next to my right wing. Its velocity increased until it was a strong wind and I heard Grandpa shout: "Go, Walter!"

I flapped my wings, leapt off the perch into the wind and tried to fly. But it was so dark inside the box, I lost my visual cues and my balance, and tumbled roughly smack into the back wall of the box.

Whirrr! The machine wound down and I dropped limply to the ground.

"Walter!" Grandpa shouted through the window. "Are you okay?"

"Warble..."

"Oh, thank goodness! Get back up on that perch. A minor setback. I'm sorry, I forgot to turn on the visual."

I slowly stood up, tested my wings, and found them stiff and a little sore. Finally, after a slight hesitation, I flew back up to the perch. What fun...!

Whirr! The machine started up again, but this time the box looked like a sunlit day inside.

Grandpa yelled, "Go!"

I jumped out into the wind and, to my surprise, flew high above a town. I could see what looked like real cars and people far below me, bustling up and down roads and sidewalks. Puffy white clouds decorated a deep blue sky above me, all illuminated by a bright noon sun. Incredible!

The town seemed to go on forever.

"Fifty knots!" Grandpa announced. "Let's try a bit of night flying now."

I warbled 'ok', but doubted that Grandpa could hear me over the wind noise.

Suddenly, it was dark, with city lights below me and bright stars above. It was wonderful! I felt like I was really flying free.

"A little faster," Grandpa called, "when you get tired, Walter, bob your head and I'll bring you in for a landing."

"Sixty five knots'" he announced.

I was flapping hard. Grandpa increased the speed until I finally started bobbing my head. The machine wound down, and I flew over to my perch and landed. I was exhausted.

Grandpa stuck his head into the window.

"Eighty knots! Wonderful!" he exclaimed. "You can go faster, Walter, I know you can! We'll work up to it. You can consider this the first day of your strength training. This machine will also teach you other things, but we'll talk about that later."

As we departed the shack, I wondered what those other things might be.

"I know that you are trying to figure out what that thing is below the shack," Grandpa said to me as he drew on his pipe that evening and puffed big circles of smoke in the air.

"I can't figure it out at all!" I typed on my computer.

Grandpa chuckled.

"Neither can Sheriff Tim," he laughed.

He took a long draw on his pipe. The sweet smell was intoxicating to me.

"I hail from a long, long line of long-lived Jeromes," Grandpa continued, "and in the fifteen hundreds, my great ancestor Michael of Jerome was considered by Rome to be a sorcerer. What he actually was is known today as a scientist. He was also a bit of an alchemist. Do you know what that is, Walter?"

"He could change the structure of elements?" I typed.

"Excellent, my friend!" Grandpa exclaimed. "Yes, he found a rudimentary way to change some elements at the atomic level. My brothers and I, along with our Science Guild, have advanced his work much further. We can change dirt, for instance, into almost any element we wish. This, of course, has also been accomplished by industry with some success, but we have taken the process to new heights. This is how we built Skynest. The structure below the shack was transformed completely from Texas dirt."

"Warble!"

"I know you must be at a loss for words, Walter," Grandpa continued, "as I would be. Here is the secret of our success. We were not creating something new, we were working with prior knowledge, as was my ancestor."

"Collective memory?" I typed.

"Bingo!" Grandpa exclaimed. "Collective memory gained from wise men who lived literally more than thirty thousand years ago.'"

"Who were they?" I typed.

"People of the last age, I suppose," Grandpa answered me, "People who passed on to us a little of their knowledge.'"

So, I thought, men do have access to collective memory. Some men, anyway.

38

I DECIDE TO STAY

I had long since given up on the notion of returning to Hawk-Watcher's flock that spring. Dottie's condition was worsening and I knew that she needed me. My mere presence gave her comfort. She looked so fragile and helpless lying in her bed, she rarely let Grandpa pick her up and move her. When he did, she cried out in pain. She even refused to wear her hair wig.

Also, the ground outside shook constantly now. I could always hear them moments before they hit. Earthquakes, Grandpa called them. They knocked Janine's best dishes off of the shelves. We had three or four a day and I just did not feel comfortable leaving at a time like this. Whatever was coming, I decided, it was coming really soon!

George and Janine spent evenings holding each other's hands on the porch swing, crying softly. I perched on George's shoulder, trying my best to comfort them. It was this crazy paradox of humanity: war...and also this! They truly loved and cared for each other! Human love was the trait that I loved the most about them, the one that drew me in. In spite of human insanity.

One morning, Dottie did not wake up. George frantically sent for the doctor.

"He is on the jet now," George told Grandpa and Janine. Janine and I stayed home from school, Janine sitting in a chair next to

Dottie's bed, holding her daughter's hand, and I perched above them both on my brass stand. Tears streaked down Janine's cheeks and she had to wipe her eyes with her handkerchief.

The doctor arrived at midmorning. He was a tall, dark, angular man with long, white hair. He was dressed in a nice, dark suit and carried an old leather case at his side. He looked so much like Grandpa, I suspected that they might be related.

"Thank you for coming, Uncle Edward!" Janine exclaimed and gave him a big hug.

That confirmed it. One of the Jerome boys.

They sent me out of the room while the doctor opened his leather case and got to work. I circled the house and landed on Dottie's windowsill, which was slightly cracked open. The voices inside her room were muffled, and I listened hard trying to hear the conversation.

"…perfectly normal at this stage, Janine," Doctor Edward was saying, "… semi-comatose … should not last long…"

"… for over a hundred years and still no cure…" It was Janine, the frantic voice of a desperate mother, "she's only eight, there has to be another answer…"

Doctor Edward hung his head.

"… I wish…" he was saying.

Janine gave the big, sad doctor a hug.

"… please, Uncle, it's not your fault…"

Later at dinner, I perched on Grandpa's shoulder. I was torn between staying at dinner and flying back into Dottie's bedroom to watch over her. She was still asleep. My curiosity had the best of me, though, and I decided to stick around to check this Uncle Edward out.

"Edward," Grandpa said, taking a sip of red wine, "this is Walter sitting on my shoulder. He is the finest and, I suspect, smartest pigeon in the world."

Dr. Edwards' sparkling brown eyes beamed at me, and he lifted his wine glass.

"To Walter," he toasted, "the Albert Einstein of pigeons!"

Talk turned serious.

"You are further along than I am, Alfred," Dr. Edward said, "I am still brewing up my final batch of nano-skin."

"You will do it," Grandpa assured him, "nano-transformation takes time. Ronald and James finished their projects even before me, so that they could go out and collect samples of plants."

"All is still on schedule then," Dr. Edward observed.

"All is well, Edward," Grandpa agreed, "but when your nano-skin develops, hurry!"

"Don't worry," the doctor said, "and let us pray that your latest visions are accurate."

"Let us pray," Janine agreed.

"Kenny comes home tomorrow," George announced, "it's spring break."

Dr. Edward looked inquiringly from Grandpa to George and Janine.

"Don't worry, Edward," Grandpa said with a strange quietness in his voice, "he won't be returning to school."

Later that night, while perched over Dottie on my brass stand, I could hear Janine quietly crying outside on the front porch.

"We'll get through this dear, don't worry," I heard George whisper as he tried to comfort her.

I joined Grandpa out back as he lit his wonderful, fragrant pipe. I perched on his shoulder, cooing for a while. When he set my computer down on the bench, I worked up my nerve.

"Grandpa," I typed, "when I pray, I actually pray to a different God."

"Oh?" Grandpa asked.

"I pray to the Great White Stork. He is the beginning, the now and the future. Every bird knows that."

"When I die," I continued, "he will hold in his giant beak the full account of my life. I don't want to let him down."

Grandpa nodded.

"I understand," he answered.

"Walter," he said after a long while, "is it possible that we might be praying to different versions of the same God? I also know that my God is the beginning, the now and the future. If he is a wonderful God, he watches over all of us. Don't you think?"

I pondered that idea for a long time.

Then, I fell asleep.

Rays of morning sunlight filtered through the east window of Dottie's bedroom and woke me. Somehow, I had ended up on my perch in Dottie's room.

I looked down to see Dottie smiling weakly up at me. She was awake! Maybe the prayers that Grandpa and I had uttered worked.

Dottie typed slowly, gingerly on her computer.

"I love you, Walter," she typed, "You are my very, very best friend!"

39

THE STAR CHART

School was out for spring break; which meant that Kenny was in his yellow Bug, on his way home to relax.

Relaxation had become a distant memory for me. While Janine sat with Dottie after breakfast, Grandpa took me to the shack.

"Now, the serious stuff begins," he told me. "I have a lot of work for you, Walter, and a lot of homework. First of all, take a look at this."

We were at his desk. My computer sat to one side while he placed a sheet of paper in front of me with strange markings on it. The letters of the alphabet were printed down the left side of the page, but next to each of them were a series of dashes and dots. For instance, the letter "A" was followed by. -, and the letter "B" had - ... beside it. The same was true for numbers.

"This is called International Morse Code, Walter," Grandpa explained, "I want you to learn it and practice it until it becomes as natural as talking in pigeon."

It sounded like a pretty tall order to me.

"For instance, listen to how I can tap out a "B", "he said, and tapped on the desk with his index finger. Loud tap, soft tap, soft tap, soft tap.

"See how it works?" he asked. I bobbed my head.

"You can do the same thing on any hard surface with your beak," he assured me, "try it."

I tapped my beak on the hard surface of the desk. Loud tap, soft tap, soft tap, soft tap.

"Grand!" Grandpa exclaimed. "Learn it, Walter. Practice it every chance you get."

He did not tell me why Morse code was so important, but I was getting used to that by now. Grandpa had his reasons.

"Now," he continued," let's talk about the stars. Do you use the stars to help you find your way when you fly at night?"

I bobbed my head yes. It was an ability that had not even been taught to me; I just knew it. I also used the moon at night, the sun during the day, and any landmarks I recognized. I navigated the same way the geese did. There were even times when I had none of those things to help me find my way. At those times, I just knew where to go.

Grandpa walked over to a dark, cluttered corner of the workshop and brought out a big colorful ball. It was mounted on a stand so that he could spin it around."

"This is called a globe, Walter," he explained, "a model of the world. You've probably seen one at school. Did you know that the world is round?"

Again I bobbed my head yes. Of course the world was round. Everybody knew that.

"Good," Grandpa said, "now, here we are in Texas."

He pointed to a spot on the ball.

"Everywhere you see blue is water, the oceans. As you can see, there is a lot of water on the world."

Again, it was something that I already seemed to know. I knew about the far lands, the oceans, and even that the white areas at the top and bottom of the globe were great areas of ice and snow. It was all of that stored knowledge in my collective memory.

"So you can tell your position by using the stars above you when you are flying, is that correct?"

I warbled and bobbed my head again.

"Do you recognize individual stars, or groups of stars?" Grandpa asked.

I typed on my computer and pecked the button.

"Both," I said.

"Well, well then, "Grandpa said with satisfaction. He stood up, rummaged through his shelves, and turned back to me while unfolding a big map.

"This is a star chart," he explained, "with groups of stars called constellations marked on it."

He spread out the chart and pointed to a group of stars linked together by thin lines.

"Now, Walter, what would you call this group?" Grandpa covered the name of the group he was pointing to with his thumb.

"We call that one three hens in a roost," I typed into my computer.

Grandpa lifted his thumb. The group was called Orion on the chart.

"Okay", he said, "how about this one?"

"Five little eggs in the nest," I typed.

When he lifted his thumb, the chart named it Pleiades! What a strange name.

"One more," he said.

"Slinking snake," I typed.

It was named Cassiopeia on the chart.

"Excellent!" Grandpa exclaimed, "We're off to a good start, Walter. You are going to go somewhere in your flight simulator today. I want you to use the stars and try to tell me your destination."

Fair enough, I thought. That should be easy.

"Do you recognize this star?" He asked, pointing to a star that we pigeons called the 'steady star'. The star chart called it Polaris. The North Star.

I bobbed my head.

"Now," Grandpa continued, "just for grins, what happens to the stars if the world does this?"

He lifted the globe off of its stand, flipped it upside down, and put it back down. Then he turned it around again.

I typed.

"It would look like all of the stars were falling, but if you still recognized the groups, I think you might still be able to use them."

"But it would be very confusing, wouldn't it?" Grandpa asked.

"It certainly was the last time it happened," I typed, "but the world did not flip quite that far."

Grandpa stopped turning the globe and leaned across the desk, looking at me intently.

"When did that happen, Walter?"

I had to think hard. This was going to take a few moments. Too bad Old Dude was not here, he could probably spit the answer right out. Finally, the answer came to me.

"About thirty-thousand years ago," I typed, "and thirty-thousand years before that!"

40

KENNY COMES HOME

Grandpa and I spent the remainder of the morning and part of the afternoon working in the flight simulator. At least, I was working. Grandpa was monitoring gauges, flipping switches and yelling orders at me. I was exhausted.

First, we did an exercise called city recognition. Grandpa set the speed at fifty knots, and flew me over great cities like New York with its Empire State Building, London, Paris with the Eiffel Tower, and Moscow. It all looked real to me; every city was different in its own way. Mexico City, for instance, sprawled out as far as I could see; a huge human nest sitting in a giant bowl of land surrounded by gigantic mountains.

Then we practiced what Grandpa called "avoidance". He sent Sky-Gods, I mean jets, flying straight at me and taught me how to duck and roll to avoid them.

"Good, good Walter," he called, satisfied, "now I'm going to fly you back over the farm. See it? Good. Here comes nighttime. Now, fly the bearing you are holding right now until I tell you to land. Use the stars overhead, and when you are finished, tell me where you think you are.

It was a good exercise. Grandpa kept me flying at a steady pace so that I did not tire too quickly, and I followed the stars for a couple of hours.

"Ok, Walter, "land now."

Whirrr! The machine wound down and I flew over and landed on the perch. Grandpa appeared at the window, holding my computer for me.

"Where did you land, Walter?" he asked.

"At Kenny's college," I typed, "right next to the school fountain."

"Unbelievable!" Grandpa exclaimed. "Walter, I really do believe that you are the smartest pigeon in the world. That's why God sent you to me."

Humility overtook me. I thought of my mother, my father, Old Dude, and my great-great-great grandfather. There was no way that I belonged in such distinguished company as those heroes.

"Grandpa," I typed, "I'm just an ordinary homing pigeon."

"And a humble one at that," Grandpa said with a grin.

We were finished for the day and I was hungry. I was also anxious to check on Dottie. I was spending less time with her and more time with Grandpa. I rode on Grandpa's shoulder as we exited the shack, just in time to see Kenny's yellow Bug rolling up the dirt driveway. A huge mound of bags and suitcases were haphazardly strapped to the round roof of the car, about half of them barely hanging on. Grandpa laughed at the sight.

As the car stopped in front of the farm house, Kenny opened his door and climbed out of the driver's side, stretching his arms. I was surprised to see Fiona emerge from the passenger side.

"Hello Walter, hello Grandpa," she said and gave Grandpa a big hug. He was so big, she looked like a child as he hugged her back.

"Boy, have I missed you kid," Grandpa told her, "you are prettier than ever."

"Warble, warble," I excitedly said to Fiona. She reached up and patted my head.

"Get me out of this sardine can!" A familiar voice yelled from the backseat of the Bug.

Surprise of surprises, Marshall un-wedged himself and climbed out, wild, scraggly hair, multicolored T-shirt, dirty jeans and all. He scrambled over and stuck his hand out to Grandpa.

"Hi, Grandpa," he said, "I've heard so much about you! I've even seen you on the tube!"

Kenny laughed as Grandpa shook Marshall's hand.

"I've heard everything about you, too, Marshall," Grandpa said, accommodatingly, "so I know how interesting you find my project, welcome to Jerome."

"There's not much to see in town," Marshall observed, "at least, not for a New Yorker. Hi, Walter!"

"Warble, warble."

Then it happened. I heard her voice emerge from the back seat of the Bug. Warbling- pigeon translation-'where did everybody go? Hey, what about me?'

Stunned, I flew over and landed in the open window of the Bug. There, in the back seat, perched in the middle of a plastic shower curtain, was a light gray, slightly plump female pigeon!

41

MARGIE

I perched in the window, speechless. The female pigeon and I stared at each other in bug-eyed silence. Out of the corner of my eye, I noticed Kenny rounding the front of the Bug, hugging Grandpa, and walking up to me.

"Her name is Lulu," Kenny told me, apologetically, "Marshall decided to bring her back from New York to keep you company."

Then Kenny leaned forward and whispered in my ear.

"She stayed with us all spring," he whispered, "and, believe me, she can be a real pain! I don't think she's half as smart as you are, Walter."

"What does he know?" I heard the female pigeon mumble sarcastically.

Grandpa walked up to the Bug to take a look.

"Hmm…," he said, and threw a big arm around Kenny's shoulder. They walked away together, talking. That left me alone with her. I worked up my courage.

"What's up?" I asked.

"Can you help me out of this chicken roaster, Cowboy?" She asked with a definite New York pigeon accent. We had a couple of New York pigeon transplants back in Hawk-watcher's flock. They definitely had the same accent.

"Sure," I said, "follow me."

We flew together to the rooftop of the farmhouse and landed in a cool breeze next to the weather vane. We, of course, maintained a polite distance from one another. She was plump and dull gray, like most city pigeons, but I could see a spark in her eyes. She started talking.

"Great White Stork, I thought I was going to cook in there," she started, "I was pretty sure I was tonight's dinner! That idiot Marshall is a complete moron! My name is Margie, not Lulu, and he never would have caught me if it hadn't been for the cream puff! Give me a couple of cream puffs, honey, and I'll follow you anywhere! Marshall figured out how to keep me around, even with his hideous music blasting out of his New York apartment window all day. Cream puffs! I was born in Brooklyn, right above a wedding cake shop. Smart girl, my mom! If a cake wasn't perfect, whoosh! Out the back door it flew. That's how I got my sweet tooth. All the other pigeons called my flock the Brooklyn Cakers. We fought everybody for squatting rights over that cake house! Try to take one of my cakes and I'll rip your heart out, pal! Vanilla and strawberry are my favorites, Cowboy!"

"My name is Walter," I offered rather sheepishly.

"I know who you are, Honey! Everybody in New York knows the story about you and that one-eyed wildcat! And Old Dude! Oh, Great White Stork, he's a big legend in New York! Anyway, some idiot finally closed the cake shop a few years back and turned it into a butcher shop. Yuck! Can you imagine? So the Brooklyn-Cakers broke up and I had to fly all over Manhattan, scavenging for sweets. That sneaky Marshall! How did he know I would fall for cream puffs? So here I am, kidnapped and dragged all the way to the wild, wild-west! Oh, look! The wonderful humans are going into the house. That must be George and Janine."

"Yep," I managed to say.

"I like that name, Janine. Kenny really loves his mom! They seem like such a sweet family. That Kenny is a sweetheart, and Fiona, what a catch! I can't wait to see their kids, they were made for each other. I guess Marshall and Kenny brought me out here to be your mate, Doll! It's not their decision, of course; even if they think it is. You aren't thinking about courting me, are you?"

"I-I'm barely a yearling," I gasped.

"That's just fine, honey," Margie continued, "because Merle, my true love, got himself run over by a yellow cab on Fifth Avenue when he swooped down to pick up a donut for me a couple of years ago! He was a good pigeon, and he always brought me sweets. I really miss him!"

"I'm sorry," I said sincerely.

"It's okay, Sweetie. It happens all the time in New York. You've gotta always watch out for those crazy yellow cabs! Insane maniacs drive them! You land on the street to pick up a chocolate that some stupid kid dropped and smack! Pigeon heaven, here I come! The Great White Stork! Well, that sneaky Marshall kept a stack of sugar donuts in the dorm room for me. Do they have sugar donuts here?"

"I don't think so," I said, "but Janine bakes a lot of pies."

"Oh, I love pies!" Margie exclaimed. "Boston cream pies are my favorite, but any pie will do. So, you're not going to be my charmer, Darling? That's a relief! I hate being forced into an arranged blind marriage scenario! Tell you what, we'll be Big Sister and Little Brother; and you can tell your Big Sister anything, anything at all!"

That sounded good to me. I immediately liked Margie. She would be good company. Just then, I heard a familiar barking overhead and looked up to see a big formation of snow geese flying south!

"Ah-honk, ah-honk, ah-honk!"

"Look at those stupid geese," Margie said, "it's not even close to winter! They're all heading the wrong way!"

"Excuse me for a minute, Margie," I said, and took off to catch the flock.

42

SNOWING IN THE BRONX

The Canadian geese were flat trucking. They were easily doing seventy knots. I was still tired from my morning exercise in the flight simulator, so I had to work hard to catch up with them.

I located a big male halfway down the right side of the V formation. I flew next to him and he looked over at me.

"What's up?" I asked in standard goose greeting.

"Nothin' much. Same old stuff," he answered appropriately.

"I'm Squeaker," I told him. He brightened up.

"Pleased to meet you, Squeaker," he said, "heard all about you. My name is Scooter."

"How come you guys are flying south in the spring?" I asked.

Scooter looked surprised.

"Haven't you heard?" he asked, "It's coming!"

"What's coming?"

"The Big One," Scooter said, "everybody is flying south, repositioning."

"What's going to happen?" I asked, truly lost.

"The Big One," Scooter said again, "that's all I can tell you, buddy."

"Do you know Henry?" I asked.

"Know of him," Scooter said, "never met him. He's a few flocks behind us."

"Could you send word to him that I'm at that farmhouse back yonder?"

"No problem," Scooter said, "but I think you really ought to come along with us."

"Can't do it," I said, "I'm helping a human family back there."

"I totally understand," Scooter said, "but be careful, you don't have much time. It really is The Big One!"

"Keep your nose on the horizon," I said as I pulled away.

"Yep," Scooter answered in the kindred reply, "watch your tail-feathers!"

Margie was still carrying on as if I had never left when I landed back on the rooftop.

"Snow geese are about the dumbest birds on earth, aren't they, Little Brother?"

I was too exhausted to answer. Margie did not seem to mind.

"That car ride was worse than the plane ride from New York! Marshall said we were going to ride in a bug! A bug? How can anybody ride in a little bug? I had to eat bugs for breakfast when creampuffs were scarce! I hate the way bugs scream bloody murder and scurry away!

"I said to myself, that stupid Marshall has a great big bug in his brain! He really set me up with that one! He said our bug was a beetle!

"Well, we have some monster beetles in Manhattan, almost as big as the freaking sewer rats, but nothing big enough for a pigeon to fit inside of! I figured that he was scheming to dump me out in this frying desert, Al Capone style! Bye, bye, Margie! Thanks to the Great White Stork for Kenny and Fiona! I think they saved my tail-feathers!

"That Kenny is the smart one, studying astrophysics and all. I perched on his side of the dorm room most of the time. You can get yourself killed on Marshall's side of the dorm room! And that stupid mermaid that swims round and round! She drove me bonkers! And that Grandpa, what a celebrity! All of my girls in New York talk about him all the time, he's always on TV! He is so handsome and he's the only human in the world who knows about The Big One! All my sweethearts are taking up residence on the top railing of the Empire State Building, Honey! High ground!"

"What is The Big One?" I managed to interrupt.

"What is The Big One?" Margie gave me a quizzical, pigeon-eyed look. "You know, The Big One! Oh, you're barely out of squeakerhood, kid! I keep forgetting because you're so famous, big and handsome, Doll! You probably don't remember back that far yet."

I could remember the thirty-thousand year earth flip that I had discussed with Grandpa. Maybe that was The Big One? I hoped not. According to pigeon collective memory, it had been a horrible, horrible time for men and birds!

"How does anyone survive The Big One?" I asked.

"Oh, geese and ducks have a fighting chance," Margie said, "they are great swimmers! Fish make out great, of course! Pigeons don't fare so well, but we wouldn't be here if some of us didn't make it the last time around, would we?"

How could you argue with that kind of logic?

"I want to go see Dottie," Margie said.

"Follow me."

She followed me to Dottie's half open window. There was plenty of room for both of us to stand on my brass perch. Dottie lay below us, sound asleep and looking as pale as ever.

"Oh, poor darling!" Margie said. "Kenny prayed for her every night. He even cried, and sometimes I cried with him."

"She's very sick," I told Margie quietly, "Grandpa's brother, Dr. Edward, said she doesn't have much time left."

"Well, they need to know about Bird Island, home of The Great White Stork!"

"Bird Island?" I asked, cocking my head at her.

"Yeah," Margie answered, "you know, Bird Island? Where The Great White Stork comes out every thirty thousand years or so? This might be a great time for him to show up. You know?"

"A great time," I agreed, "let me show you where we eat."

I flew her around the outside of the house and into the half-open kitchen window where fantastic cooking aromas where drifting out. We landed atop the refrigerator, where my original perch was still in place, newspaper, birdseed and all.

Margie glanced down at the newspaper.

"Great White Stork!" Margie exclaimed, flapping her wings as she read the news. "It's snowing in the Bronx!"

43

MARGIE MEETS DOTTIE

Before sunset, I was able to introduce Margie to Schatzie, who was totally overjoyed now to have two pigeons to play games with! Then I warned Margie about Bear, the cat. Bear was laying low somewhere, waiting for his chance.

"If he is anything like the tomcats in New York, I'll be worried, Little Brother," Margie assured me, "they can whip sewer rats twice their size. But he sounds like easy pickings to me."

Kenny had been wrong. Margie was smart, probably twice as smart as me. I did not have to worry about her. She listened with great interest as I told her about Myrtle, the milk goat, and Jack, the mean bully Billy goat.

"I always wanted to watch someone milk a goat or cow," Margie said, "you don't get that chance in Manhattan, unless you go to the zoo. And I hate the zoo! There are too many filthy, nasty animals at the zoo…like snakes! I hate snakes! Slithery and slimy, and they bite!"

"Me, too," I agreed, thinking back to the long days I had spent hiding in the tall grass next to the river, nursing my wing. There had been plenty of snakes there. I promised Margie that we would watch Janine milk Myrtle first thing in the morning.

I flew back to Dottie's room and saw that she was awake. She smiled at me and typed "Hello, Walter" on her computer. Before long George and Janine would come in and fetch her for dinner. I hopped down to her computer and started to type.

"Hello, Dottie," I typed, "I have a new friend I want you to meet."

"Who?" she typed with curiosity in her beautiful brown eyes.

Just then, I heard a loud crash and a pigeon screaming "Great White Stork!" from the kitchen. It was Margie! To a human, it would have sounded like a loud: "Squawk!!!"

"I'll be right back, Dottie," I typed. I flew out of her room to investigate.

Margie was trapped on top of the refrigerator with a look of sheer terror in her eyes. Below her on the floor, Bear stalked her. He was grinning and his giant green cat eyes glared up at her maliciously.

"What is that thing?" Margie screeched, "It looks like a weird throwback from the last ice age!"

I flew up to join her on the refrigerator and giggled.

"Margie, meet Bear the cat," I introduced, "don't worry about him, he can't get up here!"

Janine walked into the kitchen, saw Bear, and shouted, "Shoo, cat!"

Bear grumbled and slinked out of the kitchen.

"How sweet," Janine exclaimed when she spotted Margie and me on top of the refrigerator, "what a darling couple you make, you two love birds!"

"So, what's for dinner?" Margie asked me.

"Come on," I said, "follow me.

I pulled Margie away from the wonderful smells of the kitchen and back to Dottie's room. I hopped down and pecked at Dottie's computer.

"Dottie, this is Margie, from New York," I typed and pushed the button.

Margie cocked her gray head and looked puzzled as she heard Dottie's voice come from the machine.

"What is this contraption?" she asked.

"It talks for Dottie," I explained, "Grandpa built it for her. He built me one, too."

And if you think that's something, just wait! You ain't seen nothing yet, Big Sister!

"Hi, Margie," Dottie typed, "you sure are pretty!"

"Oh, she's such a Doll!" Margie exclaimed. She hopped down and tried to use the computer, but after frantically pecking at it, she did not quite understand it yet.

"Don't worry," I assured Margie, "I'll teach you how to use it."

"Margie says you are pretty, too, Dottie," I typed. Margie listened to the computer and looked satisfied. Dottie smiled.

44

THE SEVEN SAGES

Janine baked another world-class home-cooked dinner for her guests. She set the big dining room table with her finest linen, plates, silverware and glassware. It all sparkled as she lit the table candles. Then she brought in a large silver platter of honey baked ham, green beans and yams, a basket of hot rolls and butter, tea and wine, and, of course, fresh baked pies.

"Yum!" Margie yelled. She sat on Kenny's shoulder, pegging him as a sure bet for easy handouts, and she was right. I took my old familiar place on Grandpa's shoulder with the same idea in mind.

Soon, two simultaneous conversations took place at the table, one between the humans and one between Margie and me.

"Oh, that darling Dottie," Margie started, "I feel so sorry for her."

Grandpa was updating everyone on his progress and that of the whole Skynest Project. I lent one ear to Margie and the other to Grandpa.

"...over one thousand projects in all," Grandpa was saying, "that we now oversee. Unfortunately, there are less than one hundred here in the United States. The government has completely ignored my research."

"Probably too worried about their hundred trillion dollar deficit," Marshall mumbled between bites of ham. Grandpa raised his eyebrow.

"I am finished with Skynest One," Grandpa continued, "and I'm working with Walter now. Ronald and James finished their projects a few months ago. Now they are busy collecting and freezing plant DNA specimens. Lucas, Mark and Jon Lee should be finished in a day or two."

"Tell me about Bird Island," I asked Margie.

"Well," she said, "it's only a myth, mind you. You have to accept that first, Little Brother."

"How many people can one project support?" Marshall asked Grandpa while Janine passed him the basket of hot bread rolls.

"We are concentrating on saving as many children as possible," Grandpa answered with a somber tone, "so I designed each craft to hold and support one hundred adults and four hundred children. Children, of course, weigh less."

Marshall did some quick calculations in his head. "So you are talking in the neighborhood of half a million people!" he exclaimed.

"Not quite that many," Grandpa sadly admitted, "we are short of serious volunteers. Few people believe what they cannot see."

"About a hundred years ago," Margie told me, "two arctic terns showed up in New York City. Great White Stork! What a long trip! They were very friendly and quickly learned our language. We are messengers, they announced. We are here to tell you about Bird Island!"

"The hardest challenge," Grandpa continued, "was cracking nano-tube production on a massive scale. Mark is responsible for that break-through. Everything, even the balloons, make use of that material. It is extremely light, and is still the strongest material I have ever worked with. Mark also refined quantum-dot technology to the point that we are supremely confident we can generate more than enough power."

"How much room do you have left on Skynest One, Doctor?" Fiona asked.

"More than enough for both of you and your families," Grandpa assured her and Marshall.

"So they said to the pigeons, and the geese, and the sparrows, and anyone else who would listen," Margie continued, "that far, far to the south, where the air gets cold again, after you pass the hot middle of the world, you reach a giant land of ice. We're talking ten, twelve thousand miles!"

"Whew!" I exclaimed. I had seen that huge, white land at the bottom of Grandpa's globe.

"The humans call it Antarctica. Not far from it, protected by a strange current of warm water, is a place called Bird Island."

"Tell me about your brothers," Fiona asked Grandpa.

"Let me tell you about them, Fiona," George broke in, "and give Grandpa a chance to eat. He has six brothers, all doctors and scientists of different disciplines. Between them, they have acquired quite a bit of the world's knowledge."

"Like the Seven Sages?" Fiona asked quietly, setting down her fork. "I learned all about that legend."

"A fine comparison," George agreed, "although so many, many other specialists have also signed up. But as for these brothers, Edward is a physician, specializing in oncology and heart disease. He is an international leader in both fields."

"This Bird Island," Margie continued, "is something very special, the terns told us. First of all, it has all of the food a bird could eat. Not cake, of course, but shrimp, krill and creepy crawlies. No cake, but hey, if you gotta eat, you gotta eat!"

"Ronald," George continued, "is a molecular biologist. He specializes in animal and plant genomes and the cryogenic preservation of thousands of biologic entities."

"The most interesting thing they said about Bird Island was that The Great White Stork lives there," Margie continued, "THE Great White Stork! Can you imagine?"

"James," George continued, "specializes in veterinary science, animal husbandry and agriculture."

"The secret of Bird Island," Margie whispered to me, "according to these terns, lies far beneath the ground. They said that there is a fountain of living water that surges up from the heart of the world!"

"Lucas," George continued, "is a wonderful architect and specializes in civil engineering. He can literally design and build cities! Mark is our chemist and metallurgist. He specializes in nano-technology and quantum physics. He builds everything from bucky-ball nano-machines to race cars. He developed the process of converting common dirt and rock into our Skynests!"

"So they say the water from the fountain is healing water," Margie continued to whisper, "the terns told us that birds fly in from all over the world to Bird Island to heal themselves! If it's true, maybe it could help Dottie!"

"Then, there is Father Matthew," George finished, "a priest, a scientist and, formerly, a famous rock musician! And of course, we all know about Grandpa."

"Wow!" Marshall exclaimed, "The seven of you could rebuild an entire world!"

Grandpa winked at him and sneaked me a huge bite of sourdough roll dripping in homemade butter.

"I saw that!" Janine teasingly scolded him.

"How do you find this Bird Island?" I asked Margie.

"Beats me, Little Brother, most birds think that it's only a fancy myth!"

Margie and I heard it before the glasses and plates started vibrating on the table. Soon the entire house was shaking. Margie looked stricken.

45

SHAKY GROUND

"Everyone, get outside!" Grandpa ordered as he rose from his seat.

George jumped up and quickly scooped Dottie up in his arms.

We all rushed out of the dining room, through the back kitchen door, off of the back porch and into the backyard. Marshall was the first one out, followed by everyone else.

The ground literally shook and rolled beneath us, up and down.

"Stay clear of anything that might fall on you," Grandpa shouted. Even Bear ran outside into the grass, looking confused. Schatzie ran around in circles, howling and barking pitifully.

The ground shook for a full minute, and then we heard a loud "Thump!" Glasses and dishes fell and shattered inside the house. I could hear shelves of books crashing to the floor. Everybody struggled hard to stay on their feet. Then the ground shook for an additional full minute, followed by a stronger "Thump!" Finally, all was calm. Everyone was down on their hands and knees now, hugging the ground. Bear and Schatzie rolled in the grass while Margie and I flapped our wings and hovered in the air.

"That felt like about a seven or eight on the Richter scale," Grandpa told George, "you check the house for structural damage before anyone goes back in. Then check Skynest and make sure our mainframe feeds are still up. Janine, as soon as George clears the house for damage, turn on the TV and find out what you can."

"My God," Janine exclaimed, "I've never felt anything like that around here!"

"We'd better get used to it," Grandpa answered grimly.

"The epicenter could have been in Mexico," George guessed, "or maybe in the Rockies up north."

"It could have been anywhere," Grandpa answered, "Kenny and I will take the pickup truck to town to see if anyone needs help."

He kissed Dottie on the forehead and handed her to Janine.

"Be careful," Janine told Grandpa with worry, "stay out of those old buildings."

"Come on, Kenny," Grandpa said and headed for his pickup truck. Kenny kissed Fiona and his mother and followed the big man. I caught up to Grandpa and landed on his shoulder.

"I'm staying here, Honey!" Margie called to me and flew up to the roof of the house. "Be careful!"

"George, stay alert for after-shocks!" Grandpa called as he climbed into his truck.

"You've got it, Dad!" George called back.

"It's starting, isn't it Walter?" Grandpa asked me seriously.

"Warble, warble," I answered, bobbing my head.

Kenny had my computer and held it out to me. I typed.

"It's The Big One," I typed, "we're running out of time, Pilgrim!"

"George!" Grandpa yelled out of his truck window. George came running over.

"Activate the call-tree," Grandpa told him, "Launch time, approximately two days. Maybe sooner."

"I'm on it, Dad!"

"Tell Marshall and Fiona to call their families. They have to fly out here first thing tomorrow."

"Will do, Dad!"

As we pulled away from the house and started down the dirt road, Kenny sat slumped in his seat. He had a grim look on his face.

"It really is happening, isn't it?" he asked.

"Did you doubt me, Kenny," Grandpa eyed him like he was studying a disciple who had lost his faith, "did you doubt my data?"

"No, Grandpa," Kenny answered dejectedly, "I just prayed that something, someone, maybe God, would somehow intervene."

"I did too," Grandpa assured him, "I prayed every single night."

I understood that. I hopped over to Kenny's shoulder and cooed in his ear to comfort him.

The shocked townspeople of Jerome were wandering up and down the main street, talking and hugging each other. They walked up to Grandpa's truck as soon as they recognized it.

"The school and the old theater have collapsed," one middle aged, well-dressed man told Grandpa, "and thank God, no one was in them! What do you think, Alfred?"

"It's time to get ready, mayor." Grandpa said. "This is just the beginning. When I sound the siren, you get all of the children out to my place."

"You've got it, Grandpa," the mayor said, "may God be with us all!"

"Amen." Grandpa said.

We drove a few yards further and Sheriff Tim stuck his head in Grandpa's window.

"Dang it, Grandpa!" He hollered. "What the heck is this all about?"

Spit.

"It's starting, Tim," Grandpa repeated, "go get Sarah and Joey ready and listen for my siren. Spread the word."

"Now Grandpa," Sheriff Tim said, "don't you go off scarin' the townfolk over an ordinary earth-quake, you understand?"

Spit.

Grandpa gave the Sheriff a hard look that could melt steel.

"You do as I say, Tim!" Grandpa growled, "If you don't, I'll whip you over my knee, like I did the time you and your little pals stole my peaches!"

With a shamed look, Sheriff Tim nodded his head and walked away. Grandpa turned to us.

"The toughest part of this," he explained, "is dealing with skeptics!"

Then why not just ignore them, I thought to myself.

"Sheriff Tim is a good man," Grandpa said, seemingly reading my mind again, "and valuable. Trust me, we can use him."

We drove slowly through the rest of town, stopping here and there to talk to people. When Grandpa was satisfied that everyone was safe, with the newly homeless people gathered at the church, he turned east and headed back to the farm.

It was the dead of night now, moonless and clear. Kenny looked south and nearly jumped out of his seat.

"Look, Grandpa!" he said, pointing out his window across the southern plains. Grandpa looked and nodded his head.

"Just as I predicted, Kenny," he said, "the Earth's magnetic field is shifting south. You are looking at the Aurora Borealis, the Northern Lights. Bright, aren't they? I guess we'd better start calling them the Southern Lights!"

I studied what looked like ethereal green illuminated giants, roaming back and forth across the skies above the southern plains. I felt slightly sick; my magnetic sense was all askew.

"Can you sense which way is north, Walter?"

"Warble..."

No, I could not.

46

THE END OF AN AGE

G randpa explained that the molten iron core of the Earth had become unstable and now was irrevocably shifting to a new position. The Earth's magnetic field reflected that motion and was in the process of its' own relocation.

"Our Solar System is just starting to cross into a treacherous region of the galaxy," he said, "I didn't want this to happen. I prayed that it wouldn't happen. Other scientists laughed at me and trashed my data."

"We are approaching a special area of space." Kenny explained to me. "Normally, the black hole at the center of the Milky Way doesn't generate enough pull to disrupt the position of our planets; but in this particular region, a river of concentrated dark matter flows through space like one of our big rivers of water here on earth."

"Dark matter acts like a conductor," Grandpa cut in, "and it can conduct strong gravitational fields from one location to another the same way that copper wires conduct electricity. Do you understand, Walter?'

"Warble, warble."

"Good," Grandpa continued, "and concentrated rivers of dark matter actually even amplify the gravitational force of our Milky Way's black hole. Those rivers of dark matter conduct enormous gravitational force out from the center of the galaxy and radiate out like the spokes of a wagon wheel. Our Solar System is approaching one of those rivers. Everything, from our sun to our moon, will be affected by it. Over millions of years, these dark matter rivers in space have truly altered the way our Solar System behaves, and they literally wreak havoc on Earth!"

"We cross one of these rivers every thirty thousand years, give or take." Kenny added quietly. "One age of man ends, and hopefully another age begins."

"Warble, warble," I said. It has been the same for pigeons.

"Yes," Grandpa agreed, "the same for pigeons."

Was he reading my mind, or learning my language?

"We designed Skynest," he continued, "in order to save as many people and animals as possible."

"And don't forget plants!" Kenny added.

"Yes, even plants," Grandpa agreed "my mother had a vision over a hundred years ago when my brothers and I were just kids."

Over a hundred years ago? Did humans live that long? I was puzzled, looking at how young and strong Grandpa actually looked. Who were these men?

"Yes, Walter, I have lived a long time! A terrible time was coming, mother told us, and we had to prepare. We had to save as many people as we could. We each took up different disciplines and studied hard. We even tried to find any hint of lost knowledge from the past age of man."

"But almost all of the knowledge of the previous age of man was lost in that catastrophe," Kenny said, "Grandpa and his brothers are determined to not let that happen again."

"God willing," Grandpa said, shaking his head, "God willing."

"Today is just the beginning, Walter," Kenny said, "it's going to get worse, day by day, until..."

Grandpa stopped him with a sharp look.

"Hopefully, we will not witness that," Grandpa said, "if we do, that means our century old mission has failed."

We turned up the dirt road to the farmhouse.

"I hope you aren't too tired, Walter," Grandpa said, "we're staying up late tonight."

"All of us," Kenny added.

"Warble."

47

DARK FLIGHT

Marshall was the only person who actually got any sleep that night.

"He can sleep through anything," Kenny said, with a hint of envy.

While Marshall blissfully snored away, Grandpa put me through the wringer. He practiced messages in Morse code with me, and then ran me through airborne celestial navigation. It was a real brain teaser, making up origination points and destinations with absolutely no ground based references. We created directional headings for me to follow that Grandpa called 'star headings'. We used different star groups as foundations, such as an Orion based heading of 360 degrees. Orion was one of the easier constellations, because of its obvious orientation to the other star groups. Dimmer constellations like Pleiades were not quite as obvious.

"We will try to use Orion whenever possible," Grandpa decided, "or maybe the Big Dipper. But remember, Walter. It may be necessary to improvise."

"What ever it takes!" Was Grandpa's new mantra.

"Remember," he said, "when all else fails, do whatever it takes to get the job done!"

My great-great-great grandfather had used that philosophy.

It was time to climb back into the flight simulator.

"Eat this," Grandpa ordered, handing me a small bowl of gooey stuff, "I made it myself. It's supercharged with nutrients and energy rich."

I warbled and gobbled it down. Despite its gooey texture, it was actually not half bad.

"We'll start the session by giving you some light, Walter, so you can keep your balance on takeoff," Grandpa shouted as the machine wound up, "but after that you'll be in total darkness!"

I bobbed my head in understanding.

"Easy now," he warned, "use your internal senses and fly a straight bearing. If you sense a wind shift, compensate for it and maintain your original bearing. Do what ever it takes! Got it?"

I bobbed my head again.

"Ok, go!"

I launched into the wind, kept my balance, and almost immediately the lights went out.

"Keep flying, Walter!" Grandpa yelled, "Show me what you've got!"

I warbled several unspeakable words to myself. I was so disoriented, but I concentrated on that imaginary bearing. I had no idea how fast I was flying, but I was flapping extremely hard. I started to pick up on the slight wind shifts Grandpa was throwing at me.

While I labored in the box, George and Kenny worked exhaustively over a stack of checklists developed for the project. They conducted test after test on the systems of Skynest One, double and triple checking everything. Any system glitch had to be investigated and fixed on the spot.

Janine and Fiona spent the night cooking, piling up box lunches and other necessities.

"Work as fast as you can," Grandpa ordered, "the electricity will go out soon, and we will have to rely on our generators!"

We needed to preserve the generators as much as possible for final Skynest One preparation.

Margie had mastered Dottie's computer and spent the night nurturing and re-assuring Dottie. She told Dottie all sorts of stories, including stories about Bird Island. Dottie was enraptured by Margie's rich imagination. She stayed awake through the night. She finally fell asleep in the wee hours of the morning.

I flew on. The bowl of goo Grandpa had fed to me sustained me physically, but my mind began to wander, my imagination ran wild, and I quickly lost track of time.

I imagined that I was flying next to Old Dude with three hawks hot on our tail.

"We kin outrun 'em, Squeaker," Old Dude was saying, " 'cause Grandpa fed us the good stuff! Now you do what he tells you to do, Squeaker! He's one sharp cookie!"

"I miss you, Old Dude," I answered, but he was gone. I still had the hawks on my tail, so I flapped harder.

Then, I imagined that I was tiny, sitting in my nest a foot or so from the door of the coop. I had just lost my downy fuzz and my true colors were starting to emerge. A big hand reached in through the door, scooped me up, and held me up in the sunlight.

"This is the best of the new hatchlings," Rancher George was telling someone. I squinted to see who it was, but the sunlight was too bright.

"Beautiful," a man's voice exclaimed, "he looks just like his old lady!"

"Show her some kindly respect," Old George was saying warily, "She's won every award in the state!"

"No disrespect intended, sir," the other man apologized, "how much do you want for him?"

Rancher George laughed.

"He's not for sale at any price!"

I kept flying. I can fly forever, I told myself, and I even halfway believed it.

"Walter!" It was my mother's voice, "where are you, Walter?""

"Here!" I called. But she was gone, too.

I kept flying.

Whirrr! The machine wound down.

"Grab your perch, Walter!" Grandpa called as the box lit up. I landed and suddenly realized how exhausted I was. I could hardly stay upright on the perch.

Grandpa stood next to the window, checking his stop watch and mentally calculating something. I could tell by his mutters that he was adding things up.

"Amazing," he said finally, "six and a half hours at eighty knots, Walter. That has to be a record. You held a straight bearing in total darkness for well over five hundred miles! Unbelievable!"

I marveled at the accomplishment myself. Grandpa reported my work to George and Kenny, who each whistled and patted me on the head. Then Grandpa carried me outside, just as the sun was rising.

"We had two more earthquakes while you were flying," he told me, "each one a little stronger than the last. I have a feeling tomorrow will be our last day here."

I only halfway listened to Grandpa. I was distracted by the sound of geese barking out behind the other side of the barn, near the old cow pond. It was a whole lot of barking, the barking of a big flock of geese. I pecked Grandpa on the cheek and flew off to find Henry.

48

I MEET UP WITH HENRY AND JEWELL

The flock of geese were just waking with the sun. It was a full flock of over a hundred geese, scattered all the way around the perimeter of the Grandpa's stock pond.

"Hi, Squeaker," a guard goose greeted me as I approached.

As I expected, Henry was up, wide awake and standing next to Jewell near the water's edge. I hopped through a crowd of stirring geese and made my way over to him. He spotted me and flapped his wings.

"What's up?" I asked as I approached.

"Same old stuff," Henry answered, "not much going on. How about you?"

"Same here," I said, "it's great to see you, Henry, and you too, Jewell!"

"We flew back and found your farm late last night and called for you," Henry explained, "but you must have been busy.""

"I was," I confirmed, "I was inside of that little shack over there, working on a big project."

"We decided to settle here for the night and wait for you," Jewell said, "but it was a rough night, the ground shook a lot.""

"Earth quakes," I said, "and it's going to get worse. Are you heading south like the other flocks?"

"Yes," Henry answered, "we came further east than normal to find you, Squeaker. But when we take wing, it will be due south for a long, long way!"

"Based on what I've heard," I said," that is probably the best plan."

I told him about the myth of Bird Island.

"As good a plan as any," Henry agreed.

"By the way," I continued, "around here, they call me Walter."

"Walter," Jewel said, "what a pretty name!"

Just then, George and Grandpa rounded the corner of the barn carrying giant sacks of grain on their shoulders.

"Sweet cob," Grandpa said, "should keep these fella's going for a' while."

He held my computer in his free hand. Some of the geese squawked and hopped out of his way.

"Friends of yours?" Henry asked me carefully.

"The older one is my best friend," I assured him, "and the younger one is his son. They are good humans, Henry, very kind and very smart. They are my new family."

Henry settled his flock down with reassuring words. Then we watched as Grandpa and George scattered the cob all around.

"They are very kind," Henry observed, "please give them our thanks.'"

I hopped over to Grandpa and George as they finished spreading the grain. I perched on Grandpa's knee as we sat and watched Henry and his flock enjoy their breakfast. Grandpa held out my computer for me.

"This is my friend Henry," I typed, "he said that they are very grateful to you."

"Good," Grandpa said, "any friends of yours, Walter, are welcome to anything we can spare."

After a few minutes, Henry and Jewell hopped over to us. I made the introductions and Henry once again thanked Grandpa and George.

"You are very welcome," Grandpa said through me.

Henry looked at me, slightly amused.

"I knew this would happen, Squeaker," he said, "you've fallen in love with humans!"

Then he grew serious.

"Do they have any idea what is about to happen to them?" he asked.

"Yes," I answered, "that is what their project is all about. Grandpa is an enlightened human! He built a project to protect as many people as he can, plants and animals, too."

"That tiny shack will not fare well," Henry said.

"You should see what is below it," I confided to him, "a grand Skynest! Grandpa is a genius!"

"Walter," Grandpa said, "tell Henry that we wish to take two geese, preferably mates."

"Mates that get along with each other," George added, and chuckled.

"Yes," Grandpa agreed, laughing. "That would be preferable. Also, ask Henry for any idea he has about what is happening."

Jewell hopped off into the flock after I translated Grandpa's wishes.

"I'm the leader of the flock," Henry answered, "Jewell and I will stay with our kin and head south."

I typed furiously on my computer, keeping up with Henry.

"As for your other question," he continued, "we call it 'The Big One'. The whole world shakes and floods and catches on fire. Almost everything dies."

Grandpa nodded his head in understanding as John Wayne's voice laid it out for him.

"I will lead my flock deep south," Henry continued, "and hunt for Bird Island!

"Walter just told me about it, but we have always known. It's just a story we tell each other at night, but who knows, it may be real. In any event, it is probably our only hope."

"I wish I could take more of you with us," Grandpa sadly lamented, "I wish there was a way."

Henry bobbed his head.

"Thank you, Grandpa," he said, "but we need to stay together as a flock. That is our way."

"Fly south," I told him, "and fly fast and hard! Stay over land through the hot zone and keep heading south until the land is cold again. Bird Island should be south of that, across a narrow stretch of water, near a big land of ice."

"Thanks, Squeaker," Henry bobbed.

Jewell hopped back to us with a pair of younger geese.

"This is our son, Caesar," she introduced, "and his mate, Mishka. They have agreed to go with you, Squeaker. You are as special to them as you are to Henry and me."

I introduced Caesar and Mishka to Grandpa and George.

"Wonderful," Grandpa said, "and now, I have to go. I have so much to do. God speed, Henry and Jewell!"

"Keep the wind at your tail, Grandpa!" Henry answered through me.

Then Henry looked at his expectant flock and shouted, "Up and away!"

Caesar and Mishka stood next to me as the flock took wing, circling us twice forming a "V", and then headed south.

Mishka watched them for a long time and cried.

49

THE EXODUS

It was a terribly rough day. The ground shook more frequently and black clouds formed overhead, blotting out the sun. Fiona's parents, Herb and Martha, arrived shortly after noon. Janine sat them down for a quick lunch.

Marshall's mother refused to leave New York City. I saw the true side of Marshall as he sat outside underneath the front yard tree, crying. Grandpa went outside and sat down next to him, talked to him quietly and threw his big arm around the young man's shoulder.

I spent some time resting up, and then played with Margie and Dottie, who were now best friends. Grandpa fetched me to his workshop. As we went over Morse code and celestial navigation, Grandpa told me how pleased he was with my quick progress.

"You are picking it up just fine, Walter," he complemented me. Then he grew very quiet for a while.

"Walter," he asked finally, "where do you think pigeons go when they die?"

I typed on my computer.

"I have it on the best authority that we fly up to The Great Nest in the Sky, where we stand before The Great White Stork and give a full account of our lives. Hopefully, a good account."

"A nest in the sky," Grandpa said as he rubbed his beard, "Skynest!"

"Yes," I typed, "where The Great White Stork measures and weighs us and then, if we are found brave enough, and have a good heart, we see all of our family and friends who have flown up to The Great Nest before us."

"A nest in the sky," grandpa repeated pensively, "kind of like heaven for humans. Could it be the same place, Walter?"

"Of course it is," I typed," death would never separate the brave and the kind, who live forever. Animals or humans. Old Dude was certain of it!"

Grandpa smiled.

"Thank you, Walter," he said, "I want to meet Old Dude one of these days."

"You have a lot in common with him," I assured him.

By late afternoon, the sky was stormy and it started to rain. The ground rumbled. Kenny stood on the front porch and I landed on his shoulder.

"Look at that Walter," he said. I looked out to the horizon. The sky had gone crazy with bizarre whirling black clouds.

"Twisters," Kenny told me, "tornadoes, Walter. I can count at least forty of them out there."

Grandpa turned on a loud, piercing siren and lit up a bright light out next to the highway.

"Hopefully, its batteries will hold up," he grumbled.

People began to arrive in their cars and trucks, their headlights piercing the rain and wind. I knew that they came from all over the county, and that most of them were here to bring and drop off their children. I watched through the front window as mothers and fathers hugged their children, cried, and sent them to Grandpa. I cried too. There just was not enough room aboard Skynest One for everybody. Then I recognized Sheriff Tim and his family, the mayor and his. Miss Dixon, too. They were the few lucky adults who had been selected by Grandpa for their particular talents.

Grandpa looked cool as he herded everyone through the open door of the tiny shack. But I had been with him long enough to recognize that he was deeply concerned, almost panicked. Everything was happening much faster than he had anticipated. The shack entrance was too slow.

"Raise Skynest!" Grandpa shouted to George. George nodded and hurried into the shack. A few moments later, I witnessed a sight that I will never forget.

As Grandpa waved everyone back, way back, from the shack, the ground started to rumble. Out of the Texas dirt, it emerged.

It was enormous!

It was a gigantic black, shiny ship that looked like Henry with his wings tucked to his sides. The ship was at least a hundred times, I thought, bigger than the farmhouse. Its tail end disappeared into the dark night. A huge hatch opened at ground level, large enough to allow dozens to board at once. George walked out to help the children board.

The wind outside was unbearably strong now, and it was too dark to see where the twisters were.

I flew into Dottie's room to check on her. She was wide awake, sitting up in bed and looking frightened. Someone was missing.

"Where is Margie?" I typed into Dottie's computer.

"I thought she was with you," Dottie typed.

"I'll find her" I typed, "don't worry."

"I love you Walter," Dottie's computer answered as I rushed out of the room.

Caesar, Mishka and Schatzie cowered in the living room with Fiona and her mother. Herb was outside, helping Janine with the children. Bear sat simmering in a big pet carrier. He growled when he spotted me.

"Have you seen Margie?" I asked Caesar and Mishka.

"No", Caesar said, shaking his head.

"I did hear something up on the roof, through the wind noise," Mishka said, "like a squirrel scratching to get in."

Margie on the roof? In this wind and rain? No way!

Frantically, I flew all through the house and searched everywhere. No Margie.

The roof?

No way!

50

RESCUING MARGIE

Sure enough, Margie was trapped on the roof, latched on to the weather vane for dear life in the howling wind and rain.

I found Janine and, with her help and my computer, devised a plan to scale the windward side of the house to the crest of the roof and hopefully bring Margie down to safety. Janine tied a long line of thin nylon string to my left leg and carried me to the window, where the wind blew us backward as soon as we opened it. It was that good old Texas duster wind, the kind of wind that crosses the state and winds up carrying the Texas topsoil to the Atlantic Ocean.

As soon as I crawled out of the window and up the white paneled siding of the house, the wind plastered me against the wall and pelted me with dust, dirt, grass and gravel. To either side of me, I could feel larger objects slamming into the wall, but so far I was lucky to avoid them. I had to hang on for dear life as I inched my way up. One false move and I was going to end up in Georgia, hopping around on one leg. Grandpa had his hands full, directing the last arriving busloads of children as they slowly drove up the dark, dusty drive. Where were their parents, I briefly wondered? At one point, when I had progressed about halfway up the side of the house, Grandpa ran by and spotted me.

"We are running out of time," he yelled through the wind noise at me, "Walter, what on earth are you doing up there?"

Oh, just hanging around, Grandpa, enjoying this fine, calm Texas evening!

The dust, gravel and sharp bits of tumbleweed were really hurting now, pelting me like lead shot from a shotgun.

Thoughts were running rampant though my mind. What had possessed her to go up there? There was no telling with Margie. I wondered how much longer she could hang on. Janine fed out the nylon string and I continued up until I had the crest of the roof in sight.

Margie spotted me as I topped the edge of the roof. I was now totally depending on the strength of the nylon to keep me from flying off into space. The string cut into my leg like a sharp knife, and I was beginning to feel warm blood running down the side of my foot.

I could see Margie screaming at me, and I could see the sheer panic in her eyes. I knew that it would only be a matter of time before she weakened and was gone. I had to hurry and, despite the biting pain in my left leg, tugged harder on the string. Janine carefully played the nylon string out and I started creeping along the ridge of the rooftop. At first, I scratched around and had trouble gaining any purchase with my claws on the roof shingles, but I finally worked out a way to grip them.

My progress was agonizingly slow and I started to really worry about my left leg. How much blood was I losing? It felt like either my leg would break, or I would run out of blood any minute. I continued to creep, shingle by shingle, as the wind behind me blew my feathers and wings out and threatened to launch me into the air. Shingles all along the roof started to flap loudly, rip apart and spin through the dark air like deadly whirling meat cleavers.

After what seemed to me like an eternity, I reached the weather vane and Margie. The weather vane was bent crooked and flapping, obviously just about to break off and take Margie with it. She was flipping from side to side as it whipped back and forth in the wind gusts. But, miraculously, she was still hanging on.

"Oh, Great White Stork!" Margie screamed when I reached her. "Thank you, Little Brother!"

"What on earth are you doing up here?" I yelled, my beak as close as possible to hers as she flipped around.

"I missed my Merle," she screamed back, afraid to let go of the weather vane, "I always come up here when I miss him. I didn't know that the sky was about to fall!"

"It just about has!" I yelled.

Margie was in bad shape, bleeding from a multitude of wounds and missing over half of her feathers.

"Climb on my back, Margie," I yelled, "trust me; and whatever you do, don't let go! I'll get you down!"

"Ok, Little Brother!" She screamed, and reached toward me with her beak and one leg. The other leg still held a death grip on the weather vane. I could feel her claws digging through my feathers and gripping the skin on my back. It hurt like the dickens!

When I felt Margie securely aboard, I tugged hard with my left leg and Janine started playing out the nylon string again. Before I started creeping again, I yelled at Margie.

"Margie, if you let go," I screamed, "you will die!"

"I know, I know!" She screamed.

The wind howled, shingles whizzed by our heads like buzz saws, and I felt Margie's grip weakening.

"Hang on tight!" I yelled again. Margie was warbling to herself, praying to The Great White Stork.

I crept slowly, agonizingly, gripping the shingles that still held, working around the loose ones. If a loose shingle hit Margie, I knew, it was over for her.

Finally, I could see the far edge of the roof through the blowing dust. Janine played out more string and allowed me to reach the downwind side of the house and drop over the edge into the windbreak. We had done it, the wind calmed down! I hung in the air by my left leg with Margie on my back, too exhausted to do anything else.

Fiona's parents, Herb and Martha, stood waiting at the window below, with Herb leaning out to look up at us. Janine eased us down into his waiting hands and he gently gathered us in.

"Thank you, Odin," I whispered as Herb untied the nylon string from my bruised and bleeding leg. He pried Margie off of my back and handed her to Martha.

"Poor guy," Herb said, and started dabbing my wounds and dressing them.

Margie lay like a limp rag doll in Martha's hand, passed out cold!

"This little girl is going to need a lot of attention," Martha exclaimed, reaching for the salve and bandages.

Janine came running in from Dottie's room, picked me up and kissed me.

"You are my hero, Walter!" she exclaimed, beaming at me with her pretty brown eyes.

The house started to tremble with the onset of another earthquake. I heard dishes falling and breaking, and water blasting from a broken water pipe somewhere.

"This house is unsafe," Herb said, "we have to evacuate now!"

George ran in through the front door. He was dirty, sweaty and bleeding from a couple of cuts on his dark face.

"Get out of here, now!" he yelled, "Two twisters are heading straight for us!"

Without another word, he dashed straight for Dottie's room.

51

A SAD ESCAPE

It all happened so fast. Janine pushed Caesar and Mishka into a rabbit cage.

"Only for a little while," she assured them.

Margie and I were gently placed into a wicker picnic basket. Margie was placed on a small, soft pillow. She was still unconscious. I looked at her poor gray, crumpled body and sighed.

Schatzie ran around in circles, barking at the wind. Fiona's parents hoisted the rabbit cage with the geese and marched out into the storm.

I could see everything through the slits of the wicker basket. I saw Fiona scoop up Schatzie and head out the door, with the poor dog still whining and barking. Janine grabbed Kenny and handed him the picnic basket.

"Be careful" she told her son, "Walter and Margie are inside, and they are both hurt."

Kenny hugged his mother.

"Hurry, Mom!" He shouted. "Get out of here!"

Marshall took charge of Bear and grunted as he hefted the big cat and his carrier.

Outside, in the horrible dust and rain, I was expecting complete pandemonium. The truth was, everyone was working quickly, but calmly, following Grandpa's orders.

Curiously, I heard what sounded like a freight train barreling down on us, getting closer and closer.

Janine and George were still inside the farmhouse, wrapping Dottie in blankets. They ran out with her and George handed her to Grandpa.

"Crank open the helium!" Grandpa shouted fiercely, and George took off for the barn. The freight train roar was growing closer.

I looked behind the farmhouse at the gigantic black, shiny ship with huge shiny wings, nearly the size of the city of Jerome, Texas! The last of the children were climbing into its' giant hatch, holding onto the side rails. Miss Dixon was helping them aboard.

The train was roaring louder, getting closer.

"Wait!" Janine screamed, and ran back into the farmhouse.

"No!" Grandpa screamed at her, "Janine!"

Everything switched to slow motion for me. I could see Janine running slowly into the farmhouse. I could see that what I had thought was a freight train was actually a giant, dark, evil twisting mass of dust, dirt, boards, tumbleweeds, rocks and who knows what else. It materialized from the darkness like a huge monster and headed directly toward the farmhouse, just as Janine disappeared through the front door. George ran out of the barn, screaming, "No!" He ran for the farmhouse, but Grandpa tackled him and forced him to the ground.

"It's too late, son!" Grandpa screamed.

The twister ate the farmhouse. Janine appeared on the front porch, holding Dottie's computer in her hand. She looked terrified. Then, just as the twister engulfed her and the rest of the house, her face calmed down into an utter look of peace.

"No!" George howled, still down on the ground.

Kenny held the basket containing Margie and me, and cried softly.

Grandpa wore a scowl on his face.

"Get to the ship!" He ordered. "Or we all die!"

He picked up George by the shoulders and pushed him forward. George moved like an old man, crying uncontrollably.

"To the ship!" Grandpa kept screaming. It was raining harder. I looked ahead at the ship and saw three huge bundles of black shiny fabric attached to its humpback unfurling and flapping in the wind.

Kenny carried us up the stairs into what he called "the safe room." It was an enormous room, painted light green, with hundreds of seats and harnesses in it. I looked out at all of the children, strapped in their seats, their eyes red and wet. Miss Dixon was talking soothingly to them. Sheriff Tim had taken charge of Dottie and was securing her in a seat built especially for her. She was also crying.

At the front of the safe room, five steps led up to the 'cockpit,' a two seat affair with big windows, controls, screens, knobs, switches and glowing gauges

I looked up at Kenny through the slits in the basket and could see that the ceiling above him looked like a clear window. I could see one of the huge fabric bubbles expanding outside above us.

Kenny saw what I was looking at and explained through his tears.

"They are called balloons, Walter," he said, "big strong ones. They are going to save us."

Grandpa came on board with George, who was still sobbing uncontrollably, led him up the stairs to the cockpit, and sat him down in a seat.

"George," Grandpa said firmly, "Janine is gone! You have to calm yourself, now! You have to help me fly this ship! We need you, these children need you! Think of Janine! She wouldn't want you to die, she wouldn't want these children to die!"

Grandpa leaned over and gave George a big hug. Fiona, crying, hugged Kenny.

"It will be ok," she whispered softly. Her tears dropped down through the wicker basket and dripped onto my head. Janine, that wonderful, beautiful lady who had saved Margie and me, was gone.

I cried and cried.

"Janine is watching you now," Grandpa gently told George, "make her proud!"

George wiped his eyes and nodded his head.

"I can't do this without you, son," Grandpa repeated. He twisted a knob on the control panel, threw a switch and I heard a 'whoosh'! Then, I felt pressure on my ears.

"We are pressurizing," Grandpa announced. He looked back from the cockpit, and down at his passengers.

"Kenny, strap those birds down!" He ordered. "Miss Dixon, strap in. Make sure your straps are tight!"

"Balloons are full," George said quietly.

"Good," Grandpa said. He was still looking back at us. Kenny strapped our basket down on a small platform next to his seat and then strapped himself in. He looked around at all of the children and gave Grandpa a thumbs-up.

"I'm detaching the helium hoses," Grandpa said, "the barn is on fire!"

"Releasing the hold-down latches," George said, "there!"

Grandpa waved away the brave fathers who were standing outside of Skynest, manning the hold-down latches. At his signal, they released their hold on the ship. Their children were aboard and safe for now. Slowly, but surely, the giant ship started to rise. He then looked over at his son, who was still sobbing quietly. He patted him on the shoulder.

"George," he said quietly, but firmly, "you are the captain now. Skynest One is yours to command. Get us out of here!"

End of Part Two

PART THREE

Dear readers, losing Janine was one of the saddest things that ever happened to me! To this day, I still cry at the memory of that dark night. I know that my story is giving you a dreadful feeling about what is happening at this point. Doom seems certain. But in the face of doom, hope always takes a strong stand! Stay with me as I pull you deeper into the cataclysm that inevitably follows in these next chapters. It was certainly the end of an Age of Man, and everything else for that matter… but hope springs eternal! Read on, Dear ones!

52

SKYNEST FLYS!

I can remember the tumbles I took early on in Grandpa's flight
simulator, how rough they had been on me. They were nothing
compared to what I was experiencing now.

Skynest One rocketed up off the ground and immediately got
tossed around in the wind like Schatzie's red ball bouncing around
in the backyard. The higher Skynest climbed, the harder the wind
buffeted it.

"Running lights on, now!" George commanded.

"Running lights on," Grandpa confirmed.

Skynest's balloons floated directly above us and lit up like giant
light bulbs.

The ship shook and trembled hard. The women and children
started screaming and crying. Men grimaced. Margie woke up.

"What's up, Cowboy?" She asked me weakly.

"Nothing much," I managed to say, "same old stuff."

Something huge hit the side of the ship and violently knocked it
sideways. Margie closed her eyes again.

"We hit something!" George said to Grandpa.

"Probably shack debris that got away," Grandpa answered as he
studied the gauges, "she'll hold together. Nothing showing up on
the radar yet."

The ship started to sway violently from side to side.

"Warp the rudder, George," Grandpa said, "turn her nose back into the wind. We don't want to tangle the balloons."

George worked some foot pedals in front of him and I felt the whole ship turning. My ears popped as the room continued to pressurize.

Grandpa and George started to calm down.

"Ten-thousand," Grandpa said, "big storm cell dead ahead, fourteen miles, thirty miles across."

"Tops?" George asked, working the rudder.

"About sixty-thousand," Grandpa answered, "I recommend passing to the left."

"I concur," George said, "fire up the aft prop, we need some thrust."

Grandpa worked switches while George worked the controls. I could feel the big ship slowly turning left.

"That's it," George said. I could see tears streaming down his face, "that's it."

"Activating the remaining air packs," Grandpa said, "I want to be fully pressurized when we top out!"

"Concur," George answered.

And so it went. The two of them calmly conversed while the ship shook violently and four hundred children cried.

"Twenty-thousand," Grandpa said, "pressurizing nicely."

"Thirty thousand, clearing the cell... uh, uh, come right, now. Another storm cell ahead, twenty miles, thirty-five miles across."

"Tops?"

"Fifty-five thousand."

"Climbing through forty thousand."

"Pressures holding, George. Good....good, you're clearing it."

"Fifty-thousand."

"Ok, shutting down the aft prop," Grandpa said, "stowing it."

"Good."

I pictured in my mind: the giant, black shiny ship, bigger than Old Dude's learnin' school, climbing up through the clouds! The things these men built!

"Passing sixty," Grandpa reported, "we're on top."

"Any weather breaking through?" George asked.

"Uh... no," Grandpa said, "but I can see Skynest Two, balloons bright, about two hundred miles over there on the southeast horizon. Edward made it!"

"Good!"

"Seventy-thousand...steady as she goes."

I looked up again through the clear ceiling. I could see bright stars above, brighter than I had ever seen them before. And a spectacular, full moon dominated the heavens. Everything was dead calm now.

"No leaks," Grandpa reported.

"Good," George said.

"Eighty-thousand," Grandpa said, "and activating flight-leveling stabilizers."

"The balloons are made from a new nano-fabric," Kenny whispered to me, "they don't expand or leak."

I understood most of that. What I intuitively knew though, was that we were tremendously higher than any pigeon had ever flown.

"Slowing," Grandpa said, "ninety-thousand."

"Easy, girl," George said to the ship.

"Approaching one hundred thousand," Grandpa reported, "activate the final flight level stabilizers, George."

"Right, Dad," George said, "leveling."

Grandpa wrapped his arms around George's shoulder.

"You've done a fine job, son," he said as George hung his head, "I'll take it from here. You take Kenny and Dottie to your cabin. They are going to need you now."

George started to quietly cry again. Kenny looked up from the children, saw him and started to sob.

"Come on, son," George said, hugging Kenny. They unstrapped Dottie and went away through a hatch at the far side of the safe room.

Grandpa unstrapped and stood to face his passengers.

"Welcome to Skynest One," he said, loud enough to quiet the children, "I'm going to need another hour to safely anchor us at one hundred, ten-thousand feet. We can climb even higher if we need to, but for now, I think that will be high enough. I will use this time to run status checks on the ship and then I want to talk to all of you children. For now, please stay seated. Miss Dixon will help you with your straps and will give you lunch boxes and water. If you need to go to the restroom, Miss Dixon will show you where they are located. Does anyone have any questions?"

Sheriff Tim stood up.

"Grandpa, I know that we are high," he said. He walked up to Grandpa and whispered: "What happens if we get hit by a volcanic rock or meteorite?"

Grandpa looked pensive for a moment.

"It's possible," he finally agreed, "but remember, Tim, the hull of this airship is a hundred times stronger than steel, and ten times lighter. It shouldn't be a problem. If the hull is breached, it has memory. It will quickly close back up and seal itself."

"Let's hope so," Sheriff Tim grumbled.

Fiona opened my basket and, with a tearful face, soothed me with quiet tones and whispers. Margie opened her eyes again; but she was obviously suffering from a lot of pain, disoriented and disheveled.

"I'll be back in a little while," I told her, "You need to rest as much as you can, Margie."

"I'm not going anywhere, Little Brother," she said weakly, "thank you for saving my life."

Then she closed her eyes again.

I flew to the cockpit where Grandpa was busily working, landed on his shoulder and pecked him on the cheek. He paused and smiled at me.

"I've never been this high before," I tapped to him in Morse code on his shoulder, "you made it look easy, Grandpa."

Grandpa sighed.

"Get used to it, Walter," he answered, "welcome to our new home.

Home was now a gigantic ship, aloft in the thin upper atmosphere at 110,000 feet, with nearly four hundred children aboard.

Only Grandpa could pull off such a feat!

53

THE GREAT DARK RIFT

Grandpa Jerome, Sir Alfred Jerome of The Seven New Sages, was now at least ten feet tall in my eyes. He was doing the impossible and succeeding. He was a great man, almost equal in my eyes to the Great White Stork. To me, he looked like my very vision of what The Great White Stork must look like. I wanted to be with him when I died.

He worked hard at the controls of Skynest One, checking and double checking readouts, making adjustments, stabilizing the great beast with ease at 110,000 feet like we were sitting in Grandpa's living room!

The children ate bits of their lunch boxes and cried. All four hundred children that Grandpa had planned for were aboard. It was a miracle. Fiona, Martha, Mrs. Sheriff Tim and Miss Dixon circulated through the children, comforting them and taking them to the restroom, seeing to their needs.

All of the children from Janine's school were present. They were only a few of the many children aboard, most of whom I had never seen before. Their ages seemed to run from about three years old to seventeen or eighteen.

My left leg was stiff and sore, but I ignored it and flew around the children, landing on their shoulders and kissing them on the cheeks. That's right, I had learned how to kiss instead of peck, much to Dottie's delight! Through the children's tears, I elicited a brief smile here and there.

Grandpa finished his work and stood at the top of the stairs at the cockpit, facing the children. I flew up and landed on his shoulder.

"Good work, Walter," he whispered. Then he called the children to attention.

"Dear children of Skynest One," he started with a deep, but kind voice, "your parents love you very, very much! That is why they wanted you to come with me. You are going to be safe, I promise!

"All of your parents are very brave people. They chose to stay down below so you would have the best chance to live. The world is going through a big change, and they knew they could not keep you safe down below until that change is over.

"I know how much you miss your parents, how much you love them. I know how sad you are right now. But I want to tell you about the other part of my project. All over the world, high up in the highest of the high mountains, my teams have built thousands and thousands of strongholds. It took us many years to build them, but they are very strong buildings packed with enough food to last your parents for many, many years.

"Right now, all of your parents are driving to some of those strongholds high up in the Rocky Mountains. My studies have convinced me that they will be safe and sound. Other people who have listened to my warnings are also heading to other strongholds that have been built all over the world.

"You saw the terrible wind and storms when we left, but those storms will ease up for a week or two before they start again. Your parents will have plenty of time to reach the safety of the mountains.

"Your parents want us to live up here in the air until the world settles down again. If you cry because you miss them, don't worry. I cry because I miss them, too. We will pray together for their safety every day.

"Now I want every one of you to look up and pick out two of the prettiest stars in the sky. I asked your parents to do that, too. Talk to your stars every night before you go to sleep. Your parents will hear you, I promise!"

The hundreds of children gave one giant, collective sigh. Most of them looked up beyond the bright hovering balloons and hunted for their own, personal stars. Grandpa grew another ten feet in my eyes. He turned his head and looked at me with his sparkling, brown eyes.

"Walter," he said, "there is a historical precedent for all of this, you know. The holy city of Lhasa, high up in the mountains of Tibet, is not located where it is by accident. It sits high up on the site of an ancient stronghold, built just before the world's last crossing through a dark matter river in space. It is the ancient home of The Seven Sages who escaped from Atlantis with their ark of knowledge. 'Ark' to them meant a strong vessel of knowledge. They did their best to re-build a fresh, new world. Of course, their knowledge has mostly been lost to men in the cobwebs of tens of thousands of years of antiquity, but maybe not to you and your kind."

Then he called Miss Dixon over.

"Show the children to their assigned cabins," he instructed the pretty young teacher, "four to a cabin. They will be delighted when they see that they can look up through the clear ceilings and see their stars."

"Right away, Grandpa," she said, and gave Grandpa a big hug, "thank you, Grandpa, for everything!"

Then he called over Sheriff Tim.

"I want to hold a memorial service for Janine at 10:00 tomorrow morning. Will you preside over it with me?"

"I would be honored, Grandpa," Sheriff Tim said with sadness in his voice, and gave Grandpa a big hug.

Later that night, Kenny showed me something. We sat nearly alone while everyone but Grandpa and George slept.

"It will be days before I can sleep," Kenny told me.

We sat and studied the stars together.

"See the Milky Way, Walter?" Kenny asked.

"Warble, warble."

"There is a dark band without any stars cutting across the middle of it now, see that?"

I bobbed my head.

"That band is called the Dark Rift, the band of dark matter I told you about. We will enter it in a week or so. That is when the world will really start to shift."

"Warble, warble." It was a big story in pigeon collective memory. The world flooding, the terrible dark sky, the fire coming out of the middle of the world, so many things dying. Oh yes, we remembered it all too well, and now I pictured it clearly in my mind. The Big One!

"The world should be in its' most violent state right around the winter solstice," Kenny continued, "and the surface will look like a nuclear winter. That's half a year from now. Then it will take the world another three years to exit to the other side of the Rift. Then, we enter what Grandpa calls the Golden Band."

"Warble?"

The Golden Band?

"We don't know much about the Golden Band, Walter. Grandpa detected its' radiation two years ago."

I searched my memory for anything about a Golden Band, and came up empty.

54

THE STAR OF HOPE

Within the next hour, Skynest Two, commanded by Dr. Edward Jerome, and Skynest Five, commanded by Dr. Lucas Jerome, were both in radio and visual contact with Grandpa.

"It was a rough ride," Dr. Lucas relayed, "but we are in one piece."

"How many souls are on board?" Grandpa asked his brothers.

"Two hundred and ninety-one," Dr. Edward said.

"Three hundred and eighty-eight," Dr. Lucas answered, "we missed a few. They never showed up."

"Probably the twisters," Dr. Edward said, "A big one nearly took the ship."

"We lost Janine," Grandpa said quietly.

There was a long silence on the radio.

"Good work, Gentlemen," Grandpa said, finally, "I'll hold the base position, join on me."

"Radar shows you to be two hundred miles out," Dr. Lucas said, "but you look a lot closer, Alfred."

"Not much atmosphere up here," Grandpa answered, "the thin air magnifies everything."

"Of course." Dr. Edwards agreed. "We're a hundred and fifty miles southeast and it looks like we are on top of you.'"

"Bring them in slow," Grandpa ordered, "we have nothing but time, brothers."

Kenny and I moved up to the cockpit. I hopped from Kenny's shoulder to Grandpa's.

"I'm going to extend the control pod now," Grandpa told Kenny. He flipped a red covered switch and the cockpit started to move up and out. We rose about ten feet above the main deck and now sat in an extended clear, round ball. The stairs converted into a ladder of sorts, leading back down to the main deck. We had a perfect view of the sky above us, below us and all around us. Lightning streaked through clouds far below us. The feeling of total exposure in the clear ball was dizzying and disorienting to me.

"Lighting the ship now." Grandpa radioed and threw another switch. I turned around and watched as the entire length of our ship lit up with bright, white light.

"Wow," Dr. Lucas said, "a bright new star in the sky!"

"Yes," Grandpa agreed, "let's call it the Star of Hope!"

"Extending wings," Dr. Lucas said, "firing up all props."

"Take it slow," Grandpa repeated. He leaned back with satisfaction and turned to Kenny.

"The wonders of modern technology," he stated, "beautiful, isn't it?"

"The ship is fully lit up outside," Kenny explained to me, "and the light projects outward. For the children sleeping in their cabins, the windows are dark. They let in starlight, but filter out ship light."

"Coming forward toward you, Alfred," Dr. Edward said.

"Careful, gentlemen." Grandpa told his brothers. Kenny and I watched as the two new bright stars called Skynest Two and Skynest Five drifted across the glorious night heavens toward us.

55

A FLOATING CITY IN THE SKY

A month passed. One by one, like shining stars gathering to form a new constellation, ships approached us from every direction. A hundred ships arrived at first from our hemisphere. The remaining nearly thousand ships were much further out, across oceans, and would take much longer to reach us.

Our hundred ships floated in a stabilized loose diamond formation, holding a safe distance of one thousand yards between one another.

Seven of the ships were commanded by the Jerome brothers, while the others belonged to close professional peers of the brothers. All of the ships were filled to the brim with children, teachers, nurses and families of the project builders.

"I wish we had more ships," Grandpa lamented, "it was so hard to convince people of a coming catastrophe, and persuade them to take action."

Grandpa anchored Skynest One in a fixed position, triangulating off of the stars.

"The earth will shift," he said, "but we will not."

He was talking to me more and more as an equal these days.

"We will commence docking procures next week, Walter," he said, "the air turbulence zone is at least forty thousand feet below us."

During the daylight hours, the ships acted as giant solar energy collectors. Their outer skin literally breathed in the sun's rays and converted it to useful power. One big room in our ship was dedicated to what Kenny called a hydroponic greenhouse. He, George and Herb joined forces with the children to tend it and soon little green sprouts of new plants were springing up.

The main deck safe room was converted into a giant classroom, and school was conducted five days a week. I was surprised to see desktops spring up from the floor at the push of a button on the side of every seat. Miss Dixon, Fiona, Martha, Grandpa and Kenny all served as teachers. They divided the children into grade levels and started right away with their continuing education. It was heaven for me as I hopped from desk to desk and studied with the older children. Grandpa was also delighted.

"I have a lot of budding young scientists on my hands," he confided in me.

Saturdays were free days. Movies played on the main deck while all of the adults joined together cooking up their favorite recipes in the ship's galley. It was amazing how much food was stored aboard. The ship had a separate recreation area, complete with swing sets, an exercise floor and, to Schatzie's delight, plenty of red balls. All of the children learned how to milk Myrtle, how to tend the chickens in the chicken yard, how to grow food and, most importantly, the critical process of recycling.

Recycle, recycle, recycle was Grandpa's favorite mantra. Recycle everything!

"I estimate that we have enough supplies to stay up here for more than four years," he told me, to my astonishment.

"What about water?" I typed on my computer.

Grandpa took me to a giant storage room. As far as I could see, clear jelly-like blocks at least a foot square stood stacked from floor to ceiling.

"You are looking at matter," Grandpa told me, "that we can process into food or water, or even fuel. So much is possible, Walter, if you allow your mind to discover it."

I roomed with Kenny while Margie stayed next door with Dottie. The cabins were comfortable, and even seemed spacious because of the big sky windows overhead. I started to spend more and more time in the greenhouse. It contained a wonderful damp climate and a familiar musky smell that reminded me of Old Dude's roost. Little lizards and other ground critters crawled all around the plants, and songbirds sang from the greenhouse's upper reaches. Colorful fish swam among the water lilies in its' many ponds. Bear the cat stealthily hid there, and lurked around like a giant feline jungle predator. Bear always kept things interesting.

It was also a wonderful place to play ball with Schatzie, who had become one of the children's favorite pets.

I started calling Margie the "Great White Stork!" pigeon. Everything she said was preceded or followed by "Great White Stork!" She was healing quickly and her gray plume was growing back.

"Great White Stork, Walter!" She exclaimed as we looked at the seething world below us. "It's terrible, just terrible! What has become of my sisters, my friends, New York?""

I tried hard to comfort her.

"If your sisters and friends are anything like you," I told her, "they will find a way to survive."

"Great White Stork!" Margie said, "How high are we?"

"One hundred and ten-thousand feet."

"Great White Stork! That's higher than the Empire State Building!"

"I think so," I agreed, although I had only seen the Empire State Building while flying in Grandpa's flying machine.

"Great White Stork!"

And so it went.

Two more ships arrived from South America and Grandpa was satisfied that we could safely begin to dock. All of the ships, including ours, spread their wings.

"We are the center," Grandpa told me, "they will join, four directly to us in diamond formation, and spread out from there.'"

I was amazed how much the ships resembled shiny black geese in flight, suspended from strong, giant impermeable balloons. They looked so elegant to me, shining in the bright sun.

Up in the control bubble, I sat on Grandpa's shoulder as Dr. Edward slowly eased his ship closer. George was sitting in our pilot seat, his hands on the controls. Grandpa sat next to him, and the two of them talked quietly over the radio to Dr. Edward.

"Easy as you go, Uncle," George said, "I'm extending a docking tube."

"I see it," Dr. Edward confirmed. I watched as a dark, translucent tube extended out about fifty feet from the left wing of our ship. It had appeared out of nowhere.

A similar tube stretched out from Dr. Edward's ship's wing as he inched closer.

"Easy," George said, "Easy, two degrees to the left. Uh.... there. Yes, bring it in."

The tubes started moving up and down, side to side, seeking each other. Then, with a mild kiss, they connected.

"That's it!" George said with satisfaction. "Welcome aboard, Skynest Two!"

It took thirty days to connect a hundred ships to one another. At night, they all lit up and undoubtedly became the single brightest object in the night sky, next to the moon.

"We will really become the Star of Hope for the people below!" Grandpa assured me. "When the entire thousand ships are connected, we will be three times brighter than the full moon!"

The earth below us was now blanketed by a thick layer of black clouds. Occasionally, we could see a bright orange glow though the darkness, a volcano erupting.

"The earth is starting to shift," Kenny told me, "starting its slow tilt in a new direction."

Grandpa cornered me a few days later.

"Walter," he said, "it's time to continue with your training."

He led me down a long inner corridor to a door of a cabin marked 'Flight Simulator,' and opened it.

I gasped.

There it sat, as good as new.

56

MORPHIC RESONANCE

Three long years passed. The thousand ship formation formally known as 'Skynest' was now the brightest object in the sky. Skynest ships floated in from Europe, Asia, Africa, South America, Russia, and Australia; from everywhere. Weddings took place; babies were born. Great friendships were formed and people even switched ships to be closer to new friends. Over 400,000 children were growing, learning, and finding common ground with each other.

Of the adults aboard, most were doctors and teachers, specialists from every profession. On Sundays, Father Matthew Jerome held services in his chapel on Skynest Seven. But you could also find wonderful Hindu, Buddhist and Islamic areas to worship, among many other religions, if you so desired. One thing was certain, every person aboard this grand flotilla was happy to be alive.

Grandpa quietly established rules for the governing of Skynest and reigned over the project as Chief Director.

Kenny and Fiona were married at the end of the first year aloft, which resulted in my prompt eviction from Kenny's cabin. I took residence with Margie and Dottie, which was difficult. Margie talked constantly! Great White Stork this and Great White Stork that! The healthy food aboard ship had trimmed her down nicely and she was a very attractive female. But if we were the last two pigeons alive on earth, it would spell the end of our species. She was not my type!

Marshall was having trouble attracting prospective human females. He decided to travel like a vagabond from ship to ship on free days, putting on plays for the children. My favorite was his version of Treasure Island. He, of course, was Long John Silver and said things like "shiver me timbers!" Kenny played his good mate, Hawkins, and did a fine job of it. I, of course, played Cap'n Flint, Long John Silver's faithful parrot! Kenny would hold my computer up to me while I perched on Marshall's shoulder, and I would type furiously.

"Pieces of eight! Pieces of eight! Pieces of eight!" John Wayne's voice would exclaim, over and over again. The kids would howl with laughter and roll around on the floor.

We even got them involved.

"Fifteen men on a dead man's chest..." Long John Silver would sing. Then the kids would pipe in: "Yo-ho-ho and a bottle of rum!"

"Pieces of eight! Pieces of eight! Pieces of eight!" I would exclaim.

The greenhouse was now a luscious garden, full of fruits, flowers, vegetables and such a heavenly smell! I, along with everyone else, spent plenty of time there, breathing in the rich fresh air.

The intricate matrix of connected ships provided a fabulous flying arena for me. Grandpa's flying machine workouts had made me incredibly strong, and every day I flew through the docking tubes, and through all of the ships lining the perimeter of the gigantic Skynest formation. It was a wonderful flying circuit. Everyone knew me by name and waved at me as I flew past. Kids always had treats stuffed in their pockets for me.

Grandpa allowed me to attend school classes, but he was clearly more interested in my progress with star navigation and Morse code. I practiced Morse code until I could tap it out as fast as Grandpa talked! From that point on, it became my primary form of communication with him.

"Why Morse code?" I tapped out one day, "why am I learning it?"

"The earth's atmosphere and magnetic field will be disturbed for many years," Grandpa tapped back, "we have been sending down radio broadcasts for three years, Walter, with no response. I think that there are millions of people still alive down there, especially in the strongholds, but our radios can't reach them. Morse code works well in adverse conditions, so it will probably be the first type of signal to get through. We have been using it every day, but so far we've received no answer."

"Do you really think anyone survived down there?" I tapped.

"I hope so," Grandpa tapped back with a grim look on his face.

One day, Kenny strutted around the ship with a big smile on his face. At dinner, he stood up and tapped his spoon on his water glass to gain everyone's attention.

"Fiona and I are expecting!" He announced. Fiona beamed as everyone congratulated the couple. Expecting what, I wondered? Margie saw the confusion on my face.

"Fiona is pregnant, you moron!" She gently explained to me like I was probably the dumbest bird in the world. "She's going to have a baby!"

Oh, ok. That made sense.

Grandpa stood up.

"This calls for the finest brandy," he proudly announced, "from our secret, private stash!"

"Here, here!" Exclaimed George, who had just recently started spending a lot of time with Miss Dixon, the beautiful young teacher.

Later, after my exhausting lessons, Grandpa settled in to smoke his pipe and sip on a glass of brandy. The briefing room with my flight simulator doubled as his workshop, with a desk, computers and books, and a big easy chair. I perched on his desk and watched him blow wonderful smoke rings into the air.

"You know, Grandpa," I tapped on his desk, "there are still a lot of birds alive down there."

Grandpa stopped smoking and turned his gaze toward me. His crystal brown eyes regarded me curiously. That gaze, that long white beard, that strong intelligent face, still startled me when it concentrated directly on me. He was Old Dude's Odin, for sure!

"What makes you think so?" He tapped out in Morse code.

"I don't know," I tapped, "I just know."

Grandpa stood up and opened the door to the cabin.

"Go find Margie, Walter," he said out loud, "let's see what she thinks."

I found Margie in Dottie's cabin, pecking away on my computer. Dottie was propped up in her bed, smiling. Contrary to Dr. Edward's opinion, she was hanging in there. For three years counting, her sickness had stabilized. She was not getting any better, but she was not getting worse.

Margie followed me back to the simulator flight briefing room where Grandpa sat in his easy chair, waiting for us. He spoke directly to Margie.

"Margie," he asked, "do you believe there are still any birds alive down below?"

"Great White Stork, yes!" Margie answered in pigeon.

"There are still tons of birds down there!" She exclaimed. I translated for her by tapping on the desk. Grandpa nodded his head slowly.

"How do you know this?" He asked.

"Beats me, professor," Margie said, "I just know."

Grandpa turned and pulled a book from his bookshelf.

"This is an extensive study of a phenomenon known as Morphic Resonance," he explained, "different species of birds were studied for evidence of it. Pigeons tested extremely well. Evidently you two are capable of using a form of resonant communication to transmit information to other flocks across the world. Great care was taken to ensure that the test flocks never came in physical contact with each other. The methodology of how it worked was never solved, but there was plenty of proof that it did work. It seems to be some type of sub-quantum resonant communication.

Margie rolled her eyes.

"Sub-quantum spuantum! How do you think I found out about my fifth cousins in Kiev," she said, "or my Great Uncle Murray in Egypt and his secret girlfriend, for that matter?"

Grandpa chuckled as I translated.

"Alright," he said, leaning toward us, "the two of you put your heads together and try to find out where these birds are. Where there are birds, there may be people."

"You got it, Sugar-Honey," Margie said, "Great White Stork! I can't wait to get started!"

"We're on it," I tapped to Grandpa.

That night, like every other night, Margie and I prayed at Dottie's bed with Grandpa.

"Our Father...warble, warble..."

"Who art in Heaven...warble...warble..."

Then, we concentrated our thoughts on the birds down below.

57

WE MAKE CONTACT

As Old Dude used to say, *"News travels purty fast amongst pigeons!"* *"Yer can't keep no secrets to yerself, Squeaker,"* he told me, *"If'n you know somethin', purty soon everbody knows it!"*

"How come?" I asked.

"I don't rightly know," Old Dude said, *"I jest know that it makes you watch yer tailfeathers, that's fer sure! Ain't no sense in startin' up any bad gossip 'bout yerself!"*

That is how it worked, this thing called Morphic Resonance. One minute, you did not know something. Then…bing, bang, boom! The next minute you did. It just popped into your head!

Margie and I had group sessions and finally worked out a plan. For an hour each morning and evening, we took turns focusing and concentrating our thoughts to the world below. 'We are up here! We are riding in Skynest, the bright new star in the sky! We will come down. We will help you!'

And so on.

At first, it was difficult teaching Margie how to concentrate for any period of time. She thought about anything and everything but the task at hand.

"I feel like I have a bumble bee bouncing around in my head!" She confessed to me. Then, she would shake her head and scream.

I told Grandpa about her problem.

"Hmm…, that is also a human malady." He told me. "What you and Margie are trying to do is not easy, Walter. Let me see how I can come up with a way to help her."

The next morning, when Margie and I were preparing for our session, Grandpa showed up with a nice looking young man who had a long black beard and a dark complexion. I recognized him immediately as the nice, quiet guy who always greeted me as I flew through Skynest Twenty Four.

"Margie," Grandpa said gently, "I would like to introduce Dr. Mahatma. He is a world famous psychologist and also a master of Zen. He wants to try to help you."

"What's a Zen Master?" Margie asked me.

"Beats me," I shrugged my wings, "let's see what he has to say. What do you think?"

"Ok," Margie said, "But he had better be good! He'd better not try to hypnotize me or anything. Great White Stork! One time, in New York, there was this sidewalk hypnotist and..."

"Margie!" I interrupted gently.

"Ok, ok," she said, pouting, "he'd just better not try any tricks!"

I nodded to Grandpa, and Dr. Mahatma stepped forward.

"Hello, Margie," he said in a quiet, soothing voice, "you are a very special pigeon. God made you one of a kind. There is no other pigeon quite like you. God takes extra special delight in his creatures of the air. Just look at your beautiful plumage!"

"I like this guy!" Margie confided to me, fluffing up her feathers. She kept listening.

"Your thoughts," Dr. Mahatma continued quietly, "are not the real you! Your thoughts are what you, the essence of you, create for yourself and for others. The real you can watch your thoughts from a distance...as they are born...as they take form...as they grow.

"Now, Margie, relax," he continued, "watch from a distance as your thoughts take form."

"Uh, oh," Margie whispered to me, "now he's going to try to hypnotize me! Just like that stupid quack on 42nd Avenue!"

"Shhh!" I said. "He will not! Go with it, Margie! I won't let him. Now just relax and try to do what he says!"

"Margie," Dr. Mahatma continued quietly, "watch your thoughts as they grow."

Margie reluctantly bobbed her head.

"He's a quack, all right!" She whispered to me.

Dr. Mahatma smiled at Grandpa for a second.

"She's a really good patient," he said.

"Margie!" I quipped with more indignation than I actually felt. "Let him try to help!"

Margie reluctantly agreed.

"This is going well." Dr. Mahatma observed. "Margie, your thoughts form from that quiet place that is you, the real you! You can watch them from that quiet, inner place. You can control them. Relax, and nurture the positive thoughts you wish for until they are fully grown. Ignore all of your negative thoughts, they will eventually die without your nurturing. Do you understand?"

Margie slowly bobbed her head.

"Good," Dr. Mahatma said, "Margie, you are the quiet watcher now. Your thoughts are completely separate from the real you! You can observe your own self-created thoughts from a safe distance. You alone are in complete control!"

He went on like that for an hour. Margie started to look cross-eyed, but in the end I think that he actually helped her. He certainly helped me.

In the days that followed, Margie was significantly quieter and really did work hard at focusing her thoughts to the world below. So did I.

Day after day, we practiced morning and evening, forming our thoughts and sending them below. Sometimes, Grandpa sat between us, smoking his pipe and relaxing. Maybe he was trying to do the same thing, trying to contact humans.

Then one day, it happened! Skynest! It hit me like a bolt of lightning out of the clear blue. *Pigeons who ride the Star of Hope, we hear you,* the thought popped into my head. *We are down below! We wait for you!*

It was pigeon language! Somehow, pigeons below had heard!

58

ATLANTIS REVEALED

As hard as we tried, Margie and I could not locate the birds below. We had definitely cracked their information network; but all of the buzz was about us, the Star Riders. It was actually nice, being a celebrity again.

Many times during the past three years, I had told stories of my great-great-great grandfather, and of Old Dude, to Grandpa, George and Kenny.

"I knew instantly that you were no ordinary pigeon," Grandpa once remarked, "I only hope that you never have to prove it the way your great-great-great grandfather did."

Secretly, I wanted to prove myself. I had to prove myself! How was I ever going to stand tall before The Great White Stork otherwise?

To my delight, my stories about Old Dude made Dottie laugh. She enjoyed hearing them over and over again.

Margie was now completely full of herself, thanks to Dr. Mahatma. She claimed that, in addition to being an all-powerful self-watcher, she also had psychic powers.

"I'm going to beam a thought to you from the quietness of space," she typed to Dottie, "and you try to tell me what it is."

It never worked, but Margie kept trying. She told me that it was only a matter of time before she and Dottie would be beaming thoughts to each other.

For our Morphic Resonance sessions, Margie and I decided to change our tactics. We thought only of Bird Island. We described to each other what it must look like, and then we framed a picture of it in our minds. Maybe it would work.

Things were quickly changing with Dottie. As much as she laughed at us, I could tell that she was growing weaker. Her face was gaunt and sallow, almost yellow in color.

Dr. Edward visited her every day. He always walked out with a grave look of concern on his face. One day, he quietly approached Grandpa.

"She is completely out of remission," he told Grandpa, "what little remission she had. She has a month left, at most. I'm so sorry, Alfred. With all of our technology, this is the one problem we can't fix."

Grandpa didn't answer; he only nodded his head. I was in shock. One month? I loved Dottie so much. This could not be happening.

I followed Grandpa back to the simulator briefing room, where he took his seat, lit his pipe and cried quietly. I sat on his shoulder and cried, too. I kissed his cheek.

"It's ok, Walter," he said with tears streaming down his cheeks, "we are not giving up, are we? You and I are too smart to give up, aren't we? We'll think of something."

Later that day, Kenny called everyone to the radar room. Now that he was twenty-three years old, it was Kenny's job to scan the earth's surface with radar and map any changes he could detect.

He was very excited. All six of Grandpa's brothers left their ships and showed up, along with several dozen other scientists.

"As we all know," Kenny started, "the shifting of the earth's crust has been slowing for the past year. We exited the Dark Rift two years ago, but it still takes time for the world to stabilize. Well, it finally has!"

"What about the magnetic field?" Father Matthew asked.

"It's still flipping and flopping," Kenny said, "our magnetic core is still in a sloppy, unstable spin. I'm afraid that it will be a long time before it can be of any use to us."

"Can we locate and re-calibrate the GPS satellites?"

"We are developing a plan for that," Kenny answered, "but remember, the ground support structure for the GPS satellites has been destroyed. Hopefully once we land, we can rebuild ground receivers and begin a re-calibration process."

"Are we still positioned above the earth's new equator?" Grandpa asked.

"Absolutely, Grandpa," Kenny said, "that was a great call! We are smack dab above it and, lo and behold, very close to a giant land mass!"

"And that would be..." Dr. James Jerome asked.

"Well," Kenny said, "it used to be called Antarctica.

He beamed at the scientists, proud of his work.

"I caught sight of it through a hole in the volcanic ash recently," Kenny continued, "it is melting rapidly. It already has a huge, dry coastline that is increasing in size daily."

"And obviously, some other parts of the world are freezing," Grandpa remarked.

"Precisely," Kenny agreed, "according to my calculations on earth's new tilt and rotation, mid-Africa is the new North Pole and the French Polynesian islands make up the new South Pole. The good news is that the majority of the world's landmasses are temperate or tropical."

"Congratulations, Kenneth," Grandpa said, "you have just earned your doctorate, as recognized by all of your peers, present here today!"

"Thank you, gentlemen," Kenny said, grinning broadly.

"Tell us, Professor," Dr. Mark Jerome asked Kenny ceremoniously, "will you be joining us for a brandy tonight?"

"You can count on it!" Kenny answered.

"By the way," Grandpa said, getting the last word, "the big landmass below us has an ancient name, one that we will use from now on."

He looked around the room, letting the suspense grow.

"Its' old name was Antarctica, but its' real name," he said with a smile, "is Atlantis!"

59

OUR MISSION TO SAVE DOTTIE

Dottie continued to deteriorate. She lapsed into deep comas, lying in bed like a little rag doll with her arm taped and hooked up to what Dr. Edward called an IV. George, Miss Dixon, Martha, Margie and I took shifts sitting with her, listening to the constant beep, beep, beep of her monitoring machine.

Grandpa prayed at her bedside every morning and evening. Whoever was present always joined him. Even Caesar and Mishka, along with all of the ship's children, dropped by constantly. The children drew pictures that decorated Dottie's walls. There were pictures of animals, trees, waterfalls, mountains, just about anything to remind Dottie of the beautiful world below us.

When she was awake, I told Dottie about Bird Island and all of its' mysterious wonders.

"I really want to go there," she weakly typed on my computer, "Pilgrim!"

She smiled wanly at me.

I spent some of my free time in college, learning as much as I could about Antarctica. Birds had known about the landmass at the South Pole for thousands and thousands of years, but I learned that men had only discovered it in the last couple hundred years or so. What had happened to men, that they knew so little of the world?

Kenny confirmed that the entire Antarctic Ross Ice Shelf had broken away from the mainland, and was floating hundreds of miles out to the sea, melting rapidly. It was an enormous chunk of ice.

I learned that the ice at the center of Antarctica was nearly 9000 feet thick. It would take thousands of years to completely melt, if ever.

Dr. James Jerome studied alongside me. The professor of agriculture was excited about the prospect of so much plentiful, fresh water; but there would be problems to be solved.

"It's a farmer's dream, Walter," he told me, "but we have to successfully route new rivers where we want them and not allow giant ice dams to develop. Nine thousand feet of melting ice could cause enormous floods!"

Dr. James was on it, I thought. He was as smart as Grandpa.

From what I learned about Antarctica's location, Bird Island had to lie close to the Northern Antarctic Peninsula. It was a small hook of land that extended north from the mainland toward Cape Horn on the southern tip of South America.

"You have to stay over land and fly south, south, south until it gets cold again," Margie had once told me.

That gave me an entire huge chain of islands to consider. South Orkney Island, South Shetland Island, James Ross Island, Biscoe Island and a multitude of others. Men could not possibly have explored all of them, but there was a problem. The weather in that area was harsh and extremely cold.

"A current of warm water flows around Bird Island," Margie had said, "making it a great home for birds, especially fishers!"

"Hmm…" Grandpa took an interest in my research.

"God knows the way," he told me one day, "God points us in the right direction if we are quiet enough to listen to him."

I was listening, now that Margie had quieted down. She spent a lot of time in therapy with Dr. Mahatma and she seemed happier than I had ever seen her before.

Maybe the Antarctic Peninsula Islands had not been as cold as I had assumed. I read about the warm Peru Current that flowed down the south coast of South America and warmed the waters close to Antarctica.

Two weeks after Dr. Edward's sad diagnosis of Dottie, Grandpa called a meeting in the safe room of Skynest One just after bedtime for the children. His brothers attended, along with the Skynest One adults, a dozen other scientists, Margie and me.

When everyone settled into their seats, Grandpa stood up.

"I've had a vision, a strong vision," he started, "about an island that Walter has told me about. It is an island covered with birds of all species."

Margie gasped.

"Bird Island," she whispered to me.

"Yes, Bird Island," I tapped out on my seat.

"Yes, Bird Island," Grandpa agreed, looking directly at Margie and me, "it is real! In my vision, I was told to go there immediately. A voice in my dreams told me: Go with haste to Bird Island, for Dottie's sake!"

"The world is still inhospitable," one of the scientists grumbled, "we need to stay up here for at least another year!"

"Yes!" Grandpa flashed a hard look at the man. "I agree! That is why Skynest One will be the only ship to leave formation and descend. We will transfer our children to other ships, but I will take on any adult volunteers who want to come with me."

I flapped my wings and flew to Grandpa's shoulder.

"Any adult volunteers who will come with Walter and me," Grandpa corrected.

"If you think that I'm staying up here one minute longer than I have to, you are crazy, Little Brother!" Margie told me and flew to Grandpa's other shoulder.

"But it's going to be dangerous down there," I told her calmly, "the sky is still dark, the world is still suffering through the last throes of perpetual winter. Volcanoes may still be erupting, there may be more big floods. There may not yet be anything to eat."

I went on and on about the frightful state of the earth.

"If it scares you that much, stay up here!" Margie chided me. "As for me dear Little Brother, I'm volunteering. You never know, Mister Right could be waiting for me down there!"

Margie had a point, Bird Island definitely had tons of birds on it.

"I volunteered the day I arrived at the farm and met Grandpa," I assured Margie, "nothing can keep me off of Skynest One!"

"Good," she said, "then it's settled."

The away party would include us, Grandpa, George and Kenny. Miss Dixon, who I could tell had a big crush on George, volunteered. Caesar and Mishka wanted to see if their parents had made it to Bird Island. I also missed Henry and Jewell. Last of all, Fiona insisted on joining the mission. Because of her delicate state, Grandpa refused.

"It's too dangerous, Fiona," he said emphatically, "we don't know what to expect in the descent. I'll have my hands full keeping Dottie safe."

"I go where Kenny goes," she said with defiance, her arms folded.

Kenny took Fiona aside and talked quietly to her. She started to cry.

"It will be ok," Kenny told her, "as soon as I can establish radio contact, we can talk to each other every day."

There was no calming Fiona down, but she finally did agree. She, as a mother-to-be, knew that her unborn baby's welfare was at stake.

"We leave the formation tomorrow morning," Grandpa grumbled to Kenny, "move Fiona and her parents to Edward's ship."

Marshall found Grandpa and me in the control bubble. He was out of breath, as if he had run across the entire length of the formation of ships.

"Let me come along, Grandpa!" He said. He wore his long hair in what he called dreadlocks and his clothes were as shabby as usual.

"I've been studying with Kenny," he said, "I might be able to help."

"I wouldn't consider leaving without you, Marshall," Grandpa said with a smile, "you are a member of my crew, and a member of my family."

Later that evening, after dinner, Grandpa and I met in the safe room with all of his brothers, George and Kenny. The mood of the room was somber.

"I designed this project so that every ship would be self-sufficient," Grandpa began, "that way, if only one ship out of a thousand survived, mankind would still have a chance to recover. There would be a history preserved. Each ship contains its' own databank of the important elements of human knowledge and culture. Each ship carries seeds, DNA and genome samples of our animals and plant life, our sea life. Each ship is in itself a complete Noah's ark.

"We may perish on this mission," Grandpa continued, "but the rest of you certainly will not.

"So if the worst happens to us, carry forth, persevere and build the new world!"

"Who will be in charge?" Dr. Edward asked, "Who will make the final decisions?"

"If I perish," Grandpa answered him, "that will be you, Edward, until a republic, a representative government is established. You are the next oldest among us. And I expect the six of you to meet in counsel over any major decisions.

"One final thought. Teach our children. Teach them well their heritage, the foundation of our past, the founding fathers, so that they can hammer out a new world, based on freedom, liberty and justice for all!"

"Of course, Alfred," Dr. Edward said.

"Kenny," Grandpa asked, "Do you have anything to report?"

"You mean besides the fact that my wife will not speak to me right now?" Kenny asked.

That caused a chuckle from the group.

"Seriously," Kenny said, "Uncle Mark, Marshall and I have confirmed that the solar system has moved beyond the Dark Rift and is now entering the Golden Band."

"The Golden Band," Grandpa said, pensively.

"The Golden Band, as you all know," Kenny continued, "is a large ring of radiation that exists past the Grand Rift. We have been working hard to analyze and identify the radiation but it is elusive and I'm afraid that our instruments are neither sensitive enough nor sophisticated enough for the job."

"What we have noticed," Dr. James cut in, "is an unusual pattern of robust growth and longevity in all of the plants we are growing. We think that the Golden Band might have something to do with that."

Kenny shrugged his shoulders.

"But we're not certain, Grandpa," he said.

"Very well," Grandpa said, "George?"

George opened a cabinet and produced an incredibly ancient, dust covered bottle of champagne and enough glasses to go around. There was a tiny glass the size of a bottle cap for me. When the group was served, Grandpa raised his glass.

"To the success of Skynest One on her new mission!"

"Here, here!" Everyone shouted, and sipped their champagne.

"To all of you, we will eagerly await your arrival next year!"

"Here, here!"

"To Dottie, may she heal and live a long and wonderful life!"

"Here, here!"

"To the wonderful New World!"

"To the wonderful New World!" Everyone cheered.

Grandpa made one last toast, nodding to me.

"To Walter! May he show the strength and courage of his great-great-great grandfather!"

"To Walter!" Everyone shouted in unison.

60

OUR DESCENT INTO THE STORM

At six o'clock sharp the next morning, Kenny woke me gently and carried me to the radar room. The big, round radar scope was set in land map mode, and every sweep of its' antenna revealed some of the land masses of the Antarctic Peninsula.

"We are here directly above the Antarctic circle, just off the coast of Ellsworth Land," he pointed out. "We will start our descent away from the Peninsula, like this."

Kenny traced his finger in the direction that once would have been west/northwest, well away from the coast and the peninsula.

"Halfway down, Walter," Kenny continued, "Dad will execute a right or left 180 degree turn back directly toward the peninsula, depending on what kind of weather is down there."

"Warble."

"Yes, Grandpa agrees with you that Bird Island lies somewhere in this area."

Kenny circled his finger around the multitude of islands surrounding the Antarctic Peninsula. There were so many.

"I know," Kenny said, "too many islands. We are going to have to take a chance, Walter. Maybe the birds down there will guide you in. Grandpa has placed all of his faith in you. He also hopes that the island might have survivors on it, someone we can contact. I know, it's a long shot, but what else can we do?"

"Warble, warble."

Kenny looked up from the radar scope and faced me with his kind, intent eyes.

"During our descent, try hard to use your inner ability to sense the directional changes we make. We will try to help you by holding cardinal star bearings like 270 degrees and 090 degrees, if we can. But we will be descending blind, Walter, and depending on a computer that will generate its track off of our last star triangulation. No compass, no GPS, only a best guess dead reckoned track, airspeed, attitude and an altimeter."

"Warble, warble," I said, then I tapped, "I will do my best, Kenny!"

"I know you will, Walter," he smiled.

I had a feeling that I was not the only one who Grandpa had taught Morse code.

"I have complete faith in you," Kenny said, "I knew you showed up when you did for a reason. Now, listen. I dropped six radiosondes yesterday and one this morning to check the winds and weather below. It's brutal down there, Walter. I lost radio contact with all seven of them before they were halfway down. The sky below us is a huge, boiling mass of storms, high winds, and volcanic ash. There's no telling where we will end up, there are just too many strong winds and shears. It will be hard for you, Walter."

"Hard for all of us," I tapped. I thought about the three plus years of training I had under my belt in the flight simulator. I figured that I had a better than even chance of keeping track of our direction.

"It's going to be strange down there, no doubt," Kenny continued, "Dad wants to splash down in the water, which I agree is the safest way to go, under these conditions. We will cut away our balloons in the descent before we hit the bad weather, spread our wings and glide the rest of the way down. Plus, we may have some mobility once we are in the water.

"Down there, Walter, the sun is going to be blocked out. Without a solar source, we don't know how long we can maintain full power on the ship. We could have built full generators, but that takes time. We can rewire the props, maybe, and use them as wind generators, but there's no guarantee that it will work."

"The problem is time," I tapped, "Dottie is running out of it."

"That's right," Kenny agreed, "with enough time, we could figure out how to power the ship. Grandpa designed it with underwater jets to use once we are at sea. She'll do eight to ten knots as long as we have power. But there is no time. That's where you come in, Walter."

Yes, I thought to myself, that was the purpose of the flight simulator. That is why Grandpa trained me so hard. He had thought of everything.

Later, at seven, everyone gathered together for a breakfast of toast and boiled oats.

"It will help ward off motion sickness," Grandpa told the group. He served me a big helping of the goop he always fed me before the simulator marathons.

"We are planning a descent at 8:00 AM," George said as we ate, "one hour from now. At seven-fifty, everyone needs to be strapped in. I expect to lose radio contact with the formation as soon as we enter the weather, so if there is anyone you need to say goodbye to, now is the time."

"It's going to be a long, rough descent," Grandpa added, "much worse than the climb. Now remember, the safe room is special. It is programmed to change shape under certain conditions. This ship is strong and it can withstand nearly any stress; but if, in the unlikely event, we break apart in the ocean, this room will change shape into a life boat. It will do this on its first contact with sea water. If sea water breaches the life boat, your seats will change into personal life rafts, all connected together. They contain rations, emergency gear and fresh water. But remember, these are precautions. Skynest One is a strong ship. She'll hold together. I want all of you to do the same."

That was the fourth time Grandpa had given us his safety brief. After breakfast, Fiona helped George secure Dottie in her special seat. Dottie was comatose, and had been so since yesterday.

Fiona wanted to stay aboard as long as possible. I could tell that she wanted to make one last tearful plea to come with us, but Grandpa was firm. Deep in my own heart, I was sad for Fiona, but I knew that Grandpa was right. The mission we were undertaking was far too dangerous for her in her condition.

She drifted around the safe room, following Kenny like a shadow as he rushed around making last minute preparations. Finally, it was time for a tearful goodbye.

"Don't worry, sweetheart," Kenny said, trying to comfort her, "we will be just fine. We have Grandpa and Walter! And just think, a whole new world awaits us below."

They embraced hard and kissed.

I do not know if it helped, but I flew to Fiona's shoulder and kissed her wet cheek.

"Oh, Walter," she choked, crying, "I'm going to miss you so much!"

It was time for Fiona to depart through the docking tube to Dr. Edwards' ship. She would help him monitor the descent.

At seven-fifty, George placed Margie and me in our old familiar picnic basket, strapping us securely into the seat next to Marshall. The cage holding Caesar and Mishka was strapped in the seat on Marshall's other side.

"Don't worry, George," Marshall promised, "I'll keep them safe."

"I'm counting on it," George said.

Ten minutes later, George sat at the controls in the extended control bubble. Grandpa took his seat next to him and Kenny strapped into a jump-seat behind them that magically popped up out of the floor.

"We have to keep the control bubble extended," George said, "for maximum visibility."

"Concur," Grandpa said, "ok, disconnecting the docking stations."

He lifted a red guard from a switch on the console and flipped it.

"Disconnecting," Dr. Edward said over the radio from Skynest Two, "There, we're clear."

"Clear," said Dr. Mark.

"Clear," said the ship behind us.

"All docking stations are stowed," Grandpa verified.

"Ok," George said with a deep breath, "here goes nothing! Descending one thousand feet."

He fed instructions into the console computer, and helium bled from the balloons. Slowly, but surely, we dropped directly down, out of the center of the formation.

"You are in the clear, George," Dr. Edward said.

"Thank you," George said, "deploying wings."

Like a giant bird, stretching in the morning sun, our long, black wings opened and spread out from the sides of the ship.

"Beautiful," Dr. Edwards relayed.

"Activating props."

Propellers extended out and came alive; one at the aft end of the ship and one mid-section at the back of each wing. The prop that I could see, the one on the left wing, started to spin, gleaming in the bright sunlight.

"Three props spinning," Dr. Edward confirmed.

"Set descent, three hundred feet per minute," George ordered. Grandpa typed in the instructions.

"Pulling ahead at 25 knots," George said calmly, "steering star bearing 270."

"Did you hear that, Walter?" Grandpa called back to me.

"Warble, warble," I called.

"He heard it," Marshall called.

When we were well away from the enormous Skynest formation, George called for a seven hundred foot per minute descent. On a star bearing of 270 degrees, we left behind our city in the sky. The Star Riders were returning to earth. What would we find, I wondered?

"One hundred-thousand," Grandpa called out, "steady as she goes."

So far, so good. The descent was smooth and I knew that we would be in smooth air for a little while longer.

Margie huddled on the pillow in our basket. I hung by my claws upside down from the lid, trying to see as much as possible.

"Was the climb bad?" Margie asked me, her eyes wide with fear. She had been out cold during the climb, three years back.

"No, it was fine," I lied, "it was a piece of cake!"

Steadily, we descended.

"Ninety-thousand."

"Eighty-thousand."

Seventy-thousand."

"Cut away the balloons," George commanded, "I want to extend out further before we bank back and we need more speed for that. Otherwise, we might overshoot the peninsula."

"You've got it," Grandpa said, and flipped another guarded switch.

"Balloons away," Grandpa announced, and we all felt the slight jolt of their release, "Goodbye, dear old friends!"

"Ok, Uncle, we are gliding under our own power," George radioed to Dr. Edward, "we'll drop into the goo soon. Good luck to all of you."

"We'll see you in a year, Edward," Grandpa added, "we'll be waiting with a giant clambake on the beach!"

"Good luck to you," Dr. Edward radioed back, "and Godspeed, Skynest One!"

At fifty five-thousand feet, George initiated a sweeping right turn. Through the right side portals, I could see the menacing black clouds boiling below us; rising up to meet us. They looked like the multitude of twisters back in Texas, only bigger and meaner.

"Steadying up star bearing 090," George said.

"Right turn, star bearing 090, Walter!" Grandpa called back.

"Get ready!" George shouted, "Brace yourselves, it's going to get rough!"

What a statement! How the ship held together, I will never know. Everything outside of the ship went black! We were rocked, and buffeted, plunged and heaved, and I'm running out of words!

Margie glared at me.

"You liar!" She screamed. "Great White Stork! We're all going to die!"

"Just a walk in the park, Margie," I answered calmly as I flipped around in the basket.

"Try to hold 150 knots, eighteen hundred foot per minute descent, George!" Grandpa shouted above the roaring wind noise, "I'm on the radar. Heavy, severe turbulence, all quadrants!"

"Strong enough to rip an airliner apart!" George yelled, sweating and fighting at the controls.

In a voice strangely reminiscent of Old Dude's, Grandpa yelled:

"This ain't no airliner, son!"

Down and down we plummeted.

"Fifteen-thousand feet, George!" Grandpa yelled. "All three props are overheating!"

"Feather them!" George shouted. "We'll glide her in from here!"

"Feathered!" Grandpa confirmed. "Uh-oh, painting strong storm cells ten miles ahead, looks like a strong squall line!"

"Ok," George yelled, "bringing her left, we'll circle down before we hit it!"

So we glided, rolling and bumping. It seemed like too much time had passed. Then, after an eternity had passed, Grandpa called out five hundred feet.

"Ok," George said, "starting to break out; I can see big sea swells ahead!"

"Good!"

"Turning her into the wind. I'll try to set her down parallel to the primary ocean swells."

"I concur!" Grandpa said, and then called back to us. "Brace yourselves!"

"One hundred feet, son!" Grandpa called out. "Fifty, forty, thirty, warp the elevator...flare!"

"George grunted as he pulled back on the controls. Wham! The ship hit the ocean with a thunderous jolt, then skipped across the swells once or twice.

"Retracting wings, lowering rudder," George whispered calmly.

In the next moment, we rode in a shiny, black ocean vessel, bobbing like a cork in the wind, while the sea spray and the dark, heavy swells pummeled us.

And to make matters worse, I had no idea on earth where we were!

61

FLIGHT FOR LIFE

Ten o'clock in the morning. Skynest One was floating at sea, rocking in giant ocean swells beneath a black sky. She had proven her worth in the vicious swells, not even groaning as she negotiated them.

Except for Margie and me, everyone aboard was seasick. Evidently, thousands of years of perching in swaying tree branches had rendered us immune to motion-sickness problems. Grandpa hurried around, dispensing motion-sickness medicine to everyone else.

Grandpa and I then headed over to Dottie, where Miss Dixon was making her as comfortable as possible. Not that it really mattered; she was still in a comatose condition.

"She is in her last days," Grandpa said quietly, "I don't know, Walter. Will any attempt to get her help make a difference?"

"Never give up!" I tapped angrily. "Let me take the chance!"

Grandpa looked at me searchingly with tired eyes.

"You don't even know where to begin," he said, "we were thrown off course."

"I have a fair idea," I tapped, lying, "let me fly!"

Grandpa shook his weary head.

"Of course, Walter, I know you have to try. It's in your blood."

Grandpa settled me on the brass perch next to Dottie's seat.

"Rest," he said, "Kenny told me that your best chance to find the peninsula islands is past sunset, when the weather might calm down a little. I want you to be ready by then."

Miss Dixon sat in a chair next to Dottie, holding her hand, while I perched and eventually closed my eyes. Even with the strong pitching of the ship in heavy seas, I managed to sleep.

My dreams were strange. I had terrible visions of flying through sea spray black with ash. At one point, I could see my mother's worried face, watching me as I struggled to fly. I saw the funniest looking birds I had ever seen, figments of my overactive imagination, of course. They talked to me with strange accents.

"Walter," they said, "hurry, Star Rider! We wait for you!"

As the dream continued, I flew on and on. But I could not do it. I could not finish the flight. I was too tired. This is the end, my sleeping mind told me, this is the end!

I awoke in a cold sweat. Grandpa was standing next to me, carefully clipping a bright silver canister to my right leg.

"Time to wake up, trooper," he said with a weary smile.

Dottie stirred, opened her brown eyes and looked up at me. She started to smile, but when she saw what Grandpa was doing, she understood and tears rolled down her face. She reached for my computer.

"You can't go out there, Walter," she typed, "you'll die. Don't do this for me. Please Walter, please promise you won't!"

Grandpa smiled at his granddaughter.

"Walter is the smartest and the bravest pigeon in the world, Dottie," he told her, "he'll be fine."

But when Grandpa looked back at me, I could see the worry in his eyes.

I looked up and watched Kenny and Miss Dixon enter the room, followed by Marshall with Margie perched on his shoulder. George must be above, I thought, steering the ship. This was my family, the family I loved more than anyone else in the world.

"Let us pray," Grandpa said. Everyone bowed their heads.

"Lord, please give Walter the strength to fly and the sight to see his destination. Stay with him and guide him in his coming trial."

"Amen."

I flew down and kissed Dottie on the cheek. She was crying, and turned her head the other way.

"It's alright, Walter," Grandpa soothed, "she just doesn't want you to leave."

I understood, and I kissed her again.

As we headed back toward the safe room, Kenny briefed me.

"Believe it or not, Walter," he said, "we did see breaks in the clouds and watched the sun shine through. I can convert some of our blocks of matter into fuel to power the props, and we will motor toward you in case you have to turn around. But Skynest One was never meant to be a fast ocean-going vessel. I am looking at 8 knots in the water at best!"

I shuddered in contemplation of turning around in the weather outside and trying to find the ship again.

Grandpa had prepared a whole bowl of energy goop for me.

"Eat as much as you can, Walter," he said, "you will need all of your energy."

As I ate, Kenny unfolded a map of Antarctica next to me.

"We encountered some pretty tough winds in the descent," he started, "so we could be anywhere within two to three hundred miles of where we want to be. The ship's compass is spinning around in circles, Walter. Where do you think we are?"

I randomly tapped a spot on the map.

"Good," Kenny said, "that's better than I expected!"

"We are relying on your internal instincts," Grandpa told me, "give it your best guess and fly that direction, Walter."

I kept eating. I did not have the heart to tell Grandpa that my best guess was no better than my worst guess.

"Fly low," Grandpa continued, "particularly if you are going against the wind. It will be a little calmer right above the water. If you see a break in the clouds, try to get a fix from the stars; it will help us later. Use all of your training, Walter."

"I promise I will," I tapped on the table.

"When you find land, if you see humans, go to them," Grandpa continued, "you are carrying a message for them."

"I will, Grandpa," I promised, although finding humans sounded about as plausible as finding the mythical Bird Island.

The time had arrived. There were tears in Grandpa's eyes as he carried me to the hatch. He opened it up and a hard wind blew in from outside. I looked back at my crying family.

"Warble, warble," I said.

"You are my best friend, Walter!" Grandpa said to me. "Godspeed, and please come back to us!"

I flapped my wings and launched out. The hard hitting wind tumbled me for a moment, but I regained my balance and climbed. I was surprised at how warm the air was. I could see nothing but blackness ahead and the ship riding the waves behind me. I could see foam in the water from the breakers below. Where to go?

A small voice in my head told me to fly directly into the wind and hold that bearing. Great! It was not exactly what I wanted to hear; but for lack of a better plan, I obeyed it. As I turned into the wind, salt spray hit my face and stung my eyes. I flew on, leaving Skynest One far behind.

At least I was strong! I flew for hours and hours through the darkness, directly against that wind, beating my wings hard. As I flew, I pictured in my mind my mother and father, my sisters, kind Rancher George, Old Dude and Hawk-watcher. I pictured Grandpa, Dottie and my family aboard Skynest One. And then, after a moment, I thought about him! My great-great-great grandfather!

62

MY GREAT-GREAT-GREAT
GRANDFATHER, CHER AMI

His name was Cher Ami, the bravest pigeon who ever lived.
He was a gift from the British army and he served with the
brave American soldiers during World War One.

Cher Ami loved the Americans. He loved the Americans the
same way I love Americans. This was not their war, and yet, here they
were! Fighting to protect their friends in Europe and dying in the
process. How do I know this? My mother told me, just as her mother
told her. Cher Ami's memories are cherished by all birds! Even the
hawks, I imagine.

He served under Major Charles Whittlesey in an army battalion
of the 77th infantry division. It was called the Liberty Division, and
fought in the year 1918 to help free France from her enemies.

On October 3, 1918, the battalion was trapped, surrounded on
all sides by the enemy. Three hundred American soldiers died that
terrible day! Then, the Liberty Division had lost track of where Major
Whittlesey's battalion was located, and started to shell his position!

The only communications ability that the major had remaining
was the dozen homing pigeons that his signal corps carried in a special coop. Throughout the day, he sent the pigeons out, one at a time.

Every single pigeon was shot down and killed by the enemy, almost before they could even get airborne.

The battalion, which later became famously known as the "Lost Battalion," fought through the horrible night and lost more men. A feeling of impending doom set in among the men. There was little or no hope of survival. At daybreak the next morning, Major Whittlesey saw that there was just one lonely little pigeon left in the coop. It was a strong, beautiful homing pigeon, my great-great-great grandfather, Cher Ami!

Major Whittlesey's once strong battalion had been reduced to a little more than two hundred men, less than one third its original size. The enemy outnumbered him ten to one.

As the shelling from his own army grew more intense with daylight, the major had to get word of his location to the allies before all of his men were killed. He wrote a note and slipped it into a metal canister attached to Cher Ami's leg.

"Cher Ami," he whispered as he lifted my great-great-great grandfather up, "you are our only hope! Fly, Cher Ami, fly, and save us!"

The Germans watched Cher Ami take off and fly up into the smoke filled air. They fired at him with a thick barrage of bullets and hit him! He started to tumble, and the hearts of two hundred American soldiers tumbled with him. But my great-great-great grandfather was brave and strong. He flapped his wings hard, despite his terrible wound, and started to climb again. Once again, the Germans shot him and he fell.

But Cher Ami would not give up! With all of his strength, he kept flapping and climbed again! Then, he was hit again! He tumbled almost to the ground. He was terribly wounded, but he managed to flap his wings, slowly climb, and fly twenty five miles in twenty four minutes!

He reached the division coop and, with his last ounce of strength, rang the bell! Then he collapsed.

Cher Ami lay there where the soldiers found him, in a pool of blood, one eye shot out, and a hole the size of a quarter in his chest. His leg, the one that held the important message canister, dangled by a thread. But he had made it!

The division commander read Major Whittlesey's message and the Lost Battalion, with over two hundred American men, was saved. I thought about what Old Dude had said.

"Yer Great-Great-Great Grandpappy ought 'ter be the National Bird, not that stupid bald eagle! What did it ever do fer its country?"

He was right, of course. Cher Ami alone deserves to be America's National Bird, *hands down!* How many American men, women and children, descendants of those two hundred American soldiers, now live wonderful lives because of a little pigeon's unparalleled bravery? Americans obviously value good, slick, rat-eating, eagle-looks over any true demonstration of bona-fide, actual American heroism! Some Americans, anyway!

Cher Ami was nearly dead! Army medics worked long and hard to save him. They fashioned a little wooden leg to replace the one they had to amputate. There was nothing they could do for his missing eye.

The French awarded Cher Ami a medal called 'The French Croix De Guerre,' with a palm leaf. With tears in his eyes, the great General John J. Pershing, commander of all the United States Army, kissed Cher Ami and awarded him the Distinguished Service Cross.

"Brave little bird," General Pershing whispered as he put Cher Ami aboard a ship headed for home, "you are truly a great American!"

That was Cher Ami! That was my beloved Great-Great-Great Grandfather!

63

I LOSE MY WAY

I lost track of time. How long had I been flying? Was it morning yet? I could see no sunrise, the wind was taking its' toll on my strength, and it was getting harder to breathe.

Keep flying, I told myself. You carry the blood of Cher Ami in your heart, keep flying! That thought gave me strength and I flapped harder. I tried to imagine that I was flying inside of Grandpa's flight simulator, and that the exercise was going to end at any minute. Then I would see Grandpa's smiling face.

"Good job, Walter!" He would say.

But here, the black sea spray hit me over and over again, stinging me every time. If I flew any higher, the wind became too strong and gusty. Below me lay certain death.

Perseverance, I told myself, remembering what Grandpa had said. Dottie needs you. She will die if you give up!

I flew on. Where was that island? Where was land? Even with the wind, I had to be putting miles behind me.

I thought about Margie. I wondered what her vision of Mister Right might really be. I tried to imagine what New York City looked like from her vivid descriptions. She loved New York. I thought about Skynest, the Star of Hope, the big formation of ships above me. What were they doing? All of the children were probably still asleep.

I thought about red-tailed hawks and laughed to myself. They were about the only thing that I did not have to worry about. Then I thought about Old Dude and Hawk-Watcher and it made me sad. How many hours had it been? I had no way of knowing. All I could do was stay on my internal bearing.

I flew on.

I wondered if we really did evolve from dinosaurs. I had studied about it in college. Old Dude would have a hoot with that one! I seriously doubted that there was any truth to it. Walter, the dinosaur! It made me laugh.

Wicked salty sea mist sprayed me hard, forcing my eyes closed. It was raining hard, pelting me from above. I kept flying! I cannot let them down, I told myself.

My wings were growing weaker, and I was breathing harder and harder. The ocean seemed to be rising up to meet me.

For the next hour or so, I played a game. I flapped my wings hard and the water sank below me. Then, I relaxed a little and the water rose up to meet me like a liquid monster with a life of its own. Up and down the water went. Sea spray hitting me. Up and down!

I was way beyond exhausted! I flapped harder and harder, but the water continued to rise up toward me. I've failed, I thought. I've failed Dottie. I've failed everyone. My wingtips were skimming the surface of the water. It was over!

64

A MIRACLE!

"Yer done a good job, Squeaker!" I heard Old Dude's voice say. "But yer quite a bit too far off course! We decided ta come over an help you!"

Old Dude? I opened my eyes. How long had I been unconscious? A bright glowing, golden pigeon flew next to me, looking at me and grinning.

"That's right, Squeaker!" He said. "It's me, Old Dude! I done ended up in The Big Nest in the Sky, after all! What do yer think 'bout that?"

He looked so young and strong and had a golden glow surrounding him. Something else was strange. I was not flying anymore, I was huddled up, riding on the back of another bright glowing, golden pigeon. He was even bigger than Old Dude, and so strong!

"Yep, looky who I decided to bring along," Old Dude said to me, "took me a'while to find his durn hide! But when I seen him, I knew who he was. He's the spittin' image of you, Squeaker!"

The pigeon carrying me on his back turned his head around and looked at me. I froze.

"Hello great-great-great, and then some, grandson," he said, "I am so proud of you!"

Proud of me? I thought. But I failed. I'm probably dead.

"Cher Ami?" I croaked.

"That's me," Cher Ami said, and laughed a merry laugh, "and you aren't dead, son. You almost hit the water. Don't worry, any one of us would have! But I want you to rest, now! Sleep deeply, Squeaker, and leave the flying to us for a while. We have you!"

The Great White Stork help me, I did what he said. I huddled down on his back, feeling his incredibly strong muscles flex as he flapped effortlessly through the air. As we climbed away from the water, my eyelids grew heavy. As I fell asleep, I heard Old Dude.

"Jest in time!" he exclaimed.

"Yep, just in time!" Cher Ami agreed.

65

THE LUCKIEST PIGEON ALIVE!

Later, when I woke up, I was riding on Old Dude's back. There were breaks in the clouds ahead and the day was growing brighter. Still, the immediate area around me was mainly illuminated by the glow of the two golden pigeons.

"Go ahead, admit it, Squeaker," Old Dude called. "You ain't never done seen two more handsome pigeons than Cher Ami and me, have ya?"

"That's for sure!" Cher Ami laughed beside us. He winked at me.

"I have to agree," I admitted. I felt so refreshed, like I had slept for weeks.

"So's, we was a'thinkin,'" Old Dude said, "we was a'thinkin', we'd sure better catch ya and turn ya round a'fore you reached the Horn of Africa!"

Cher Ami laughed heartily.

"Old Dude is one funny son of a gun," he said, "you've got good friends, Squeaker, and that tells me everything I need to know about you! I could have used both of you guys in the great war."

"An' git all my tail feathers shot off?" Old Dude asked with a laugh.

"Did you really receive all of those medals?" I asked.

"As sure as I am flying next to you now," Cher Ami answered, "it was a great honor! I really loved my soldiers! I loved every single one of those brave young American boys! How do you feel, son?"

I stretched my wings and flew into a position between Old Dude and Cher Ami. We were flying perpendicular to the wind. This course was much better.

"I feel great!" I exclaimed. And I did! I felt completely rejuvenated!

"That's the old mojo workin," Old Dude said, "looky here ahead!"

The clouds opened up ahead of us, the sky was clear, the water calm and blue, and the sun shone directly overhead. Right in front of us, glistening in the mist under a giant rainbow, sat a large, lush island. It was beautiful, with high cliffs and a long, white beach, thick vegetation, and multitudes of birds of all kinds.

"Ain't that a sight, Squeaker?" Old Dude asked, "that there is Bird Island!"

My heart leaped. I had made it.

"For now, pass over the island," Cher Ami instructed me, "and maintain this course. In an hour, you will reach the mainland beach where some humans desperately need you."

"Then you do ever' thing you can to git Dottie to Bird Island with the help of those humans on the beach," Old Dude said, "trust us on that, Squeaker!"

I trusted him, alright. I trusted him with my life.

"Thank you, Cher Ami." I said. "Thank you, Old Dude!"

I dropped my head for a moment.

"What's wrong, son?" Cher Ami asked.

"I couldn't do it alone," I said, "I couldn't live up to you, Cher Ami. Without you and Old Dude, I would have failed. I wasn't good enough."

Cher Ami laughed. Old Dude laughed, too.

"Son, you have flown farther, and you are stronger than any pigeon I ever knew," Cher Ami told me, "and you are certainly the bravest pigeon who ever lived! Let me tell you something, Squeaker. I was

never alone, not even in my darkest hours. There was always someone there to guide me! And you will never, ever be alone, either!"

I looked from Cher Ami to Old Dude, but Old Dude was gone. I
looked up, down and behind us, no Old Dude! Then I turned back to
say something about it to Cher Ami, but he had vanished, too!

I sighed.

I'm the luckiest pigeon alive, I realized.

Thousands of birds squawked up at me as I crossed over Bird
Island, calling me to come down and join them. In a little while, I
thought to myself. It was a big island, covered with lush green hills,
trees, waterfalls and rivers.

I crossed over and then I was out to sea again, thinking about my
rescue by Old Dude and Cher Ami. So there was a Valhalla, after all!
Old Dude had been right!

After nearly an hour of flying, I could see the coastline of the
mainland ahead. It was fronted by a long, straight white beach. As I
flew closer, I could make out tents and small buildings.

66

FRIENDS ON THE BEACH

Down in front of the tents, out on the white beach where the heavy surf came rolling in from the ocean, about a dozen men and women wearing shorts and t-shirts braved the rough surf, casting out nets. It was a sight so strange to me that I did a double-take as I flew over.

The tents and buildings were set on higher ground, where sprigs of green grass were starting to sprout. Out to the side of the buildings, three square patches of ground were furrowed and staked out; the beginning of a farm, I guessed.

Strong, huge, beautiful waterfalls raged down ice cliffs about a mile off to either side of the colony, roaring down from incredibly high ice cliffs I could see melting in the far distance.

I circled the place once or twice to scope things out and noticed that one of the women on the beach was pointing up at me. She was wading into the strong surf, casting out her fishing net into the boiling foam. One of her companions hauled in a big, wiggling fish. I could hear him hooting and laughing.

I worked up my nerve, flew down and landed on the woman's shoulder. She was fair skinned, wearing sunglasses and had her long, blond hair tied back in a ponytail away from her sunburned face. She was pretty, definitely what Margie would call a 'catch!'

"Hello, little dove," she said in English with an exotic accent, "Did you fly in with the sun this morning?"

"Warble, warble," I said.

"Kiersten, that is no ordinary dove," a blonde, bearded man said as he waded over, "that is a homing pigeon! See the canister on his right leg?"

"Oh, yes," Kiersten exclaimed, "oh, my!"

The man kneeled close to me. He had a kind look on his face. He also had bright, intelligent eyes, like Grandpa's.

"Don't be afraid, little one," he said gently, "my name is Michael, you can trust me."

He smiled warmly, and I did trust him. I looked around and saw that all of the people were pale and thin, like Dottie. Obviously, there was not much to eat around here. But Michael was not licking his lips. I decided that I was not going to end up as lunch, so I hopped over to his knee.

"There, there...easy, little fellow," Michael whispered in Kiersten's beautiful accent. He gently removed the silver canister from my leg.

"Take your time," I gently pecked on his knee in Morse code. I looked him directly in the eye.

Michael shuddered.

"Odin as my witness," he swore to Kiersten, "this little bird is trying to talk to me! He's using some kind of code!"

Odin!

He snapped the canister open and carefully extracted a roll of very thin paper, which he unrolled and held up in the sun.

"Don't mind Michael and his swearing," Kiersten laughed to me, "lately, he has been having strange dreams that he is a Viking warrior."

I could not be happier. By now, everyone had walked up and stood around us, including the man holding the big, wiggling fish. I counted five women and seven men. Then, another woman and two more men ran out from the metal buildings.

"What's going on, Michael?" One of the arriving men asked. He definitely had a North American accent.

"The little pigeon brought us a message, Steve," Michael answered, "with very small print. Do you have your bifocals with you?"

"Certainly," Steve answered. He slipped his hand into his shirt pocket and pulled out a pair of glasses, which he slipped on. He was wearing a hat, and had a long, white beard, just like Grandpa's.

"Greetings," he read aloud to everyone, "the bird who brought you this message is Professor Walter Pigeon. Please extend to him the same courtesy and respect you would extend to any one of your colleagues."

Steve stopped reading for a moment and glanced over his glasses at me.

"Welcome to Camp Shackleton, Professor Walter," he said. Everyone cheered! He continued to read.

"Professor Walter is an expert at International Morse Code and Star Navigation. We have included a copy of the Morse Code on the opposite side of this note. Please use it to communicate with him. He will tell you everything about Project Skynest. If you have an operative computer, he can also type in English. Best regards, Sir Alfred Jerome."

Steve looked at Michael and then at me.

"I should have paid closer attention to Sir Alfred's work," he said, "Professor Walter, I am Dr. Steve Conroy, of the U.S. Antarctic research team. You have met Dr. Michael Thorden and Dr. Kiersten Thorden from the Norwegian research team. We banded together out on the Ross Ice Shelf after everything came apart three years ago.

"When we realized that Antarctica was shifting to a warmer region," Michael explained, "we abandoned the ice shelf and moved to solid land. Quite a few of us died. We weathered terrible, terrible times."

"Tsunamis," Steve continued for him, "black, fire-rain from volcanoes, incredible earthquakes. Then, just as it says in the Bible, the stars slowly dropped from the sky."

"The world shifted," Kiersten broke in, "which I'm sure you already know. We were lucky at first to be out on the ice shelf, it withstood the worst of quakes and tsunamis. But when it started to fracture, we knew we had to move."

A tear rolled down Kiersten's cheek.

"We started with over forty scientists," she said sadly, "we are now down to fifteen."

I flew over to her shoulder and kissed her on the cheek.

67

A FLYING MACHINE

The position of the bright sun told me that it was noon. Steve carried me into the small, metal building he had come running out of. On close inspection, I could tell that the buildings were all big metal boxes, like steel refrigerators lying on their sides. They contained hatch-like doors and small, round windows.

Sitting behind the buildings were some of the strangest vehicles I had ever seen. They were boxy and fully enclosed, and had tracks like a bulldozer, instead of wheels. Then, I saw one machine that I did recognize. A helicopter!

"If you do find people, try to locate a helicopter," Grandpa had briefed me, "that is what we truly need!"

It was a beautiful, bright red flying machine, shining brightly in the sunlight.

"First thing, Dr. Walter," Steve said to me as he entered the building, "is we have to get some food and water in you. Then, Mike and Dawn, our pilots, will meet with us. They are both familiar with Morse Code."

Inside the small building, there were stacked beds, three to a side. A cabinet sat beneath a small window, next to a small table and three chairs. Steve opened the cabinet and pulled out a box and a bottle. Soon, I was dining on crackers and water.

"We started out with enough provisions to last us a year," Steve explained, "so far, we've made them last for three."

I pushed the extra crackers back across the table to him and pecked at only one. Steve smiled.

"You are my kind of guy, Professor," he said.

"Call me Walter," I pecked on the wooden table top as the hatch to the building swung open wider.

"He said, 'call me Walter,'" a dark haired, bearded man said as he entered. A short, red headed woman followed him in.

"Walter, my name is Mike," the man said, and then gestured to the woman behind him, "this is Dawn. We're pilots."

"It's always a pleasure to meet pilots," I tapped.

"Amazing," Dawn gasped. Mike grinned.

"A little slower, please, Walter," he tapped back on the table very slowly, "we aren't quite up to your speed."

"Do you have a computer?" I asked.

"We used to," Mike said, "one of the quakes destroyed it. Beat up most of our equipment. But the chopper, we got lucky. She's just fine."

"The burning question of the year is," Steve broke in, "where on earth did you come from, Walter?"

It reminded me of that first night that I spent with Henry's geese, telling my tale at story time. I tapped for two solid hours while Steve asked questions and Mike translated my answers loud enough for everyone standing outside to hear.

"The bright star we've seen moving across the sky at night through breaks in the clouds," Steve exclaimed, "I always had the feeling that it meant something good. We named it the Star of Hope."

As did the birds of Bird Island, I thought. How interesting! I told Mike about the island.

"We saw it as we were flying in," he said, "covered with birds!"

"The clouds are moving back in," someone called in from outside.

"Come on," Mike said to me, "Let's get to the chopper. Maybe we can contact your ship before the weather blocks us out."

There was room in the chopper for six adults. Mike had rigged its batteries with solar panels in an effort to keep them charged.

"It works ok, as you can tell by our sunburns, we've been getting a little more sun lately," he explained to me, "they are almost carrying a full charge now. Morse code shouldn't drain them too much."

"We do have a full tank of fuel," Dawn said, "and we have some fuel in the Arctic snow cats. We could probably reach your ship to get to Dottie, I just don't know if we can make it back."

Mike was messing with the radio.

"Do you have an ADF?" I tapped.

Mike and Dawn raised their eyebrows at each other.

"Yes, Walter, we do," Mike said.

"Grandpa is monitoring channel 88," I tapped.

Mike flipped a couple of switches and twisted a knob until the number 88 showed in the little, square window next to it. I heard the whining of the radio as it warmed up. Mike held up his microphone and clicked out Morse Code.

"Skynest One, Skynest One, this is Shackleton Base," he clicked.
No answer.

"Skynest One, Shackleton Base," he clicked again. With the ensuing silence, Dawn explained the problem quietly to me.

"The magnetic field is trying to regenerate," she said, "and before we lost our most sensitive radiation monitoring equipment, we detected some kind of new radiation, that along with the bad weather..."

"Radiation," I tapped, "the Golden Band."

"The Golden Band?" She asked.

"Hush!" Mike said.

"What is the Golden Band?" Steve whispered from the back seat.

"Shh! I'm getting something," Mike whispered.

It was very faint, but it was definitely Morse Code.

"Shackleton Base, this is Skynest One, how do you read?" It clicked.

Mike answered.

"Weak, but readable," he clicked, "We have Professor Walter with us."

"Hallelujah!" Came the response.

Everyone cheered.

68

ANOTHER DANGEROUS FLIGHT

The sky was darkening. We could see the boiling black clouds rolling in from the ocean, ready to engulf us.

Mike was arguing with Steve.

"We are going to fly anyway!" Mike stated ardently. "We've done it before, in worse weather than this!"

"I can't afford to lose you," Steve said, shaking his head.

"You heard Sir Alfred," Mike persisted, "they have plenty of fuel and tons of food. We are that little girl's only hope! I promise I will fly out for six hours and turn back if I don't see them."

"From the star coordinates they gave us," Dawn added, "they could be closer."

"But we aren't certain," Steve argued.

"It's a whole new world, Steve," Mike said firmly, "nothing is certain."

"If Walter made it here," Dawn argued, "we can certainly make it back. Besides, Sir Alfred promised to fire up his props and cruise toward us.""

"Look, Steve," Mike explained, "our ADF has the capability to point directly at them. Watch!"

"Skynest One, please give us a twenty second tone," Mike tapped, then switched the ADF knob to its' ADF + G position, for automatic direction finding bearing capability. We heard a long, low tone over the cockpit speaker and watched as the ADF needle came alive and pointed to the number 295 on the ADF compass.

"See?" Mike said to Steve, "that is their location, bearing 295 from us for about three hundred miles, I'd guess."

"And Walter insists that we are the only hope for that dying little girl," Dawn implored emphatically.

"This is all based on a myth," Steve argued, "about some island full of birds!"

"Yes, based on a myth," Dawn agreed, stubbornly folding her thin arms, "and when was the last time you talked school with a professor who happens to be a pigeon?"

Steve shook his head. Then, slowly, he grinned.

"I do have to admit," he said, "it's been a while."

He sat quietly for a minute, mulling things over in his head.

"Ok, Mike," he finally said, "it's your call."

Mike grinned.

"Turning rotors in five minutes," he exclaimed, "me, Dawn, and the Professor here. What about you, Steve?"

"Are you kidding?" Steve said. "I wouldn't miss this ride for the world!"

Five minutes later, as the group gathered on the beach to wave goodbye to us, we lifted off and immediately plunged into the black clouds.

The helicopter was horribly loud and the ride was rough. I sat on Steve's lap and watched his salty beard grow wet with heavy sweat.

"Our compasses are useless!" Dawn shouted back at us. She and Mike wore black helmets.

"But we do have a great radar altimeter," she continued, "and Skynest One is giving us a great signal. We'll maintain our altitude at one hundred feet above sea level. We'll keep her steady at one hundred knots, unless the weather deteriorates further."

We flew on.

After a couple of hours, Dawn turned around again.

"Two hundred and fifty miles so far," she shouted above the rotor noise, "we have to be getting close."

"Grandpa will be monitoring frequency 121.5 on your VHF radio," I tapped on Mike's shoulder.

"We have it tuned in," he assured me.

After two more hours, Dawn turned around and looked at me with concern. She tapped the fuel gauge. "We've had the wind at our tail the whole flight!" she shouted, "we have thirty more minutes, and then we must turn back!"

Now I was sweating. Steve looked down at me and patted my head.

"We'll give it our best shot," he assured me. Ahead of us, I saw nothing but blackness. After another thirty minutes, Mike and Dawn looked at each other.

"I have to come around," Mike shouted sadly, "I'll tell Skynest that we did our best. We will have to fly a reverse bearing off of their signal to get home."

Steve looked down at me again. There was genuine sadness in his eyes.

"We'll try again in a few days," he said.

That will be too late, I thought to myself. Dottie did not have that much time left.

"Hello, Shackleton flight," a scratchy voice erupted over the speaker, "How do you hear?"

Dawn grabbed her mic and answered.

"Two by five," she answered, "how do you hear?"

She looked at Mike.

"They can't be far," she said. Mike was already turning the copter around again.

"We have you the same," Grandpa's voice answered, "painting you forty out at 015. Descend to fifty feet and watch for our lights!"

69

BACK TO SKYNEST ONE

Skynest One was lit up like a Christmas tree! The ship appeared directly below us, pitching up and down in the turbulent water. Its' upper surface had converted into a flat directionally lighted landing pad, complete with a lighted, railed walkway that led up to a hatch that had popped up. Grandpa had thought of everything.

"Sea swells steady at twenty feet," Grandpa reported calmly over the speaker. Mike and Dawn gave each other that professional pilot 'here goes nothing' look that I had seen George and Grandpa give each other before.

"Check the white wind sock as you approach," Grandpa said.

"Easy does it," Dawn said to Mike as we descended.

"I'm going to time the pitch," Mike said.

"Wind, ah.... 28 knots, directly on the bow," Grandpa reported.

Plunk!

We were down. Tendrils snaked up from the surface of the ship and wrapped around the helicopter's pontoons.

"Great job, Mike!" Grandpa exclaimed happily.

We boarded and Grandpa immediately led us down to the safe room. He was delighted to find out that Steve was a climatologist and was eager to trade notes with him. Kenny and Miss Dixon had prepared a sumptuous feast for the Shackleton crew. They could hardly eat it, having starved for so long.

"Tell me all about it, Sugar," Margie said to me with a look of pained concern in her eyes. I described my marathon flight to her, going hour after hour into gusty, thirty knot winds. I told her about my exhaustion, the water creeping up on me, blacking out. Then I told her about Old Dude and Cher Ami.

"They really saved me!" I said excitedly. "And Old Dude, he looked so young! I would have died without them."

If a pigeon can truly cry like a human, Margie was crying her eyes out. Then she was quiet for a long time.

"We should never have let you go, Little Brother," she finally said with a sad quietness to her voice, "we almost lost you."

Dottie had lapsed into what Grandpa feared was an irreversible coma. She looked so tiny, sad and pitiful in her bed, surrounded by all of her stuffed animals.

"We have done everything we can," Grandpa lamented.

"I am terrified," Grandpa continued, "that she might not survive another day!"

"It really exists!" I insisted to Margie. "I saw it with my own eyes. Bird Island!"

"How could you tell it wasn't just an island with a lot of birds on it?" Margie asked suspiciously.

I puffed up my chest.

"Because Old Dude and Cher Ami told me it was Bird Island!" I said with certainty.

Mike held a quiet discussion with Dawn. He walked over to Grandpa.

"Can Dottie wait until early morning?" He asked, "The weather is getting rougher, but there might be a break just before dawn. She needs a smooth ride."

Grandpa rubbed his beard.

"That may be at the very edge of her ability," he said, "follow me to your quarters, folks and get some rest. George is refueling your chopper. Let's compromise and plan to leave at three o'clock am."

"Tell me again how you make the fuel?" Mike asked as we headed for his cabin.

"My brother developed a method using bucky-ball technology," Grandpa explained as Steve gasped, "we build nano-machines that can re-arrange sea water molecules into fuel, or fresh water, or even fruit juice for that matter."

"What a brave new world!" Steve exclaimed.

70

BIRD ISLAND!

t three o'clock AM, the weather broke just as Mike had predicted. Sea swells were only half the size of what they had been the night before and the wind had calmed down considerably. After an early, hearty breakfast that left us all stuffed, Mike and George delicately loaded Dottie on a stretcher aboard the helicopter.

"Look, there's Project Skynest," George exclaimed, pointing up into the night sky. Everyone, including me, looked up to see the incredibly bright star shining through a large break in the clouds.

"The Star of Hope!" Mike exclaimed wistfully.

"That's funny," George said, looking perplexed, "that is precisely what we named it."

Morphic resonance, I thought to myself.

"Grandpa is on the radio with Skynest right now," George continued, "Updating them and telling them our plans."

Dottie was securely strapped in the back of the helicopter. I perched on the stretcher next to her small, unconscious body.

The away party included me, George and Grandpa. Steve decided to stay aboard ship with Kenny and Marshall and help them steer her to shore over the next week. At the last minute, Margie threw a fit and insisted on coming along with me.

She did not take up any room, so Grandpa agreed to bring her along.

As Mike and Dawn climbed into their seats, Grandpa hugged Kenny at the hatchway.

"You are captain of Skynest One now," Grandpa told him, "and you have your orders. Good luck, son!"

"Good luck, Grandpa," Kenny said back, "don't worry about us, we'll be fine."

Grandpa turned to Steve, who was standing next to Kenny.

"It has been my pleasure to meet you, Doctor," he said, shaking Steve's hand, "if you run into trouble, we will be a flight away. Kenny is fluent in Morse Code."

"Thank you, Sir Alfred," Steve said in return, "I admire a man who covers all of his bases."

"Don't ever call me Sir Alfred again," Grandpa reminded him, "Everybody calls me Grandpa."

At precisely 4:00 am, the helicopter lifted off. Grandpa and George sat on either side of Dottie. Margie perched next to me.

"Destination, Bird Island!" Grandpa shouted above the noise. Mike gave him a thumbs-up.

Grandpa turned to me.

"So did you really see Old Dude and Cher Ami?" He asked me. I hopped up on his shoulder.

"They saved my life," I pecked on his shoulder, "I would not have made it without them. They actually carried me on their backs."

Grandpa closed his eyes, smiled and nodded his head.

"They must have been the two glowing pigeons I saw in my vision, so long ago," he said.

Having made this trip twice now, I could sense the course corrections that Mike needed to make. I tapped them out as necessary on Grandpa's shoulder.

"Three degrees left," Grandpa called up to the pilots who, with a spinning compass, were flying blind in the darkness of the early morning.

"It's great to have an authentic avian navigator aboard!" Dawn called back.

We made much better time than I had made two nights before. At six o'clock am, we could see the red and golden glow of sunrise reflecting across the water at us. What a wonderful site! In no time at all, I could see Bird Island!

The island was magically covered with green plants and trees. Birds were everywhere!

"This place defies logic," Mike called back to us, "how can it be so green?"

"It must contain a deep hypothermic heat source," Grandpa called back, "to keep the plants alive. And the recent sunlight has probably helped boost photosynthesis to help green everything up."

"If we had known it was this nice," Dawn yelled, "we would have moved to it. It was dark every time we crossed over it!"

"Not so fast," Grandpa warned, "it belongs to the birds!"

"Amen," Dawn called back.

Grandpa frequently checked Dottie's condition. After each check, he nodded solemnly to George.

Mike carefully set the helicopter down on a bare spot safely inside the cliffs that towered perilously above the beach. As Grandpa and George lifted Dottie's stretcher out, thousands of different species of birds gathered close around. The bird noise was deafening. The vegetation was dense all the way to the edge of the cliff, and led up a tree covered hill. I saw pigeons, ducks, swallows, bluebirds, hummingbirds, storks, seagulls, kingfishers, pelicans and many, many more.

Suddenly, the birds quieted down and a pair of snow geese waddled down the pathway toward us.

"Henry!" I cried out, "Jewell! You made it!"

"And so did you, Squeaker!" Henry honked, and laughed out loud, "and Grandpa, too! Oh, this is a happy day!"

Henry explained that the Great White Stork had been expecting us for a long time. He had been patiently waiting for the Star Riders!

"Let's waste no time," Grandpa said.

The erupting chatter of thousands of birds was deafening. The humans covered their ears.

"It's always loud here," Henry yelled, "but believe me, Squeaker, this is a wonderful place!"

We walked toward the hill, through the bushes and trees, with Grandpa and George carrying Dottie. Dottie lay still, with a sad look on her sleeping face.

"She doesn't have long," I sadly told Henry.

"We'll see about that," he said.

I could not help but notice several pigeons standing near the path. A couple of them were large males, but there was one young female who was obviously a homing pigeon. She looked like my mother, strong, smart and beautiful. I thought that I saw her smile at me.

"Hello, hello, Boys!" Margie cooed to the big male pigeons as we passed.

We reached a low, green fern covered entrance to a cave in the side of the hill, wide enough for Grandpa and George to enter if they ducked down. Just inside the cave, a giant, old white stork approached us. He glowed snow white so brightly I had to squint to see what he looked like. He had a huge beak and kind, gentle eyes that held great intelligence and the wisdom of ages upon ages. He stopped in front of me and I instinctively knelt before him. Henry, Margie and Jewell, Mike and Dawn, followed my lead. Grandpa and George, holding Dottie, slowly bowed their heads.

The entire interior of the cave glowed and sparkled in a rainbow of magnificent colors, illuminated by the bright shining light of The Great White Stork!

"Walter, Margie" The Great White Stork spoke with a deep, ancient voice in pigeon, "Riders of the Star. Long we have awaited you. What is it you desire?"

"Thank you, Holy One," I answered, "we carry a little human female. She is dying. She needs your help."

"Follow me, Star Riders," The Great White Stork answered.

We followed him into the cave, which grew in size as we proceeded. The rock below our feet descended sharply into the earth. As we went deeper, the cave walls continued to glitter and glow, lighting our way.

"This is The Great White Stork," I tapped to Grandpa, "he will help Dottie."

"For thousands and thousands of years, this cave has been guarded, "the Great White Stork said in his deep voice as he waddled ahead of us, "it is one of the holiest places on earth. Men knew of it once, in another age, long, long ago."

Again, I tapped out the translation. Grandpa nodded his head. His eyes sparkled.

Down we walked, deeper and deeper into the cave. We looked like a ceremonial procession, The Great White Stork first, followed by Henry and Jewell, then Margie and me and finally, Grandpa and George carrying Dottie, and Mike and Dawn.

After what seemed like an hour, I could hear the sound of a rushing stream ahead. We rounded a sharp corner in the cave and stopped at a large pool of dark, red-tinted water. On the far side of the pool, a great red waterfall cascaded across smooth cavern rocks.

"Behold," The Great White Stork announced, spreading his beautiful white wings, "this pool holds the sacred life-blood of the earth. Bring the little girl!"

I translated to Grandpa, who dropped to his knees and uttered a quick prayer of thanks to God. George hurriedly unstrapped Dottie from her stretcher.

Then, Grandpa and George gently lifted Dottie in their arms, and waded into the red water.

71

THE POOL OF LIFE

"Let's go swimming!" Margie yelled.

"Shh!" I scolded her, "I don't think the sacred pool is meant for a casual swim!"

The Great White Stork overheard us. I expected him to be offended, but I was wrong.

"The pool of life is here for everyone!" He announced joyfully. "Please, everyone. Join us in the water of life!"

He waddled into the water, followed by Henry and Jewell. Margie flashed me a sassy "told you so!" look and jumped in after them.

"Come on in," Grandpa called with a smile, "the water's fine!"

I looked at Dottie, and saw that her eyes were opening. Color was returning to her face. George was splashing the water and laughing. Mike and Dawn gave each other an 'Oh, well' look and jumped in. They immediately started laughing.

So in I jumped. The feeling of the water was indescribable! I felt a surge of joy and pure life wash through me, melting away all of the worries of the past few days.

Dottie started laughing and splashing water at her dad.

"Thank you, Lord!" Grandpa shouted with glee.

Afterwards, as we sat by the pool and dried off, Dottie spoke out loud for the first time.

"Thank all of you for bringing me here," she said in a beautiful, sweet voice that I had never heard before this wonderful day, "I love all of you!"

She looked at the Great White Stork.

"Thank you so much, kind sir," she said, bowing her head. He bowed back. Then she looked at Margie and me.

"I was in a coma," she said, "but I saw so much! Walter, I saw Old Dude and Cher Ami flying next to you in the dark. I saw your beautiful mother, Maria, and your father, and all of your sisters. They all told me to tell you they are safe and happy! Margie, I could see all of your sisters and friends, and even Merle! He was busy eating a gigantic cream pie! And my mother, she has been watching over all of us all along! Grandpa, I could see Grandma, always standing next to you and hugging you! It was so wonderful! They all asked me to tell you that they are happy and fine, and they love you very, very much!"

Dottie's bright brown eyes beamed with happiness. This is the past, the present, and the future, all wrapped up into this one incredible moment, I realized.

Dr. Mahatma would be proud of me!

72

A BRAVE NEW WORLD!

Bruno, a big gray pigeon from Queens, was completely smitten with Margie. And I had never seen Margie happier.

Their initial conversation went something like this:

"Yo, Babe, I'm Bruno, from Queens!"

"No doubt about it, Handsome!"

"Yeah, Sweets! One day, a bunch of snow geese fly by, headed south in a hurry. I join up with them and I says 'yo, so what's the big hurry? And they says, 'if youse wanna live another year, come with us, Queens!' It ain't every day snow geese invite youse along, so I know something big is going down! So I go with them. I didn't know they was goin'' halfway around the freakin' world, youse know?"

"It takes a big, strong pigeon to fly this far south, Honey!"

"Yeah, that's right! That's why I got these big muscles, little girl. Check these out!"

"Ooh, let me feel those muscles. Wow!"

And so on. As a devoted disciple of Dr. Mahatma, Margie was performing therapy on Bruno within a week.

"Now try again, Honey," she instructed, "find that quiet place, that place that is the real you!"

"Anything for youse, Cream-puff!"

"Oh, I love cream-puffs, Sugar Honey!"

As for myself, I located that beautiful young female homing pigeon who had smiled at me when we first landed. Her name was Lily, and she was truly a vision! Our first conversation went something like this:

"What's up?"

"Same old stuff, not much going on. How about you?"

"Same here. I'm Walter."

"I'm Lily."

"I'm a Star Rider."

"I know."

"Did you know that I'm a real, actual Professor?"

"So I've heard."

"I know three languages."

"I know, oh, about twenty. But when you stay on Bird Island for three years, you can't help but learn all of the bird languages."

"You are very pretty!" I dance around, trying to keep her interested.

"Thank you, Professor Walter. You are very handsome."

She coyly coos.

"You want to fly around the island with me? I can tell you all about that big star in the sky!"

"Sure, why not?"

Lily became my lifelong mate. We almost single handedly repopulated the world with homing pigeons. Margie and Bruno also mated. They hatched brood after brood of little pigeons who warbled with a Bronx accent.

New Atlantis slowly, but surely, melted. Kenny succeeded in bringing Skynest One ashore and everyone feasted at Thanksgiving. Within a year, the entire Skynest Project landed from the upper atmosphere and serious building began on a new city.

There were many marriages and births during the following decades. Kenny and Fiona's firstborn baby was a girl, whom they named Janine. Their next baby was a boy, and they named him Walter, after me.

The ships of the Skynest Project were converted into long range surveillance aircraft and searched the new world, especially the strongholds, for survivors. They found multitudes! Almost all of the children of the Skynest Project were re-united with their parents.

High up in the Andes Mountains, Grandpa and I located a teacher, an old Peruvian Quechuan woman who had saved the lives of every one of her students, seventy children in all. Grandpa fell in love with her and married her.

The Golden Band was the real deal. God's gift, Grandpa called it. Just like the red pool of living water on Bird Island!

New Atlantis slowly, but surely transformed into a fabulous tropical garden. Dr. Ronald Jerome started his project to re-introduce many animal and plant species to the huge continent.

It was evident when the ice receded further away from the coastline that a tremendously advanced civilization had once existed here. Within a few hundred yards of our city construction, past a hill that emerged from the ice like a huge burial mound, a great, colorful city of crystal and glass thawed and sparkled in the bright sunlight.

"An ancient city of the Atlanteans!" Grandpa whispered in awe. As the acknowledged leader of our project, with thousands of excited kids running around, he forbade anyone to approach the ancient city until the ice fully melted and more could be learned about its' structural soundness.

Lily and I snuck flights through the crystal city whenever Grandpa was busy elsewhere. We were the ones who discovered a beautiful golden glass dome at the center of the city, now known as the Shining Dome. One day, at about noon and under a warm sun, we located an open side window framed in red and blue flowers and we were able to fly directly into the dome. What an amazing place! Objects were scattered around like toys left on the floor by a messy child, strange objects that held little meaning for me. A giant, shiny pipe-like metal cylinder with glass ends lay directly across the middle of the floor. Who knows what it could have been, but my breath caught when I spotted what stood next to it. A golden perch, undamaged, still standing as it had for thirty thousand years! Birds had lived here! I wondered what they might have been like, what manner of people had they lived with? I would never know, of course, unless I could somehow access that ancient memory.

As engrossed as I was with the golden perch, Lily nudged me and caught my attention.

"Listen," she whispered, "do you hear it?"

In the quietness of the dome, I did hear it, ever so faintly. It was the most beautiful deep, low harmony of music I had ever heard, an almost unworldly song.

"We must tell Grandpa," Lily decided.

"If we tell Grandpa that we were even near this place," I argued, "he'll fry us for breakfast!"

Lily huffed and pouted.

When everything had melted, Grandpa finally relented and allowed the archaeologists and engineers to enter and study the ancient city. Kenny and I tagged along.

"It's incredible," Kenny uttered in amazement, "everything is perfectly preserved. It all looks like it could have been built yesterday!"

"Beautiful," Grandpa agreed, "and this crystal is as strong as steel! We need to discover their methods of smelting."

Kenny examined a smaller, pyramid shaped dwelling, similar to many others in the city.

"I see no wiring," he observed, "no obvious power source; and yet the entire city lights up at night!"

"And it will be your job to discover that source, Kenny," Grandpa said with growing enthusiasm, "the Atlanteans left us a magical land to explore."

We approached the golden dome at city center and found the main entrance open, as if someone had quickly fled the building without bothering to close the door. I glanced across the dome at the open window Lily and I had entered a year before.

"Here, Walter," Grandpa said, pointing to the golden perch we had found before, "rest on this. Ah, look at this wonderful giant telescope lying on the ground, with the lens still intact!"

I sat on the perch, and a separate feeling vied for my attention. Once again, I heard the faint, low octave, mysterious, wonderful music. I leaned over and tapped on the perch.

"Do you hear it, Grandpa?" I tapped.

"Hear what?" Grandpa asked.

"The music," I tapped. Grandpa gave me a strange look.

"No," he answered, "I don't hear anything, Walter."

But he scratched his beard and continued to listen.

The archaeologists were overjoyed at what they were discovering. They found writings, strange characters etched on thin sheets of glass.

"There are probably cities like this across the entire Atlantean continent," they told Grandpa, "we must form expeditions and hunt for an Atlantean Rosetta Stone. We have to discover their language!"

"We will," Grandpa agreed, "in good time. But first, we must build a suitable city for ourselves."

The archaeologists had years and years. The Golden Band made certain of that. Everyone lived extraordinarily long lives.

A by-product of Dottie's miraculous healing in the living waters of Bird Island was her personal enlightenment; she literally lived in the Peaceful World that Grandpa and I had talked about years ago.

To my astonishment, she was also completely fluent in pigeon language, something that she would eventually teach to her children and grandchildren. Listening to Margie all of those endless hours must have had an effect on her.

Late into the evening, Margie and I would sit with Dottie and talk about everything we could think of. Dottie's peaceful state of mind calmed both of us, to the point that Margie would finally quiet herself and just gaze into Dottie's serene brown eyes.

Like her mother before her, Dottie decided that she wanted to be a teacher. She had a strong desire to pass history and knowledge down to the generations to come so that the same lessons would not have to be re-learned over and over again.

One night, Dottie sat next to Grandpa on his new porch swing as he smoked his pipe, looking up at the stars. I perched, half asleep, on his left shoulder.

"Just think, Grandpa," Dottie said, "if we can pass along our knowledge, the next time the world goes through a dark rift, everyone could be ready for it. They might even be living on other worlds by then."

"Perhaps," Grandpa said hopefully. Dottie leaned over and kissed him goodnight, and then stroked my head.

"Goodnight, Grandpa, goodnight, Walter," she said to us.

"Goodnight, sweetheart.!"

"Warble, warble!"

"Warble, warble," she sweetly chirped back to me.

"I love you!"

After Dottie left, Grandpa turned to me with a sad look in his eyes.

"Walter," he said, "I sincerely hope that our knowledge is passed down to future generations, but I doubt that it is possible. Thirty thousand years is an impossibly long time. Men will always be prone to forget the lessons of the past and I fear that next time will be as great a surprise for them as this time was for us. If only we could be more like you and sharpen our collective memory, but I fear that it is our destiny to forget again and again."

He quietly puffed on his pipe after that and I wanted to comfort him, I just did not know how.

Several years later, Dottie married a fine young man from Skynest Twenty-Six who totally adored her. In no time at all, they had a whole flock of little 'uns running around, screeching in pigeon, and climbing up on top of everything.

Grandpa was elected Mayor of our new city, which was built using wonderful solar, wind, and ocean-wave power, and even new power sources created through nanotechnology. Our meager city eventually merged with the enormous ancient Atlantean crystal city by the sea, and people inhabited those incredible structures as well. In a grand ceremony, Mayor Grandpa waved his hand in a broad gesture toward the combined cities, a blend of the new and the ancient, and named the new whole city Port Skynest.

"A fresh start," Mayor Grandpa proclaimed, "for people and animals together. May we ever hereafter co-exist in peace and mutual love."

None of the humans of Project Skynest lived less than five hundred years of age. Most of them lived well past six hundred. Grandpa, who lived to be seven hundred and thirty three years old, eventually became the first president of The Republic of New Atlantis. His first official act in office was to proclaim the pigeon the National Bird of New Atlantis!

Before he died, Grandpa commissioned a large gold statue to be built above the center of a huge fountain in the central park of Port Skynest. It was a statue of three glowing pigeons flying side by side through a dark, turbulent storm. Below the statue, the inscription read: "You will never be alone!"

And so, dear readers, or may I call you 'dear old friends', we come to the end of my story. I must rest now, and tomorrow I will travel one last time to visit dear old, ancient President Kenny Jerome and his sister, Dottie, in the capitol city of New Atlantis.

Then, I am ready to embark on my final journey. I am ready to enter the Great Nest in the Sky! I want to stand tall and state my claim of worthiness before The Great White Stork! I want to join the great circle of all of my people... my mother and father, my sisters, Old Rancher George, Old

Dude and Cher Ami, Hawk-Watcher and his flock, George and Janine, Marshall, Margie and Bruno, Henry and Jewell, and of course, my greatest love of all time...Lily. And above all else, to once again perch on the shoulder of Grandpa, my most beloved human friend, and to share legendary stories with him as he puffs away on his pipe.

AUTHOR'S NOTES

Fact: *Pigeons have the ability to hear sounds 11 octaves below middle C. (Which gave Walter the ability to hear the low harmonic hum of the Atlantean crystal city.)*

Fact: *Advanced studies at the University of Montana conclude: "Pound for pound, columbia livia (the pigeon) is one of the smartest, most physically adept creatures in the animal kingdom.*

Fact: *Cher Ami really did live and really did save the "Lost Battalion" during World War One. Many generations of Americans owe their very lives to his heroism. His body is on display at the Smithsonian Institute. Because Cher Ami and other brave pigeons like him, sacrificed their fragile lives to save so many of us, the pigeon really does deserve to be declared the National Bird of the United States of America! Humans should make this happen!*

I personally met my Walter at my home in the spring of 1975. He was a beautiful, intelligent pigeon who had flown into my brother's dorm room at Texas A&M University. Kenneth brought Walter home at the end of spring semester and our mother, JoAnn, a science teacher, decided that Walter could stay in the house as long as he stayed on top of the refrigerator. He made it a game to sneak down any time she wasn't looking.

Walter amazed us! He could hold long conversations with us, obviously understanding that we were talking to him and asking him questions. We could not understand his answers, but we knew that he was trying his best to communicate with us.

Walter really did play ball with Schatzie, the family dachshund, and we really did have a huge, clumsy cat named Bear. It was not unusual to see Walter in the hallway or in the backyard, pushing a ball up to whoever was around to play with him, including us.

Walter walked on the sidewalk next to my mom to school, obeyed the street crosswalk guard, and quickly became my mother's class's favorite. He loved school and constantly flew from classroom to classroom throughout the school. He played with the elementary school kids, pulled their hair, and knocked their pencils off of their desks.

Later, when I drove to college, Walter wanted to ride along with me. He flew up onto the roof of my little Ford Pinto and crossed from side to side as I tried to shoo him away.

My mom always stressed that Walter was free to come and go as he pleased. One day, after a week's absence, he showed up with a female pigeon and stayed up on top of the roof of the house for the day. She evidently wanted a different starter home, and the next day they were gone. We never saw Walter again, but we always wished the best for him. He truly is the inspiration for this story!

S. A. Mahan

Other books by S. A. Mahan

Chrissie's Run - *Finalist 2015 Chanticleer's National Dante Rossetti's Young Adult Fiction Award*

The Baby Sea Turtle - *Finalist 2015 Colorado Children's Book Award*

ABOUT THE AUTHOR

S. A. Mahan is a fiber artist who loves to knit, spin wool, and weave fabrics the way she intertwines her story plots. A rancher and barista, she loves to travel to far-off places and hear from her readers.

Mahan is the author of *Chrissie's Run*, a young adult thriller and finalist for the 2015 Dante Rossetti Young Adult Fiction Award, and *The Baby Sea Turtle*, a young children's picture book that is a finalist for the Colorado Children's Book Award.

A mother of three and a grandmother of six, she currently lives in the Colorado Rocky Mountains with her husband.

CPSIA information can be obtained at www.ICGtesting.com
Printed in the USA
LVOW07s1703310816

502664LV00010B/1021/P